Breakfast Will Never be the Same

Dale Rogers

CROSSBOOKS
PUBLISHING

CrossBooks™
A Division of LifeWay
1663 Liberty Drive
Bloomington, IN 47403
www.crossbooks.com
Phone: 1-866-879-0502

First published by CrossBooks 04/07/2011

Scripture taken from the King James Version of the Bible.

ISBN: 978-1-6150-7735-9 (sc)
ISBN: 978-1-6150-7736-6 (dj)

Library of Congress Control Number: 2011922980

Printed in the United States of America

This book is printed on acid-free paper.

I would like to dedicate this book to my three girls-- Penny, Lori, and Lana. They have loved me and encouraged me in this endeavor. I love you all.

Acknowledgments

I would like to thank everyone who helped me on my project.

Betty Magee, your special gift of the English language and how to place this language on paper was so much help. In fact, I could not have finished this book like I wanted it, without your editing. You are a creative person with the ability to teach. How fortunate for your students.

To Lana, and Lori, you two girls, helped in more ways than reading and rereading. I know you tired in reading the same book over and over, but I want to thank you both for using your time, encouraging and helping your old dad do this project.

Thank you, Penny, for my inspiration.

Laura Horn, I'm amazed that someone can visualize a scene and place it on canvas. Your expression of my characters for the cover was so special. Also to Brooke Lepard, who used her camera and her eye of photography to move this canvas to the digital photo for the cover.

Last of all, the beautiful people of my hometown, who have given me the best place to live and some of the best folks to live with. I love this small town and people with all my heart. Everyone should get the chance to live in a small town where everyone knows you by name.

CHAPTER 1

John Reed entered rehab unknowingly, and as usual a loving family member arranged for his help. Why did he need rehab? He was an addict. John was addicted to work and as all addicts he loved his addiction. John knew he was blind-sided when Susan his older sister convinced him to come to one of the most beautiful spots in the world to help remodel her home in Hawaii. She felt she had a stroke of luck when John arrived, and his cell phone rarely worked.

She knew he wouldn't be calling every minute checking in at his office, but his email and text did come through. This turned out to be a blessing because Hazel, a trusted employee sold John out to his sister earlier when Susan came to her about John's rehab. Hazel, wanting him to have a life outside work, screened all messages keeping his involvement at the office to a minimum. John, not completely naive about all that was happening, had avoided every party he had been invited too since he came to the island and this was irritating his sister. With her allies, Susan kept up with every invitation offer and by the same conspiracy she also knew every event he refused. Each defeat was disappointing and she could only quietly retreat to plan for the next move. The reason for rehab was to remove the addiction from the addict. The smoker has to want to throw the smoke away, the drinker has to desire to leave the drink, but the work-alcoholic has to long to do something other than work. He wasn't in denial, or rejecting help like most addicts tend to do at first. John was finding he enjoyed playing this little game with his "shrink". John wanted to help his sister with her renovation because it was a challenge and he not only loved a challenge, he loved the project of doing something special for his sister. He knew she was up to something, and he knew she knew that he knew.

1

As John raced toward his breakfast with his thoughts only on food, a change was coming. Timing, fate, the efforts of a sister/therapist, John's life was about to change for better or for worse.

Timing placed John late for breakfast for the first time in ages. He started every weekday the same way for 12 years. John began with a short run, a shower, and then breakfast. He had learned if his routine was changed, he wouldn't run at night. However, he let his guard down this morning accepting that today's routine could be out of whack. If he had known the next phase of therapy, not only would he have omitted breakfast, but he would also have packed his bags and returned home this very instant.

It was a long drive to the Hilton, but oh was it worth the 20 bucks for breakfast. His mouth was already salivating with the thought of the pineapple, papaya and mango so sweet and juicy the fear of choking in public made you suck on the fruit before you could chew. He thought he would have the cream cheese Danish this morning, or maybe he would try the cinnamon roll dripping with cream cheese icing. John thought about home, if he was running late at home he would omit his normal breakfast or be content to be late for work. Back at home, he would order at Michael's drive thru, a hometown fast food restaurant located on the way to work. John detoured 2 tenths of a mile for a plain biscuit, two apple jellies and a Coke, only three bucks. He wanted to be ahead of schedule each day, on the road for work before, but no later than seven. Why seven? John did not have a personality disorder, he developed his routine because he lived 50 miles from work, but he was also a man of habit. If he left Carthage no later than 7:00, he would be at his office in Madison on time. If he left five minutes later he could be as much as thirty minutes late due to increased traffic.

While here on the island, John drove 15 miles one way to eat at the Hilton Hotel's outdoor breakfast buffet and like home, he encounters some increased traffic. It only took a few days to cope with the time difference, but then his internal wake-up clock took over. He didn't have to be so deliberate with his routine, but he was afraid to break this schedule because he knew one day he would return home. He took more running time each morning before breakfast, a luxury he would not allow himself at home. Nonetheless, he still wanted to be at the Hilton by 7:00 A.M. when the morning buffet was served. He wouldn't make his appointed time this morning, but he wasn't in a rush to be at work either. He enjoyed this wonderful treat the first morning after his arrival. His sister Susan and her husband Jeff brought him for the brunch on the terrace before they left for a work-related stay in Europe. The first few weeks of his long stay, John came only on the weekends to brunch. However, now that his sister's kitchen was gutted, due to the renovations of which John was in charge, he reasoned he could come every day. The reason for being on the island in the first place was to design and oversee the renovations of his sister's house. The kitchen couldn't be completed too soon for John. Even though he liked coming to the Hilton for this beautiful morning getaway, it did consume a good portion of morning time, but after all, he only had one job to do here: his sister's house.

John felt he had accomplished his morning rituals even if he had to give up a few minutes here and there. But, if he had been on time, John would have missed his rehab encounter. He arrived at the Hilton parking lot a few minutes before eight. Finding a parking space at this hotel was not a difficult job and John couldn't figure that one out. The traffic was always heavy, but reasoned the guests at the Hilton, must be using public transportation.

John shut the door to his sister's Jeep Grand Cherokee Limited. He, remembering he didn't do any stretches after his run stretched his arms over his head and groaned as he slowly twisted his body back and forth. Reaching back into the Jeep to find his clipboard of checklists, he felt his back stiffen. Walking to the front of the Jeep and putting his right foot on the bumper, he leaned forward and stretched his back and leg muscles then did the same with the left before he ran up the walkway that led to the open café area which overlooked the beach.

John gazed at the ocean from the mount of cuisine. He waited in line for his turn, another thing he did not do when on time. The buffet table was on a section alone a couple of steps above the sitting area. The added height helped him find a place to sit on a crowded morning like today. The courtyard below was perfectly designed.

"Good morning, guys. Rough night, frankly I was afraid you might have skipped the outdoor spread this morning," John said to the servers in hearing range as he reached for a plate.

"Good morning, Mr. Reed, couldn't let the guests down on a day like today."

John filled his plate with different pastries and fruits; he loved all the choices of fruit. He usually would return for the more traditional food. He asked one morning if they had any grits, then after trying to explain he promised to produce a package one day to show them first-hand what grits were like. With his plate full, John paid with his debit card, and he turned to find a table. "Now, this is my kind of spring morning," he thought to himself.

"Sit anywhere you like, Mr. Reed. Will you want a soft drink?" asked a familiar voice.

"Yes, Adam, a Coke please."

"I'll be right out with it."

John had befriended several different people during his short stay. Most of the waiters were friendly native islanders although their work kept them too busy to visit; John did know a couple of their names. Adam, on the other hand, usually gave John a few tidbits of his life each day. He told John over the past few days that he came to the island from California. He had studied two years at Berkeley when he decided he wanted some adventure before he finished college and started a career. He left school at the disappointment of his mother and the blessing of his father.

A beautiful morning like this was expected on a vacation island, but it was hard to imagine especially after the terrible storm that raged through the island last night. John was somewhat surprised that everything on the patio was in place. The sun was blazing. He could feel the warmth on his skin even with the brisk, cool, stiff breeze. It was blustery and unusually brisk, even for an island morning, warm in the sun, if you could block the cool wind, but too cool in the shade. There were only a few clouds left from the night's intense storm. They appeared as torn angel hair scurrying across the sky, too thin and airy to have any form to them. John thought of Bob, the artist on ETV that always painted happy clouds. How would he place these clouds in a painting? How could he express their true image on canvas? These frightened little clouds were left behind and were scurrying to catch up with the scary monstrous clouds that passed through the night with speed and might.

He searched the area for an empty table and spotted one away from where he usually sat. Fate placed John at a different table. Not having his usual table was almost too much change to withstand. John had placed his plate on the only open table he saw, when Adam returned.

"Anything else, Mr. Reed?"

"No, Adam, this is all I need for now. Thanks."

"Sure thing, give me a sign if I can get you anything else."

John certainly would not dine indoors. The exterior of the Hilton was a modern structure and the courtyard led from the restaurant and also from the lobby of the hotel. He took his seat beneath one of the large colorful umbrellas, all of which were flapping and popping with the wind. It was refreshing to be outside, and obviously everyone else thought so. All the tables were round and now occupied. Sitting closer to the glass wall of the hotel than he wanted, John could not see the beach for all the planters of flowers and other people who blocked his view. At least he could use the wall of the hotel to position his seat where the sun would warm his body that the constant breeze was trying to chill. If he were closer to the exterior wall of flowers and greenery that encircled the outside of the terrace, he could watch the early sun-lovers clothed in what must be the skimpiest swimsuits in the world as they found the choice places on the beach. He might not be able to see the foam and the sea, but still he could at least hear the sound of the ocean crashing onto the island's coastline. The sounds with no vision of the ocean made the morning seem lethargic. John stood for a moment and looked out at the ocean. He watched the waves build, and crest, and then explode into white foam and spray. John sat back to enjoy his food.

His thoughts were of the first time he visited the beach on the Mississippi Gulf Coast. *As he played in the water, he was constantly pushed and pounded by the waves as they knocked him back toward the beach. He asked his father, "Why are there waves in Biloxi and not in the pond at home?" His father replied, "The pond did have waves, but the ocean was so deep and wide that when the water approached the beach, it was so glad to see land that it would heave and jump for the sky. The bigger the wave the longer it had been away from shore."* John smiled to himself; it was funny all the places and things he had retained throughout life. These memories triggered by a smell, a sound, a view or the face of an old friend. His memories of his childhood most always brought a smile. The thought of his father's answer seemed so logical at the time. His father always had an answer, no matter what the question, even if the answer was a fairy tale so it would be easy to understand and not bring on a hundred whys.

John enjoyed this beachfront experience. He loved the smells of the fresh salty ocean air, with all the breakfast foods mixed together along with that tropical oil he never seemed to get away from. That is why he returned here every day. Plus his sister's kitchen was not useable and would not be for several more days. He studied the people sitting around him as he broke apart a sweet roll. The outside wall of the patio was a planter of flowers, and this flowerbed looked more vivid and brighter than usual. But somehow the flowers were outdone by the greenery that boldly stood behind, between, and in front of the colorful blossoms. The Tuscan design of colors and stone made the courtyard so inviting. The use of stone planters, holding all the vegetation encircling the dining area is what blocked John's view. The flowers sparkled with bright vivid colors, and this bright day following the rain made it appear as if a fresh coat of paint had been applied to all plants. Ah! He could smell the fragrance of coconut and tropical oils every beachcomber was wearing. Even if he had to settle for a different table today, how could he possibly eat anywhere else?

John was not a loner even though he was alone most of the time. He liked people, and he really liked being with people to observe what others were doing. John was taking in all the beauty this morning had to offer as he checked his email from his phone. He looked up from his email as a couple of girls wearing skimpy swimsuits walked past. He thought, "They must be cold." His eyes stuck to them until they were out of sight. He was told one time by a friend if you look twice it was sin, so you take one long look. John was scanning across the crowd when he noticed her.

She was standing on the top step that led to the dining area. She was stunning! Where did she come from? She stood holding her tray of food searching for a place to sit. John took a bite of sweet roll and studied her as he chewed his food. She wore a white cotton dress with short sleeves. It had a camp shirt collar and a button-front that was buttoned above the knees. The hemline was below the calf, but the wind was showing at least one of her beautiful legs. She wore more clothes than half the women on the terrace combined, and she was by far the sexiest female there. Tall, slender, elegant, she had a soft look to her. She seemed annoyed that the breeze was tossing about her short brown hair. She turned her head into the wind, and the wind moved her hair away from her eyes. Her hair was all one length, cut above her shoulders, and it turned under slightly. Her skin wasn't snow white, but creamy like the froth on a cappuccino although she could use some sun. John guessed that she had not been on the island long. He swallowed, and then stood waiting to make eye contact. She looked past, and then noticed him standing. John motioned with his hand to offer her a seat at his table. She looked around one last time not too eager to sit with a stranger and walked toward the table where John stood. She had her tray in her hands and a black leather binder under her arm. The way she was dressed and the notebook made John think she was not a tourist. He remained standing to help her with her food as he introduced himself.

"Good morning, sort of crowded this morning. My name is John Reed, please join me."

She made sure the zipper on the notebook was closed, placing the leather binder to her right. As she positioned the tray of food directly across from John, she offered her hand to him with a smile that made his heart skip, "I'm Patti Scanlon, thank you so much for sharing your table. I was about to go inside when I saw your offer."

John would not need the sun anymore for warmth; he had her smile. Her eyes were as brown as her hair. It was impossible to tell where the pupil and the iris separated, deep brown surrounded by white. They were so dark he could see his reflection, but he thought they seemed to twinkle as she talked. John had never noticed the color of anyone's eyes before.

His mother was always referring to someone with a certain color eyes. She would often ask, "John, did you see that pretty girl at the ball game? You know the one with those big blue eyes." He would never know whom she was talking about, nor would he care.

"Eyes are not like fingerprints," he would tell his mother. "Mama, how many girls at a ballgame do you think might have blue eyes?" he would ask.

Patti said, "I thought I would get a head start on the day and have breakfast out here. I never thought this many people would be up this early. Is this wind always like this? I will leave my papers in the binder. I cannot bear the thought of what might happen if I tried to work out here. Why are there so many people up at this hour? I thought this was a vacation place? You would think everyone would take advantage of time off to sleep. I know I would if I didn't have to be up."

Patti was maybe a bit hyper this morning. She kept talking as if John had answered all her questions. He thought she was so cute. When there was a brief pause in her inquiry, John said, "Look around, notice the faces. Most are elderly; there are a few sunbathers. My guess is since it is Tuesday. Yesterday was a travel day, or at least I came over on a Monday. This may be a fresh bunch of tourist ready to get a quick start on the fun and sun. Getting your money's worth when you sun as you eat, and it is a great place to eat. I feel everyone that takes advantage of the early morning is enjoying the best the island has to offer. I love to come here in the mornings and work. To think under the clear sky while I listen to the clamor of people and the waves."

Patti asked, "What kind of work do you do?"

"I'm an architect, I am taking some time away from my work on the main land to design, overlook, and remodel my sister's house. She and her family live here, but they are away this summer. I guess I'm taking a working vacation."

"How do you work out here?" She asked making a reference to the wind.

John held up a plain clipboard with a common rubber band at the bottom, "My checklist."

She nodded and smiled at John's remedy.

"The wind blows all the time although I would say not always this hard, and I've never been this cool before. Now you, what brings you to the island?"

"I live and also work for a company that is based in Chicago. I am in the process of negotiating a deal with a corporation that has its headquarters, as well as their research and development, here on this island. The CEO and principal owner lives here on one of the islands somewhere. This will be the largest sale of my career."

John thought to himself as he listened. She could not be more than twenty-five. She looked younger. How long could she have been working to be in a position that sounded like a major sale? Yet, she was talking about this sale like a seasoned salesperson. John thought about her name. Surely Patti was a nickname. She looked more like a Victoria or a Dominique or maybe even Elizabeth.

Patti said, "I've been working on this account for months. I want to close this deal as quickly as possible. I'm booked on a return flight in two weeks, but I hope to close sooner. It would be great to be able to take a breather for a few days and get some sun."

"Then you will be here for two weeks?" John asked.

She rolled her eyes back showing a grin and a cynical laugh, "Yes, that is my plan. I'm not glued to this schedule. I feel this is enough time. With what I know about Jack Marshall, the man with whom I'm working, he'll probably keep me in research until it's time for me to leave. Then he will meet me at the airport my final hour here to sign the agreement. As long as I get his signature, then whatever it takes will be all right by me. The odd thing is, Marshall is the Chairman of the Board and I've been told he's the only one I have to please. This could be good."

John had only known Patti for a few minutes, and yet he felt he had always known her. He was amazed at the way she talked and the way she expressed herself. No wonder she was handling what must be a major account. He could see she never met a stranger, plus she beamed with confidence. Even if the deal took the entire two weeks she was confident in her success. He could not help looking at her face, her big brown eyes, and her snow-white teeth. Her skin was so smooth and silky. He was wrong about her needing a tan; she had plenty of color, even without sun. John worked with lines and angles. He had always wanted to be able to draw without drafting tools or the computer, like his friends George and Liesa. He could not help thinking of them; both are always looking for that different scene to draw to make that special picture that would catch a buyer's eye or please their own. They can change a white piece of paper into a flawless portrait with a pencil. He thought about his living room and of a cat lying on a tile floor that George sketched with a pencil. John remembered how George used an eraser to make the sunlight seem to reflect off the tile. He would be hard pressed to put Patti's face on paper.

John let his thoughts run as Patti talked. A portrait would have to start with the shape of her face. Those big brown eyes, then her nose, and her lips were thin, but beautifully shaped. Her face surely had never seen a blemish, not one line or wrinkle. He loved the way she talked using her dainty hands. She wore pearl earrings and they made her look perfectly adorable. She was Barbie in the flesh. Yeah, a Corporate Barbie, she could be packaged in a three-piece suit along with a briefcase. A great idea! She would be a hit. She could be in every toy store in America, CEO Barbie? What about Ken, oh yeah; he's in the mailroom.

John received a text message from Gus; he glanced at his watch. They had been talking for almost an hour. He stood, "Patti, will you excuse me? I'm, uh, I'm late for a meeting with my carpenters. I guess I let the time get away from me."

Patti looking up at John, "Please forgive me. I've kept you."

"No, not at all, there's plenty to do. I asked that all the workers be there this morning for a meeting of the minds, to go over any problem that might need my attention, and to plan the rest of the week. It was a pleasure having someone to enjoy the morning with. I hope we run into each other again."

Patti looked at her watch to check the time. That's when John noticed the ring; it was as big as life itself, third finger, left hand, and a chunk of an engagement ring. It was pear-shaped, but he knew what it was the moment his eyes fixed to the ring.

"I do too. It was nice meeting you, John."

"Good to meet you. Enjoy your stay." As John walked away, he noticed that nothing was left on her plate, and he did not remember seeing her take a bite. He left the veranda and walked to his sister's Jeep. He spoke to himself as he walked, "Oh, man! She could make a glass eye cry." He could not believe there could be a girl like her. It was truly a pleasure meeting Patti Scanlon. He knew he would never see her again, but some lucky guy back home certainly had a prize.

Patti sat a few minutes longer. She traveled quite extensively. She always was talking to someone, usually the person in the next seat, on a plane, in the airport, or in a waiting room. She enjoyed talking to interesting people and finding out where they lived, their occupation, and their families. She thought about John, she could tell he was from the South by his speech. He was a true Southern gentleman, who made this breakfast interesting. She liked him; he was pleasant, not like the man she would be meeting this afternoon. Patti wanted nothing more than to do a good job for her company. She was afraid that Jack Marshall wanted more from her than the products she offered.

CHAPTER 2

John stood looking into the mirror and didn't know if he liked what he was seeing in his face and hairline. A few short hours ago he met a stranger, but she didn't seem like a stranger. In fact after a busy day this girl was still on his mind.

"John, you're not too old for a young lady like Patti Scanlon from Chicago. Oh sure, your hair is beginning to pull back a bit here."

He played with his hair trying to find a better look. John tried to fluff it with both hands, pulling some bangs down over his forehead with his fingers.

"Beginning to have a wrinkle or two around the eyes, ole boy."

He then searched though the cabinet and found some lotion.

"Oil of Olay, you should have been doing this all these years," speaking to his image. He rubbed the lotion on his hands like he did with after-shave and then onto the face.

"Yeah, that's better. I've seen the ads. In a couple of days I'll be looking ten years younger, well maybe two anyway."

As he stared into the reflection of his eyes, his mind took him back twenty-six years and thousands of miles away. He was back in his hometown at his Uncle Andrew's farm. *John and his uncle were looking and discussing his uncle's new purchase. John was standing on the bottom rail of the gate looking over the top rail with his arms folded and cupped over the top rail of the gate. He wore his usual barnyard garments a white tee shirt, overalls, black rubber boots with the legs of his overalls tucked down in the top of the boots. Standing next to his uncle, who was propped against the same gate, they gazed at the new Black Angus bull. John's Uncle Andrew traveled to Georgia a couple of weeks earlier to buy this new animal. He was delivered earlier that morning from the Peach State in a long covered cattle trailer.*

"Uncle Andrew, why did you get a new bull, you still got Big Boy?"

There in the outer stall next to the newcomer was Ole Big Boy himself. Big Boy had been excited by all the commotion of the day. He had an open pen that joined an enclosed stall so he could come and go as he pleased. He was a grand champion Black Angus bull, and it almost seemed as if he knew he had that title. No one knew how much uncle Andrew gave for Big Boy, but it was thousands of dollars in a time when people didn't pay thousands of dollars for a bull, or at least around Walnut Grove they didn't. Uncle Andrew had one of the finest herds in the state. He always said that a grand champion does not eat a bit more than a scrub. Uncle Andrew let out a heavy sigh, "Well Johnny, Big Boy is getting old, and he's just about had it. I have other bulls, you know. I have them to breed with all of Big Boy's favorite daughters that I keep every year. I have over thirty brood cows I've hand picked just for the new guy. That will be his duty here: to finish the work ole Big Boy started."

Age didn't seem to effect Big Boy's actions on this day. Could a bull know he has competition? He was pacing back and forth in his outer corral doing his best to let the new comer know who the best bull in these parts was. After all, a king is king until death and Big Boy's sons and daughters were the calves that brought buyers to this farm. The new bull could not have cared less about Big Boy or his daughters. He was glad to have his feet on solid ground again. Big Boy's years were beginning to show. His long stout body that he carried for years was now looking a tad bit worn, and his belly seemed to put a strain on his back.

John remembered asking, "What are you going to do with Big Boy?"

"Most folks would probably sell Big Boy, 'cause he's out lived his usefulness. Not me, he's got a home and all the food he wants. There is still some work he can do here. Yep, everybody wants to keep living, but no one wants to get old doing it."

With some sadness in his voice, John asked, "Is Big Boy gonna die Unc?"

"Not today, Johnny. Big Boy's days are numbered, but I can assure you he will get the best treatment of any animal on this place." *Andrew reached over and placed his hands on John's neck,* "and if something happens to me, you can sell them all, but Big Boy, I'm expecting you to take care of him."

"Are you sad, Uncle Andrew?"

"Johnny, there are only two things that make me sad. One is thinking about the past, and the other is thinking about the future."

"Are you afraid of dying, Uncle Andrew?"

"No, son, I'm not."

"But you're getting old, Unc."

Laughing just a little, Andrew looked at John as he patted his back. "Yes, I am, and I can feel it creeping up on me some mornings. But it's satisfying getting old. Do you think you would enjoy it more if you died young? Nope, Johnny, I think that's the one thing you can only enjoy if you're old and worn out, and I do mean old."

"Why aren't you afraid? I am, and I'm only nine years old."

"Well, Johnny, I believe if someone is prepared when we leave this world, we go to a better one. Think for a moment, which is the prettier? A sunrise or a sunset?"

"I don't know."

"Let me see if I can help. You happened to be with me when I experienced maybe the best of both. Do you remember that fishing trip we went on a couple of weeks ago with your dad? You woke up just as we were leaving to run the lines before breakfast. It was still dark enough we needed a flashlight when we left the camp. We were going up the river, and it was beginning to lighten up. Just as we turned a bend, it looked as if the sun was coming down the Pearl River itself. As many times as I have fished that ole river, I don't remember ever seeing the sun in that way. Do you remember, Johnny?"

"Sure, I remember. I guess a sunrise is the best."

"Now wait a minute. That was 'bout the best I ever saw. The sun was so bright and looked three or four times bigger that morning, almost frightening. Now, I want you to keep that image in your mind. Now think back with me. Do you remember last fall late one evening, when I rode with your folks and you to Jackson? We were going to eat at that catfish place your mom loves so much. Do you remember? There were some thunderclouds in the sky, but a lot of sky too. The sun was sort of orange, and the clouds were tall and white but looked dark and heavy on the bottom. As the sun began to sink behind the clouds, we could see the light making all kinds of colors from behind the clouds. It was dark on the under side of the clouds. Remember, Johnny? You asked if it was going to rain."

"Yeah, I do remember."

"I know you do; I recall talking with you about the sun changing sides of the road as we went toward Jackson. Suddenly the sun seemed to just fall and was then under the clouds instead of being over them. The clouds turned from a dark grey thundercloud to an orange glow of light as the sun peaked between

and reflected off the bottom of each scattered clouds. We all discussed what color the clouds were. I said orange, you said red, and your mom said terra cotta."

"Yeah, I remember, Uncle Andrew."

"Now, to me that was the best of both that I can remember. Now, tell me with the picture of the two in your mind, which is the most beautiful?"

"Hands down, Uncle Andrew, it was the sunset."

With a softer voice Andrew continued, "Well, Johnny that is where Big Boy and I are at the moment. We are at the sunset. Here is the reason I made that comparison. The very moment the sun goes down here, its coming up somewhere in the world just like we saw it do that morning we were fishing. I am a born again Christian, believing in Jesus' promise of a life after death. I believe the very moment my time on this earth is up, at that same moment, it will just be starting brand new, fresh as a sunrise in heaven."

John had always thought his uncle Andrew was the neatest guy. He was John's best friend growing up. John walked over to his bed and checked his alarm to make sure it was set at the right time.

"I sure don't want to be late for breakfast," he said aloud.

He lay in bed and could not keep his mind from thinking of the fascinating young woman. He would close his eyes and see her sitting across the table holding her fork in her hand almost talking with it, those big brown eyes, that incredible smile.

CHAPTER 3

John Reed was from a small town in central Mississippi. Walnut Grove was an old sawmill town that was a booming place in the 1920's and 1930's. John lived there all his life except during his time at college. He was brought up very conservatively, Southern Baptist, in the middle of the Bible belt where all social events circled around the church and the activities outside the church were second. People always went to every event at church: weddings, funerals, Vacation Bible School, revivals, and every regular service Wednesday night and twice on Sundays. John probably never missed a handful of services in his life. The only meeting a young boy was not expected to attend was the WMU, (Women's Missionary Union).

Somehow through the years, Walnut Grove evolved into its destiny as a small town. There were hundred year old houses and new houses on the same block. The school where John attended first through twelfth grade was located east and little north of the business district. It was in the city limits, but town was regarded where the stores were located.

The name Walnut Grove High School, never made much sense to John, because first through twelfth grade classes made their home inside the one H-shaped building. The enrollment was about four hundred students, kids started first grade with the same girls and boys with whom they graduated.

John's parents owned a business in the city of Walnut Grove. One unique thing about Walnut Grove was that the town was built around a triangle, instead of a square, even though people called the triangle a square most of the time. The story goes that two men were going to donate the land to form the business part of town. One of the men backed out of the donation, and it happened to leave the layout of the town in the shape of a triangle. John's dad started a furniture store that evolved into a furniture, hardware, appliance, and floor-covering store. Their store was located at the base of the triangle on the south end between the Five and Ten Cent Store and Leake Seed and Feed, a diverse style of stores put together by the needs of the small town. As a young boy, John, worked in the family store, his daily jobs consisted of things like taking out the trash, sweeping the floor, dusting, and answering the phone. John was asked to help with customers during busy times. He enjoyed the store and business life, people coming and going, and many stopping in to browse and speak. The character of some individuals was so interesting to learn. People like Ms. Annie, who did not care what his dad charged her for something she wanted, as long as he did not charge her sales tax. John's dad always treated Ms. Annie fairly, but he also learned to figure the total price he would take for her purchase with tax included before he would present the bill to her. Store hours were long for his parents. Many times deliveries were made after regular store hours.

John could always go to the back of the store and watch TV or have a snack in the small quarters his mother called a lounge. As long as he let his mother know, he could amble around the triangle in the middle of the day to catch up on things with the town folk. Sometimes he would hang out with his friends, that is, if his chores were done. Most of the time his friends liked being with him at the store, and this was also acceptable as long as they did not get in the way of doing business. If they got loud, his mother would say, "John, I think you boys need more space, don't you?" This question was not a question. It meant go outside, go get a Coke, or just get lost. John knew how long to stay gone. Most of the time as long as it took to get rid of his companions. When he was allowed to run with the boys around the town, they would go exploring by walking the railroad tracks. West tracks lead to the wilderness and Tuscolameta Creek and east lead to a nearby pond for a swim. Swimming unattended was not permitted, but it was so much fun to go off in the middle of the day. The summers in Mississippi were so hot and muggy that walking the tracks and then across one of the fields to a pond would be exhausting. Getting hot and sweaty was inevitable, and every time the intention would be to wade in and cool off. With the muddy bottom of all ponds being slippery, it was unusual that at least one boy would not slip. Then there would be the mud fight at the shallow end of the pond, and this would make it a necessity to move into deeper water to clean off. Other things the boys enjoyed doing included pitching a baseball or playing a game of touch football in the triangle. Bike riding was considered play although each kid's bike was the only means of transportation, other than walking, and was not necessarily something to do for fun. Playing in cardboard boxes in the small lot back of the store was fun too. After the boxes were demolished, every boy would choose one sturdy piece of cardboard and head to a favorite hill out of town that had some pine trees at the top. The pine straw from the large trees would cover the hillside. John and his friends would take the cardboard lay it flat, kneel on the cardboard, then roll the front edge up over their knees, and hold it back to make a cardboard sleigh to slide down the hill.

John's favorite thing to do was to sit around town in front of the stores and listen to the old men talk. It was something to see them gather at different times of the day. In the mornings, they would assemble in front of the bank. The summer afternoons were mostly spent in front of the grocery store. The grocery store faced the east and had a large overhang for shade. Plus, there were refreshments, which was also part of the reason for gathering there. The bank and the other stores in town had benches in front of them, and they were put to good use. All the benches were old pine church pews, painted dark green, except the bench in front of the grocery store. It was made of oak, probably forty inches high and had a wooden rail along the bottom front to rest their feet. There were six arms on the bench, one at each end and four in-between that made a place for five seats. It was made of one-inch slats that covered the frame to make the seat and back. The seat curved slightly down where bottoms rested. The back had a slight curve toward the lumbar. The slats ran the length of the bench. This design made it the most comfortable bench in town. The bench at the bank was the preferred bench for the old men especially in the mornings probably because of the traffic in and out of the bank. John was somehow drawn to the deliberations that went on each day. The conversations were exciting; more than once these grown men would get to shouting and someone might leave mad, only to meet up the next day as if nothing ever happened. Topics mainly consisted of bowel movements, politics, and general gossip.

John and his friends learned everything from sex, politics, and the dangers of drinking, smoking, and running around with women. They were told to stay away from these things that all would lead to destruction of any man over time. How did they know all this? They all talked with so much experience. The only thing confusing to an adolescent was the fact that some of the things John and his friends were strongly warned to stay away from were the things that made up the stories told with the most excitement, laughter, and vigor. Then the lesson would come or point would be stated straight-faced and expressionless. The men would also cover the latest gossip that was going around town, the rumor that no one was supposed to know about, the secret stuff that usually went along with the lessons, on the issues mentioned. John took everything these men said as truth. He loved to sit and listen. The men would go on and on covering many different topics at one sitting, often forgetting the young men who sat in front of them. That is one reason John liked to sit around the old men. They did not hold any topic back. If the boys happened to be around, they got to hear the conversation first hand and uncensored. Well, every now and then if the subject matter got too tough, or if the language too bad, someone would notice and remind the gentlemen of the young ears. The conversations did indeed get bad at times, and these men did not make a habit of bad talk.

John was dismembered from the daily convention for a while, simply because he asked his mother one night at the dinner table why the bench in front of the bank was called the dead-pecker bench. John's father and sister laughed as his mother offered him no explanation, just scornfully forbid him to go back to the bank anymore. Then his bewilderment multiplied when he overheard his mom talking to Uncle Andrew on the phone about his predicament. She fussed at Uncle Andrew, and before she hung up she burst out laughing. Uncle Andrew tried to explain to John a few days later why his mother had reacted the way she did. He did not understand at the time how he got into so much trouble from a simple question. Andrew also told John he could return, after promising John's mother that he would see to it the subject matter would stay clean when John and his friends were there. John asked Andrew how he managed to make it okay with his mom.

Andrew asked John, "Son, you know what a pecker is."

"Sure, I know that."

"Well, Son, ladies don't like to here about men's private parts. They think that is bad language. Between men it could be considered bad talk if we started talking about ladies privates. Do you understand?"

John made a face, "I sure do."

Andrew rationalized with John, "I asked your mother on the phone if she had ever heard anyone make that statement, or had she ever made the reference herself. I also, pointed out that I didn't think the bank was where you heard the expression. That is not something we men would have a conversation about, nor would we ever label our bench with a name like that."

John remained quiet after the discussion with Andrew because he began to understand about keeping his mouth shut. It was at that very bench where he had indeed heard the expression. The men were laughing about it. John Henry told the other men about the name after his wife asked if that was where he was off. She called it that out of frustration, after asking him to help her with a flowerbed, and he refused. They had a great laugh about the name, reassuring each other, there would not be a woman who could offer proof to this name.

Andrew warned, "Now, Johnny, when you don't understand something come and ask me first. I will explain if I can, and everyone will remain happy."

As John understood politics better, he was always shocked at the political predictions of these untrained men. Probably because they sat at the two busiest places in town, plus that was all they discussed in a political year. They also involved every patron of the bank, grocery, or passerby that would stop and give an ear to this opinion poll. The poll was very seldom denied an answer. It seemed that everyone had an opinion and did not mind divulging how they stood on a political issue or candidate.

John was a good athlete although he never played a varsity sport past the tenth grade. He had a minor problem in high school with teachers or anyone in authority. Even with this problem, he was seldom in any trouble. He struggled in his first two years of college. Then he turned it around and became the model student. He loved design and longed to get out of the school grind and start work.

He started to work for his father's brother. His Uncle Larry had two children, both were doctors, and had zero interest in their father's architectural business. Without a child to follow in dad's footsteps, the business was offered to John. He bought the architectural firm from his uncle. He took a productive business and turned it into a lucrative business. John's team had the vision and exceptional talent that fit with a growing mainstream city.

John was a good listener and always wanted to use his ideas to achieve what the customer wanted. John often referred to his first job that was completely his design as the hardest and yet the most fulfilling he ever completed. Not only did he have to please the person that was to own the home, but he also had to please himself. The client was satisfied long before John was. The day of completion finally arrived. John was invited to an open house that took place a few weeks after the family had moved into their new home. John sent a large bouquet of flowers to say thanks. When he went by, the flowers were on display in the foyer. The owners were more enthused over the flowers than the house, and because of their reaction, this became a tradition for John's firm. He later changed to only red roses. His uncle Andrew told him once that red was a rose; any other color was just a flower.

CHAPTER 4

John was still in bed wide-awake his head on a pillow, only inches away from the radio-alarm clock, but wouldn't move from his pillow until the music started playing. He looked at the numbers counting down the time and finally music started releasing him from his detention. He instantly jumped out of bed and into the bathroom for a shower. He dressed as quickly as possible. He had not even thought of his usual run. His first thought of the day was the same as his last thought the night before, Patti Scanlon. He could not get this beautiful stranger off of his mind. Patti was the kind of girl men dream of all right, if they could stop thinking about her long enough to sleep.

John had not taken time in the past several years to think of any girl. He couldn't wait to start work. He finished his exams on Thursday and moved home from college on Friday. He reported for work on the following Monday. At the age of thirty-five, John had tunnel vision when it came to his career. In the past twelve years he had been on more vacations than dates, and he seldom went anywhere. He ran out to his Jeep and raced toward the Hilton Hotel to have breakfast with someone he barely knew. Would this Patti Scanlon even be there? It really did not matter and maybe that would be best, but John wanted to get to the hotel, get his food, and wait to see. If this girl didn't show up this morning and he never saw her again that would be all right, too. As John turned into the parking lot, he glanced at the clock 6:57. He parked in a space and ran up the terrace to his food and destination. The buffet tables of foods were not all in place, but a few people were already beginning to assemble. He would eat and not even worry about time this morning. John felt sure he would be ready in case she did return and by chance he could see her again. He nervously stood back and let several people go before him in the food line. The attendants were busy working, but as soon as the plates were in place, the line started to move. John placed fruit on his plate instead of eggs, a couple of bagels instead of croissants, and finished out his tray with cream cheese, jam, and juice. He stepped away from the food to make his way to the courtyard of tables, and there she was sitting at the same table they enjoyed the day before, smiling and drinking a cup of coffee. Yesterday it had not been his choice of seats. From where Patti sat the view of the beach was nonexistence, but with the present company, it was now the view of choice. Patti waved for him to come and join her. She was wearing a long sleeve, deep navy blue, velour-jogging suit with a zipper jacket and navy blue flats. The only jewelry she wore was a pair of silver hoop earrings. John walked gingerly over to the table.

Patti spoke first, "Please join me. I thought you might be an early riser. I got out early to catch up on some work. All they had available thirty minutes ago was juice and coffee and I got that inside."

Patti proudly lifted her clipboard to show John as he placed his plate on the table.

"You were listening; I see you are ready for the beach," John making fun at Patti's attire.

"It's not as cold today as yesterday morning, but I do feel more comfortable."

John wondered if she noticed how much he was grinning. Patti began telling John about her day yesterday as if old friends were meeting for coffee.

"I told you I had a meeting with the owner. His name is Jack Marshall. This was our second meeting. The first was with him in Chicago a few weeks ago, and he was very aggressive. I feel sometimes that executives see a woman in the work force, and they think anything goes. I really thought his forward actions were because he was away from home. I didn't know what to expect from him here on the island, especially on his own turf, but I know there are some men who will play while they are away and be gentleman at home." She continued, "So far, I'm impressed with his behavior. He's coming at me from a different direction. Now he wants me to have dinner with him."

John asked, "Does this happen often?"

"It happens too much," she confessed. "Most is harmless, I guess. I would like to finish up my work and enjoy the island for a few days or hours. I didn't seem to accomplish anything yesterday other than a personal visit. I know I'm not having dinner alone with him. That's not right." Patti smiled, "John, he knows, as well as I, that our product meets all of his requirements, the price is right, and our company's quality is unsurpassed. I somehow feel he's toying with me; he really hasn't talked business."

John could see her confidence and determination. As Patti talked he wondered if anyone who worked for him had ever been put in similar situations. Sure he noticed the women at the office. A couple of the girls are knockouts, one married and one single. Maybe he was too busy to notice. He was sure of one thing. If anything improper was going on, he was sure his office manger Hazel Stoddard wouldn't miss it. She came along with the business, as did some of the other staff. John sometimes wonders if he doesn't work for Hazel. She is all business and keeps up with the entire firm, and she has the type-A personality to address something like this, if it ever did happen.

He thought of his first date, and the conversation he had with his parents. His mother and father had a strong, positive meeting with him and explained how he was expected to behave toward a girl. He was to treat every girl as a lady, and if she turned out not to be one, he was to act toward her as if she were a lady and take her home. He smiled to himself remembering his mother's reinforcement of this conversation before every date. As John would leave on a date, his mother would remind him, "Treat her like you would your sister." His mother was always trying to fix him up with some girl. John would tell his mother she gave him a complex: who would want to kiss his sister goodnight?

Patti broke out that wonderful smile that shocked him back to the present. The same smile he hadn't been able to get off of his mind. The one he thought of all night and all the way to the hotel this morning. He nibbled on his food, listened contently to her speech, and watched her every motion. Everything she said was interesting, and even the way she moved in her chair as she talked. She soothed him with her very presence. He could see why anyone would want to spend time with her. He couldn't visualize anyone mistreating or taking advantage of her. John had been in relationships before, but he hadn't been close to a lasting relationship since college. John dated all along, but seldom longer than a few weeks. At this moment, he realized why. Until now he had never been truly attracted to any woman. Sure, he noticed beautiful women. What he noticed was how beautiful, smart, poised, witty, and sexy they might be, but outside of those attributes there was nothing more.

Patti giggled softly and said, "I have to change clothes; I do have a ten-o-clock appointment with Mr. Jack Marshall." She laughed again and added, "I don't' know if I should wear running gear, or business attire prepared to work."

John asked, "Will you be here tomorrow? I eat here every morning."

Patti stood and John followed, "Sure, I'll see you tomorrow. After all, I'm staying here for the next couple of weeks. I want to ask you how you eat here every morning and not be a guest at the hotel."

"All they ask for each morning is my credit card."

John remained standing as Patti walked away and into the lobby. He returned to his seat feeling completely drained. He could hear the ocean now; and listening to the ocean's sound made John feel lonely for the first time in a very long time. He sat for a few minutes, closed his eyes and listened to the sounds all around him-- the waves crashing on the beach, the umbrellas popping, the utensils touching the plates, the hustle and commotion of people, talking and laughing. The same sounds he enjoyed a few days ago were different now. John had not felt like this the past few weeks. He had enjoyed his time alone here. Now he felt claustrophobic. He opened his eyes, left a tip, and hurried off to his work. How could he let this happen? How did he let himself get derailed? Sure it started innocent enough.

Susan, John's sister, called him one day at work, "Hi, John. This is Susan.

Jeff and I are going to remodel our home. We want you to draw the plans, and this is what we want."

Then she proceeded to tell him her basic wants and needs. John had been to their home before and was familiar with her house. He knew what she liked, and he felt he could prepare a plan for her. Susan sent a detailed blueprint of the house. They talked often about changes. John was careful to keep notes and emailed her constantly with ideas.

In reality John's sister knew her brother needed time away from work. She felt that no one should work nonstop for twelve years. Susan's overall plan was to entice John to come to the island to do a special favor for her by being in charge of the renovation. She knew she could get him to consent. She called John one day to chat about new ideas and to start her sequence of problems she would have to face. New dilemmas in Susan's life seemed to pop up with every call.

After a few weeks of labor, John sent the first draft. Susan changed things, and he modified the changes. Susan, feeling the timing right, called one night about midnight. John was at home sleeping.

He fumbled with the phone and tried to answer with a normal, "Hello."

"John, are you awake? This is Susan."

Lying and trying to sound awake, "Yes, I wasn't asleep."

"John something big has happened, and I couldn't wait until morning to call you. Jeff is being sent to Europe for the next four to six months."

Jeff was a private citizen who worked for the military. Susan knew of the European trip all along, but pretended it came up at the last moment. She knew if John thought that she were in a predicament, it wouldn't take much to convince him of her need.

"John, I want to go with Jeff, and we've already signed with a contractor. John, you've needed to get away for sometime now. Will you come and oversee the house? You know what I want. After all, you might just want to stay."

Wide awake now, "No way! Sis, you know I can't leave everything here for that length of time. It might take months. I don't know your contractor. Plus, there will be people with special trade skills you will need. I don't know anyone. Can I count on your contractor to supply these people?"

"John, we live on an island, not a deserted island. We know most of the different people we want to use, so that should not be a problem, and our builder has the best reputation on the island. We have waited for him to do our construction for months. I just feel like I have to have someone here to oversee the work. That's all I need. Now, you tell me what better person than my brother, who just happens to be one of, if not the best architect in the world. John, you couldn't be saying you want me to leave this project in the hands of someone I don't know. Even if he is the best carpenter on the island, things will come up won't they?"

John had to admit, "Yes, they will."

"I plan to live in this house the rest of my life. You are the only one that can do this the way I want. If you can't come, I'll have to wait until we get back. Maybe our contractor can go somewhere else and put us on his waiting list for later."

Maybe it was the hour, but John made a big mistake, and he knew it as soon as he said, "I don't see how I can, Sis." He knew this was like saying, "I don't know how to tell you no."

"Then you will think about it won't you, John?"

There was a moment of silence. John closed his eyes in pain. She had him. He knew it. How could he say he wouldn't think about it? Why even the worst of brothers would say he would think about something. Susan was a master at leading John up to a point, and then she could push him off the edge with her little finger.

"John? You will think seriously about this won't you?"

"Okay, I'll think about it. Don't fire the contractor until you hear from me."

"Great! I'll let you get back to sleep. I love you. Goodnight."

There was no sleep the rest of the night. John, a workaholic, had too much going on in Mississippi. He didn't see how he could leave his work for an extended time to remodel a house, even if it was for his sister. He knew he wouldn't do it for money, but this wouldn't be for money, it would be for his sister. He started the list of pros and cons.

The next morning he started planning his trip. After all, the time away would be nice. Living in paradise would have to be enchanting, or why would it be called paradise. It took him several weeks to move around all his work to the other architects in the office. Some groundwork had begun on Susan and Jeff's home before John got to the island. When he arrived, he found his sister had left him in good hands. John adored Gus, the contractor, and his crew. They were all skilled craftsmen.

After he settled in and before Susan and Jeff left for Europe, Susan had a party so John could meet some of Susan and Jeff's friends. She made arrangements with all of her friends and neighbors that John would be included if there happened to be some kind of dinner party or anything that might get him out of the house. The ladies were told in confidence to be on lookout for a girl whom John might be introduced. This was not uncommon to John and he learned to avoid this unwanted help. It seemed as if every married woman in his circle of friends and acquaintances had one ambition, which was to find all single men a wife. John liked his independence. After all if he had been married, he couldn't have done this favor for Susan. The oddity of all this was, Susan was doing this for John. If he had a life outside of work there wouldn't have been a plea from a desperate sister. John liked living alone; actually, he had never felt alone. He had always been happy doing as he pleased.

John's thoughts were all over the place, why would meeting a young pretty girl like Patti Scanlon be confusing. He turned into the driveway, and as he walked into the house, he mumbled out loud, "I was perfectly happy before I met her. Now, when I am working, I think of this girl. I can't get my work done. There's too much age difference. What am I doing thinking about her. She's engaged!"

John walked inside the house where the crew was working. Nick and Mark were working in the kitchen. An electrician was working on the wiring changes. Gus, the foreman, was talking over something with his son Josh. They had the blueprints in front of them on a table of plywood and two saw horses.

John spoke to everyone, "I thought I would go out after work tonight and relax a bit. Go somewhere to get my mind off of this project." Off of this girl, he thought to himself. He asked, "Do any of you have any suggestions for where a guy from the mainland might go to accomplish something like this?"

Nick answered before anyone had a chance to think. Nick, a stay-over from the military, had worked for Gus part-time while he was stationed at the local base and could not bring himself to leave when his hitch ended. He was young and single and probably knew all the places in town. All the other workers were married. The question caught the attention of everyone. They all stopped to listen to this conversion. This had been the first non-work related question that John had asked since he started the project.

"There's a club in town that has a great house band. They play pretty good music. You know the kind you eat and dance to. They have great food, and there are always some good-looking babes hanging around waiting for someone to dance with. Hey, it's also a good place to take a girl. They seem to love the idea that a guy could enjoy dressing up and listening to or dancing to live music." He flipped his hammer in his hand, and pointed the handle at John. "Got a dance floor if you know what I mean."

John responded, "No dancing, just need a place to get my thoughts together. Where is this place, and what kind of music?"

"You know what kind of music. Sometimes jazz, sometimes pop, some older stuff, new songs too, but played the way a stage band would play. It's easy to find, it's right on Ocean Front Drive."

"What's the name?"

"The Night Club. It makes me think of an old movie with a nightclub scene. Waiters in tuxes, full service, they like for you to dress up. Although I doubt they would turn you away if you didn't dress the part. It's on the side opposite the beach. You can't miss it; the name is written out in big neon lights from bottom left to upper right. You might have to wait for dinner, unless you get there before seven."

"Oh, I'll get there before then. Anything else I might need to know?"

"Yeah, take your plastic or a big bill, the place is expensive."

John nodding that he understood then turned, "Now, with my evening all planned, what do we need to accomplish here today, guys?"

Gus motioned for John to come over to where he was looking at the blueprints.

"Here's a minor problem we have, John," as Gus pointed to the plans.

CHAPTER 5

Later in the afternoon, John finally found his white dress shirt with the French cuffs, tied his favorite tie, and then slipped into the dark charcoal coat with the light chalk stripe. The only suit he brought on the trip and one more than he thought he would need. He felt he could be a bit early, so he drove more deliberately. He drove by The Night Club and saw a parking place; he stopped and parked his Jeep only a couple of spaces from the front doors of the restaurant. The entrance from the outside was level with the sidewalk. The front of the building was plain, stucco with large neon lights protruding from the fascia just above a black and silver-lined canvas awning. Once inside, John was greeted by one of several hostesses.

The hostess asked, "Do you have a reservation?"

John answered, "No, do I need one?"

"No, sir, not this early you don't, but we do take reservations. Are you here for drinks, dining, or both?"

"Dining only."

"Will you be dining alone?"

"Yes."

Walking with the hostess away from the door, John realized they were on a balcony, high above the dining room. This was not the picture he had in mind after Nick's description. Located on this level were three large chandeliers lighting the top floor. Recessed lighting was used for the rest of the building and spotlights for the stage. A typical lounge with several seating arrangements was located in the middle of the large balcony for the guests to watch and listen to the band. An unusually embellished bar was to the right side and an unexpected twist on the left side was a coffee bar. Here guests could wait for a table in comfort or enjoy an island drink as they visited with friends. Get hammered and then sober up at the coffee bar. The impressive wrought iron banister that guarded the customers' safety continued beyond the upper level to two stairways, one on each wall that led to floor of the dining hall. The customers could be led down either left or right side stairs. There were several oval shapes to the room that stood out from the upper level. As the stairway descended from the balcony to the main floor, the last several steps of the stairs not only faced the opposite stairway, but they also fanned out broadly, arching at the last few steps.

John was escorted down the left side stairs. Then he and the hostess walked up several levels of terrace-like landings to his table; place settings for four were on each of the tables. The waiter removed all of the extra tableware on John's table. John was given a menu and asked if he cared for a drink.

"Water is fine for now, thank you."

People were steadily coming into the dining area as he looked over the menu. It always bothered him to see a menu without prices. He had finished ordering dinner and was getting ready for the entertainment, questioning why he had gone to the trouble of getting dressed in a suit to come to a place like this. There were plenty of places he could have eaten a great meal dressed in jeans and a pullover. He felt out of place in this big dinning hall.

He let his architectural blood flow, there were rows of tables arranged on eight terraces that made a slight curve from one side to the other. The terraces insured that everyone would have a clear view of the stage. The only way a table would be considered better than another would only be if it were closer to the front. John could see the stage and a section in front of the band that was an apparent dance floor. It was accessible from both stairways and the dining area. Six tables were stationed in the front section next to the dance floor. The tables were large round tables that had eight place settings and reserved cards on them. They were on the same level as the dance floor, but sitting on carpet to mark the difference in the two areas. The dance floor sparkled with a high gloss finish with several different wood tones used to create a starburst design with the center point coming from center stage. Two walkways from the bottom floor to top tier of terraces made three pie-shaped sections with tables sitting in groups on each of the clusters. The middle pie section was the largest and had the most tables. John was seated facing the stage on the forth level, far right section, but next to the aisle. He counted eight tiers of tables, not counting the tables on the floor. One other table accompanied him in his grouping. The stage had a half-oval shape, and was a couple of feet higher than the dance floor. Several different waiters served the entire area. Also under the stairs and on each side were doors that came from the kitchen. John noticed the traffic was going into these doors, but no one was coming out. Three doors that opened to a large walkway behind the last tier of tables concealed the kitchen. Food was served from these doors. He noticed everyone returned through the side entrances.

John was still checking the arrangement when someone caught the corner of his eye. He looked again toward the front and opposite stairway. Walking across the dance floor, to the last section, where John was sitting, was what looked like a fashion model. This gorgeous gal was wearing a black dress that had thin shoulder straps. The satin dress bodice flowed to the waist and combined with layers of ruffles. Each layer looked like rows of gathered crepe paper, crinkled, but not puffy like a tutu. She carried a little black purse that wouldn't hold John's car keys. She turned to the hostess, said something, and then made a slight motion in John's direction. The hostess nodded and left her. The woman, dressed in satin and ruffles, turned making her way up the aisle; her eyes fixed on her destination. She was heading straight for John; his heart moved from his chest to his throat. His heart rate increased with every level she climbed. She was focused on John and was smiling. Oh! He wished he could put her in slow motion just so he could watch her longer. She approached his table. John, holding his napkin, stood.

He somehow managed to ask, "Are you alone?"

She laughed slightly, standing across from John, and answered, "No, my children are with me, but the cab driver offered to ride them around while I had dinner." John came to this place to get Patti Scanlon off his mind, and now he was elated to be in her presence, to smell her perfume, to watch her, and to be with her.

"Well, why don't you join me then?"

"I would love to."

John helped Patti with her chair. She sat across the table from him just as they had each morning. It should be an exercise to look at something of her beauty. John thought if it were, he would never have to jog again. The waiter brought Patti a menu and motioned to one of the bus boys for a table setting.

"Would you like to hear the specials we have tonight?" The waiter asked Patti as he handed her the menu. She took the menu but never opened it.

She asked the waiter, "What did John order?"

"Filet, large portion, medium, topped with lump crab meat and butter cream sauce, steamed vegetables," was his only reply.

Patti handing the menu back said, "Sounds good to me. Could I have a six ounce, medium rare, and maybe a salad?"

"Would you like a fruit salad, a Caesar, or a tossed salad?"

"The tossed salad for me."

"We have two wonderful dressings if I might suggest. The house dressing is shrimp vinaigrette, a basic that's always great and a sweet and sour made with fresh fruit that's nice."

"The shrimp vinaigrette sounds great!"

The waiter replied, "Very good, madam, and to drink? The gentleman only wanted water.

"How about iced tea."

"We have regular tea and flavors, if I might suggest one?"

"Please."

"A mango tea is one of the house favorites."

"Then that is what I'll have."

John asked the waiter, "Could you bring my meal with hers?"

"Certainly, Sir."

An elderly lady in an evening gown began to play the piano. Patti turned to look, "She's plays beautifully. This is a lovely place. They walk you down the stairs, then back up to a table."

"It's really a good idea. It's harder to leave if you don't like the menu. How was your day?" John asked.

Patti said, "It was awful. I was caught off guard when Marshall invited me to his home to spend the weekend, and I told him a lie. John, I don't lie, and I knew as soon as I told it that it was going to catch up with me. He said that he was having a weekend celebration. Most of his people in the corporate offices would be there for a fun week, and this weekend is to be the grand finale. I thought to myself yeah, right." Patti closed her eyes for a moment then looked at John.

"Here's the lie. I told Mr. Marshall I was on the island with my fiancé, and I couldn't come. He called my bluff and invited my boyfriend as he put it to come along with me. John, I know you can't lie yourself out of a lie, but would you go with me and pretend to be my fiancé?"

John could not believe it. Of course, he could not. If John Reed is one thing, it's a straight forward, no nonsense guy. A charade like this was certainly not John's style. He shook his head unknowingly and thought he could never do something so ridiculous.

Patti's big smile diminished. John saw a hint of disappointment in those big brown eyes, he nodded, stammered, and said, "Sure. I'll do it, why not?"

"Great!" Smiling again with spirits high, she reported, "We leave at four, Friday afternoon on a company plane that will meet us at a small airport that handles tour flights for small planes and helicopters. I have directions to the airport, but I can't remember the name."

"I bet I know which airport you are talking about. Let's say, I pick you up about two-thirty at the hotel."

"Then, it's a date?" Patti asked just to hear John's answer one more time.

"Yeah, it's a date."

The band members took their places as the pianist played her final tune. She finished her piece and stood taking a bow to sparse applause. A skinny man in a white double-breasted dinner jacket took her place. He began playing softly as the other band members readied themselves to play. There was a brief pause in the music when the waiter returned with Patti's salad. He was placing her plate on the table when the music started. They played the original "Tonight Show" theme. Patti's back was to the band, and the abrupt sound of the band's first note surprised her. Patti jumped. "That caught me off guard," she admitted as she turned to see the band playing.

"Why don't we move around one chair to the right so both of us can see the stage?"

Patti stood, and before John could do anything to change the table, a bus boy was motioned by the waiter to help. Then the waiter and his helper pulled back the chairs and lifted the table turning it a quarter round, without moving anything. He had quickly solved the problem. John helped Patti with her chair as the bandleader spoke, and the band played at a subdued level.

"We hope you enjoy your visit to The Night Club tonight. We will play a mix of lovely songs, some you've loved in the past and maybe some songs you fell in love listening to. If this is the first time for you to hear these wonderful melodies, then I must warn you. They are still as enchanting today as they were when they were heard for the first time. Sit back, enjoy

33

your meal, and let us entertain you." He turned back to the band. They instantly picked up the beat and the volume. Then the conductor led the theme song to its signature ending. The bandleader started the music with an old melody.

The rest of the meal was placed on the table. The waiter made sure everything was right before excusing himself.

John asked Patti, "Do you know the name of that song?"

Patti listened for several bars. "Yes, I know the tune, but I can't say I know the title." She started to cut her steak, and then she looked up at John. He was doing the same. Patti stopped eating. John looked at her, and he paused too.

She asked, "Well, what's the name?"

"I don't know. I recognized the tune too, and that is the reason I asked you."

They continued talking through the show. When one or the other knew a song, he or she would quickly name the tune before the other could guess. The sax started to play a tune when John and Patti at the same instant said, "In the Mood." They laughed, and Patti admitted that she was not one hundred percent sure that was the right name for that piece of music. They both knew that some of the songs could not have had the names they labeled them, but who could question the counterfeit name.

"Have you seen any of the other islands so far?" John asked.

She sighed, "No, I would like to get this contract signed, and then I could relax and enjoy the sun, the beach, and some sights. I love some of the nightspots, but I am going to be angry if I go back to Chicago, and everyone there has as much of a tan as I do. I'll have to go by one of those salons that spray on tans. This weekend is work related for me. I'm told not to expect to do anything but have fun. Now how are you supposed to have fun and focus on work? I'm not against having fun. Well, what I'm trying to say is, I need to get this project sealed first."

There had been one or two couples dancing, but this new song seemed to pump up the people sitting near the dance floor. They may have finished their meals, or they could not pass up a song for which they had been waiting. They all gravitated to the dance floor simultaneously. All the men were dressed in tuxes, and the ladies in formal gowns. John watched Patti as she watched the couples dance through the song, and when it finished, all the couples stopped and applauded. As a few made their way back to their table, and other couples that ventured onto the floor waited for another song. John couldn't help remembering what Nick said, "There are always babes waiting for someone to dance with."

John said a silent prayer, "Please, God, don't let her say she wants to dance."

Patti turned to John, "I love to dance."

John waiting and thought the best thing was to keep quiet. He thought maybe I could say something to get her mind off of dancing. He could ask her if she had been to the beach. He could tell Patti was beginning to tan; she must have found some time to lounge in the sun. Then he remembered a view, "After the show, I would like to show you a place that's near here; it's one of my favorite places on the island."

She turned to John and said excitedly, "I'm ready when you are."

"Well, let's go."

John asked for the check; they argued over who would pay. John was handed the folder with the dinner bill. He left cash instead of a credit card so he would not have to wait for the return. He felt good buying Patti's meal. She took his arm as they walked up the stairway, across the balcony, and out the door to a gorgeous night. They could see every star in the sky. John unlocked the Jeep and opened the door for Patti. He heard the door lock pop as he was making his way around the Jeep. He opened the door and slid in behind the wheel.

"Thanks."

"For what?"

"For unlocking my door for me, I don't like using the keys. I drive a truck most of the time to and from work, and it has keyless entry. This is my sister's Jeep, and she has everything on it one could want, even satellite radio and a navigation system with a DVD player. Many things I would like to have. Why she doesn't have keyless entry is beyond me.

"She has a remote."

"Why do you say that?"

John pulled the seat belt and buckled up in the same motion as he turned the ignition. He pulled from the curb and started to their destination.

"Look, this is a sensor." Pointing to a button like item on the dashboard. "I bet she has a set of keys at home with a remote fob for this vehicle."

"I'm impressed. How do your know so much about cars?"

"I have always had a love for automobiles. My dad and I like to window shop for different cars, and we try to make every car show that comes to our area. Plus, I have a key on a nice chain similar to what you have just to give to the detail shop when I have my car detailed. Also, if I go somewhere valet parking is available they get the single key. My guess is your sister has probably done the same. Men don't think about little securities that give women piece of mind. She must be a smart girl to convince a top-notch architect to come all the way from Mississippi, even if he is her brother."

What a rush of adrenalin for Patti to say something like that. John is one of those drivers, if he's going to the store two blocks away for a paper, he's one who wants to get there and back as quickly as possible. Even if the trip was made for relaxation, he would hurry, but not tonight. Tonight was different. He was waiting for cars that he would normally pass and speed away from. Instead of weaving in and out of the traffic, he got in the right lane and was content to stay there letting other drivers take their turn zigzagging around cars. It was a short drive from the busy section of town to the two-lane road they would travel to get to their destination. The further away from town they got, the backdrop of stars seemed to be more plentiful and bright. John never knew why anyone needed a sunroof until this very moment.

When Patti looked up at the starry sky, she said in a soft voice, "I've never seen so many stars before. They are so brilliant we could drive without lights." She turned on the radio that was set to a golden oldies station with mostly rock and pop music from the 60's and 70's. Patti looked at John and asked, "You don't mind if I turn on the radio, do you? I like to listen to music when I drive."

"No, not at all. What kind of music do you like?"

"I'm a connoisseur of music. I like all kinds. Classical, rock, opera, and I like some country music. It depends on what kind of mood I'm in and what artist. I see you like the old stuff." Meddling through the CD's in the console, "Let's see, we have a Peter Framton, Boston. Ah, the Beatles, good one Rubber Soul, Steppenwolf and Botti. Chris Botti, you like Chris Botti? I like Chris Botti, but looking at this collection of CD's, it comes as a little surprise that you do."

"Now, remember, this is my sister's car and CD's. I do like Chris Botti. I really enjoy good music when I'm working, or trying to unwind, or read. Music without lyrics is calming. Don't you think?"

"Oh, yes, I agree. Nothing is more pure than a single instrument playing with a light backdrop of the right accompaniment. Do you work when you drive?"

"I do some of my best driving when, I mean thinking when I drive."

She laughed at his mistake. "I hope you do your best driving too."

"I like different kinds of music. I must admit I do prefer the old stuff."

"Oh, you like classical too?" She laughed again at John.

"Yes, some, but I wasn't referring to that old of music. My favorite is the old rock and roll stuff. The depth of music is better, richer sounding. I guess what I'm trying to say is the music sounds like real instruments."

The next song on the radio was an old song cut by a female artist. She had a sensual voice that added a new twist to a great old song. "You're just too good to be true, can't take my eyes off of you. You'd be like heaven to touch I want to hold you so much. At long last love has arrived, I thank God I'm alive."

The song played. They listened, and John drove on to the spot he found a few days ago. It was about the same time of night but not nearly as radiant as this night. John was driving to kill time when he found this little site. The bay was visible long before John pulled the car off of the road and stopped at an overlook. He placed the transmission in park. They were the only two present.

Neither said a word for several minutes. It was the first time Patti had been quiet since they met. The bay was aglow with the reflection of a disfigured moon. The moon appeared to be emerging from the ocean. The top was peaking out in the distant horizon as this huge orange sphere quickly pulled itself from the depths. The top half of the ball was spherical, but the bottom part was flawed. Then, in what seemed only a few seconds, it was two moons glimmering. One hovered above the other, brighter, clearer and almost perfect in shape. The bottom moon, not as bright, had a tail that reached into the bay. Patti and John were on an overlook, a small peak that jetted out from the road. The hillside that sloped down to the valley of water below was visible. This picture of rocks, flowers, and overgrowth that clung to the steep earth was distinguishable, but gave somewhat of a negative effect. The hues of this portrait were grayish, a subtle color with a silver-tone, only a hint of what would be there in the bright sunlight, only this portrait had to be better because it was live. Patti opened the door and stepped out of the car. She walked to the edge of the overlook. John went to the back of the Jeep where he reached in for a windbreaker for Patti. John walked up behind her and placed it on her shoulders.

Patti never taking her eyes off the view broke the silence, "This is a lovely view. There are so many beautiful sights in this world, and I have been amazed at many, but this view rates with the best. Did you know there would be a full moon tonight?"

"No, honestly, it never occurred to me."

Walking back to the front of the Jeep, they leaned back on the grill. It was nice to feel the warmth of the engine on the cool night. John stood with Patti and enjoyed the panorama of the night. He thought of how he enjoyed this view a few days ago, but not like tonight. He never noticed the moon a few nights ago. John thought he would never be able to enjoy something this magnificent alone again. Would he always think of Patti?

"Would you like to live here, John?"

"I'm not sure. I like my work, and I like the setup I have at home. This place does have a way of growing on you. I live in the country and work in Madison. I commute everyday to work. The island life is special. It's captivating, and I'm glad I decided to do this job for my sister so I could have this time to see what living here is like. The island never seems to have a cycle I'm told. The weather is pretty much the same year round. I like the green vegetation and flowers, but I don't know about living here. I've heard that people get a bit island crazy sometimes. What about you? Would you like to live here?"

Without a moment of hesitation she said, "I would love to live here. I didn't really think about it until I saw this picture. I love this place. Thank you for bringing me here."

"It was my pleasure. Do you have to work tomorrow?"

"Yes, but I don't have to be there until two. I have to meet with a technical team. What about you?"

"I have a busy day tomorrow. It's one of the more fun things to do. I'm buying the fixtures for Sis's kitchen so the builders can finish that part of the house. It will start moving in the right direction in a few days. We can't, or I don't want to start any of the others projects until we finish the first phase of the house. Would you like to see her house sometime?"

"Sure! How far is it from here?" "It's only about ten minutes."

"What about tonight? No better time than now."

This excited John. It meant more time with Patti. He opened the door for her and almost ran around the Jeep.

CHAPTER 6

John explained as they drove, "Susan refers to their house as in the mountains. I guess it's as close to what you would call the mountains here. It's kind of funny that neither of us has ever really liked the beach, and now she lives on an island." John turned off the main road onto a paved curvy county road. Then one more turn down a street and then into Jeff and Susan's drive. The front of the house looked normal except for a covered trailer and lumber that sat at the driveway next to the garage. John and Patti used the circle drive to the front entrance. There was a soft dull glow from the accent lighting that outlined the walkway to the front door the much brighter light was now about to clear the treetops. There was more than enough light to find the door and the right key. John opened the door and switched on the light for the inside of the room. He held the door as Patti stepped cautiously into the house. Now there was plenty of evidence of construction. The foyer or landing was level with the small porch and a nice area large enough to greet guests. Two steps down and to the left of the landing was the great room in the middle of creation. At the end of the landing, were two steps up and to the right that led to the bedrooms. John walked across the floor of the great room to switch on all the lights. He turned to address Patti who was standing on the landing.

"I know this is all a mess. Can you imagine living here with all of this chaos going on? Yet, it's perfect for me. If I need to change something, I walk from the bedroom to the worksite. We are going to finish the living area before we start on the upstairs rooms. We will make structural changes in only one bedroom, doing away with it to make two bathrooms for the adjoining bedrooms. That way every bedroom will have a private bath. I feel if the budget can stand it, every bedroom should have its own bathroom. The rest of the changes will be cosmetic, with some extras in the master suite."

Patti stepped down to join John. The smell of sawdust and paint filled the room. John continued, "I would have liked starting and completing the bedrooms first, but the need to change the main room caused us to begin here instead. This large space where we are standing was several different rooms. We began by changing the roofline on the back of the house to widen the room. After that, bracing in the attic had to be altered, and then all the interior walls had to come out."

John described in detail what the construction crew had accomplished. He depicted the most intricate details, the type of insulation and the type of glass in the windows. He realized everything he had been describing might be of little interest to Patti, and he stopped.

"Forgive me, Patti. You don't want to hear about boring characteristics. If you will permit me to start again," John walked to the middle of the room. "This room is the heart of this home. My sister loves to be with her family and friends, so we have opened this entire space for the simple purpose of interactive living. This open area where we are standing will be a combination of living, dining, and kitchen. Sis loves to cook and entertain." John directed Patti to take the short tour, "We were very lucky that our existing ceiling height was twelve feet in this part of the house. This gave me the opportunity to change floor levels to make different zones. The kitchen will be my favorite part of this living area. I like to cook and visit with my guests at the same time. I guess I like to have my company watch me cook. Maybe I could get a job on a cooking show one day. The next step is installing the cabinets, and then I'll have all the built-in appliances delivered and installed. The granite is black with gold and brown inflections. This entire end of the room will be the kitchen. I have integrated every new gadget I could fit into the space we have to work." John walked to a window, "There will be cabinets starting on this side of the window." He tapped his foot on a caulk line, "From here to the corner, then to the opposite corner will be cabinets and built-ins. I've marked where each cabinet and appliance will sit, by width, and depth and height because all the cabinets are being custom built. When they are delivered and set in place if one, by chance, is wrong, we will know then; otherwise we would find out the hard way. When the appliances are delivered, the cabinet installers should only take a couple of days to place the finished product. They will also help complete the placement of all the built-ins."

John used his hands, his feet, and his heart to show and describe his work. Patti, very intrigued with John's information, smiled at how a quiet man placed in the comfort of his element transformed himself into this extraverted designer. He paused as he walked across the floor to the outside wall.

Patti asked, "John, could you show me to the ladies room?"

"Sure, Patti. I'm sorry I haven't been a very good host. Go to the foyer and down the hall; it's the first door on your left."

When Patti returned John was somewhat calmer. He finished the tour very quickly. "The outer surface around the pool will have a new look, but outside of extending the roofline, that's the tour for now."

Patti, realizing the tour was accelerated, noticed a good portion of the wall to their right was torn out.

"What's happening over there?"

"Well, that part of the house is the bed and bath areas." John led Patti to the courtyard and continued with the visit. "We are adding a bay window in the master bath. A garden tub, overlooking the garden and pool area will set inside the window. The neat thing about the window is that it will have an electric sensor that changes the glass from clear for the view, to a frost for privacy with a flip of a switch. I think I mentioned earlier we are doing away with one bedroom to enlarge two bedrooms giving each their own bath. Well, we are using some space in the master suite also."

Patti raised her hand to stop and ask a question. "You said a sensor to switch the window in the bath area from frost to clear. If the electricity is off, is the window clear or frosted?"

John thought for a moment and a bit stunned from the question. "Patti, I don't know the answer to that. My guess, the electricity would provide the frost; I just don't know."

They walked back to the inside. "I don't know if it was by the original design, around the pool has plenty of sunlight from mid-morning to late afternoon, but the family room doesn't get direct sun any part of the day. When I realized this, it made sense to have all the doors across the back of this room. I wanted the people in this room to feel they are poolside even if they are sitting reading a book. At first, it didn't feel right with all the open space. This is what Susan wanted, and I must admit I like it more every day."

"Well, I love it. I wish I could be here when you finish. I would love to see that window when it is installed."

In all the years of working in all the houses he had completed, John never before felt the satisfaction he was feeling standing before Patti. Her approval was most satisfying. All she said was, "I love it." It was all John needed.

"John, what time is it anyway?"

"It's ten minutes till twelve."

"I probably need to get back to the hotel. I do have to work tomorrow. This has been so much fun."

They drove back to the hotel; the moon that shone so bright a short time ago now had an occasional cloud with which to contend. They stopped for a moment at the overlook. Heavy clouds covered the view of the moon. Yet, they could see the reflection of the moon bouncing around in the ocean. Even with the clouds, there was plenty of light. John walked Patti to the hotel lobby and then returned to the Jeep. It hit him again, the loneliness. John had known this feeling before. As he drove home, his mind was full of Patti Scanlon. His drive back home took less than half the time it took to drive Patti to the hotel. He started undressing and noticed the answering machine had messages. He walked over and started the machine. He walked away and continued to undress. The first message was from Susan.

"Hi, John, will call back later. Hope things are going well."

Second message, "Me again, what's going on? Is it something with the house? Are you dating? I've sent emails with no reply. I texted with no reply, and now I phone my home with no answer. If I haven't heard from you by morning, I'm calling the hospitals."

John knew Susan had the contractor's phone number as he waited for the next message. It was another familiar voice, "John, some guy called today, ah, this is Gus. The granite will not be ready until the end of next week. He said he told you this week. Ah, I called the cabinet-maker to let him know we are ready when he is, and he said he could start as soon as you give him the word. I didn't give him the go ahead, but I think we are ready. If you will inspect the kitchen, then call if everything is okay. Remember, I don't plan to be back to the house until Monday unless I hear from you. See you Monday."

"Great! I didn't have time for all this anyway." John, making a note to call for cabinets on Monday, stopped when the fourth and last message played.

"John, this is Patti. I had a wonderful time tonight. I forgot to thank you for dinner; also for the friendship you have shown me, and your willingness to help a stranger with a big problem. I didn't have your cell number, so I looked up your sister's number. See you Friday if not sooner. Bye."

John mumbled, "I know I'm setting myself up for something which I'm not accustomed. The truth is I don't care. Maybe she is only here for a few days. Maybe I won't be able to get over her, but I like the way she makes me feel. How can I deal with something I can't control? I'll just take what time I can have with her and that will have to do. I'll be happy to be with her for as long as I can. At least, I won't have to deal with the builder tomorrow. I can get my running around done and be ready for Friday."

John couldn't sleep. He kept seeing Patti, gazing at the ocean in the moonlight. He did everything possible not to think of her, but how could he get her off his mind. He tossed and turned. There was no use. He gave up, got out of bed, and went to the drafting table. He started to work on the patio and pool area, but he sat holding his pencil not concentrating on the plans. Nothing would work the way he wanted it on paper. The basic plans were in front of him. He knew what he wanted, he told Patti only a few moments ago all he wanted to do. Now his pencil wouldn't work. His mind was on the next day. He switched on the TV and returned to bed. He went through all the channels several times. Really the only good thing about having sixty-four channels is that it gives a person something to do. Frustrated, he switched off the set with the remote and tried to rest. Then he thought if I can't get her off of my mind, I will do the opposite: I'll try to think about her.

CHAPTER 7

Patti Scanlon was the third child born to Elizabeth and Patrick James Scanlon. Patrick's family was the definition of success. They always seemed to have the Midas touch. Even through the Great Depression, Patrick's father prospered in the wholesale grocery business. Patrick, not wanting to fall into a position with the family business, set out to find his own niche in the world. He jumped into the computer business mainly because he was fascinated with this new tool. His curiosity paid large dividends although he attributed his success as being in the right place at the right time.

Patrick's sister, Anna, went to Broadmoor a private girl's school. It was a privilege to go to Broadmoor and all students had to apply for admission. Only the best and brightest attended Broadmoor. Invitations were extended to Alumni, but even their children had to be chosen each year. For a child to begin her education at Broadmoor was certainly an honor. Many children stayed on a waiting list sometimes for years to have the chance to fill a vacancy in a class. Anna's dearest friend was Elizabeth Noble, and these two shy little girls bonded their first day of school. Patrick met Elizabeth through this friendship of Anna and Elizabeth's.

Patti and her older sisters attended Broadmoor. Patti broke tradition after prep school by attending college at the University of Illinois instead of the family heritage of attending DePaul. Patti could have chosen anywhere in the world to study, but her desire was to experience going away to school, and to have the feeling of leaving home, without being that far away from family.

Family events were very important to Patti. She had two sisters; both were named after each parent's mother. There was thirteen months difference in Patti's sisters' ages. Christine was the oldest, then Emily, and Patti who was four years younger than Emily. Patti was clearly her father's pet although Patrick loved all his girls. He and Patti seemed to love all the same things.

Patti graduated business school with honors. After finishing her MBA, she landed a job with OMC, short for Opportunity Manufacturing Company Incorporated. The company bought factories that made quality products but were in financial trouble. Then OMC dropped anything that was not profitable. Each venture started with the focus on quality and efficiency first, then quantity and growth. This made OMC strong and diverse. The local communities were helped with industry providing jobs and in return, OMC received tax incentives. From textiles to micro-circuitry, OMC maintained superior products, competitive pricing and high morale with employees. Patti was intrigued with the company's concept. Patti did not have to look for work. She could have plugged into her father's company in any number of positions. Not Patti, no she was too much like her father. She felt she had to be successful on her own before she could work for her father. If Patti had been born a boy, her name would have been Patrick James Scanlon III. This name had been chosen for the first male child. When this new baby was presented to her father, Elizabeth Scanlon holding her said to Patti's father, "Patrick, I'm sorry she wasn't a boy, but she's just like you."

Patrick took his daughter's little hand and kissed his wife. "Elizabeth, can I name her Patrick anyway?"

"Well, she is a little Patrick, but I don't think she would like that name over time."

"I know! We'll name her Patti," spelling her name for Elizabeth.

"Patti, it's not much of a name, but it somehow suits her. What other name could we put with Patti?"

Patrick picked up his new daughter. "Nothing else, Patti is enough. She can be Patti Scanlon, and one day if she decides she wants to marry, she, of course, will keep the Scanlon name as her middle. Patti Scanlon Rockefeller. That has a good ring to it."

Patrick would tease Patti as she grew by telling her he intended to name her Patrick James Scanlon, III, but no one would let him. The idea of her father's name never upset Patti. She couldn't understand why she wasn't named what her father wanted.

Patti and her father did many different things together in which the other family members seemed uninterested. Patrick enjoyed cars, and he seldom kept any car for a long period of time. He was always buying one, but he never wanted to collect them because he detested collections. His idea, why have a bunch of anything he would never sell. Patti soon developed this love for automobiles. Patrick would take her to see a new model or maybe a classic that had special intrinsic worth. Then the two would talk and research the car. The most fun was the test drive. Although they didn't buy all they test drove, they were always truly attracted to the vehicle. They spent weeks looking for her first car. Patrick had the most input because it had to be safe. Patti dreamed of a red Corvette, but settled for her father's choice a Mercedes C-230 sedan. Patti loved it, although she was disappointed about the Corvette.

Patti was assertive and a very able salesperson. Her poised, confident attitude was never arrogant. She would have fit perfectly in her father's corporation, but she wanted to find a job on her own merit and succeed or fail on her own. This attribute ran throughout the Scanlon family and the main reason for their success. Grabbing the bull by the horns was not only to hang on and ride, but it was also the only way to maneuver the bull in the right direction.

Elizabeth Scanlon never liked her daughter's profession and she didn't hide her feelings. Patti traveled with OMC extensively and her mother didn't approve. Elizabeth loved being a housewife and mother and she didn't necessarily think a woman's place was in the home, but she never liked the travel obligation Patti had with her company. Elizabeth had made her misgiving known to Patrick and Patti, when Patti was offered this employment. Patti's impending wedding was giving Elizabeth the opportunity each time she and Patti talked about wedding plans to urge her to look for different employment. Elizabeth knew not to press hard; she referred to Patti as being independent since age five.

Patti was engaged to Ronald William Stockwell. Ronald was an off and on boyfriend all through high school. Patti and Ronald grew up in the same neighborhood, and their families were great friends. Everyone who knew Patti and Ronald thought they looked good together and were a perfect match.

Ronald's family was a big part of the Chicago society scene, and he felt his importance. His father owned one of Chicago's oldest ad agencies. Ronald, who was not ashamed of good fortune, had an elevated position in the company provided by his father. He never worked at his skills as an advertiser; he was content with the job of entertaining clients. He was a handsome young man in charge of a communications department running over with exceptionally talented people to do the bulk of work, while he enjoyed all the benefits.

Patti on the other hand was competitive in sports, games, and work. She loved to ice skate and play tennis. She also appreciated cars, opera, and ballet, yet she had the personality of a tour guide at a theme park. She was pretty enough to be a fashion model. Patti made sales all along, but she never called her dad unless it was something unusual. She loved to see his delight, or hear the tone of his voice when she told him of her accomplishments. She knew his look of pride, and she also had the memory of his expression in disappointment.

When Patti was in the ninth grade some of her friends were at her house for a visit one fall afternoon. They were in the basement of Patti's home listening to music and talking about everything from makeup to guys when one of the girls, Carmen Warner started passing around cigarettes to everyone. When she got to Patti, Patti shook her head and held her hand up to say no.

"No, I don't think I should take one. I have never smoked."

Carmen looked at Patti, with one hand on her hip and the other hand holding the pack of cigarettes in Patti's face. "How will you know if you like them or not if you don't take one and try it?"

Patti reluctantly took one and played with it trying to pass the time by holding the cigarette. All of the girls lit up as soon as they received their gift. The girls turned their attention to Patti who was contemplating her dilemma. After some prodding from each person, she looked hard at the cigarette, feeling the pressure from her friends, placed it in her mouth, and lit the darn thing. Patti, careful not to inhale, had just mastered the technique of puffing when her father walked down the stairs. Her father was never home this hour of the day. In fact, no one was supposed to be home that afternoon. She, holding the cigarette between her fingers like all her friends, was sitting in her dad's favorite chair, with her right leg across the arm of the old leather club chair. The stereo was playing louder than normal; the girls were laughing and talking all at the same time. No one heard Patrick open the door to the basement and no one saw him until he was halfway down the stairway. Patrick didn't smell the smoke until he was in sight, and everyone knew his presence. He paused midway of the stairs. His eyes and Patti's locked. She was frozen; everyone was silent. The only sound now was coming from the stereo that seemed to get louder. The only movement was from the cigarette smoke drifting upward. Patti's father stood there for what seemed to her like an eternity. Then, without a word, he turned and walked up the stairway at the same pace he walked down. Patti got out of the chair and picked up an ashtray. She placed her transgression in the ashtray and tapped it in the dish until the smoke was gone. She held the ashtray in her lap as she sat down hard in her father's chair with her head bowed in silence and shame.

Mary Margaret Chadwick nervously said, "We had better go. Can I call my mom, Patti?"

"Sure, go ahead." Patti in a trance-like state continued twisting and turning the cigarette in the ashtray as she pressed the two objects firmly together tearing apart the paper leaving nothing but the residue of tobacco and a stained filter.

Almost in a cry Mary Margaret turned from the phone without dialing, "I need to pee first," and she ran to the bathroom.

In just a few seconds, the room transformed from a room of independence and exploration into a room of chaos and fear. All the girls moved around nervously straightening and cleaning up, everyone except Patti. Dazed she remained in the big chair.

Carmen sat beside Patti in her chair and with a sympathetic voice, "Patti, I'm sorry, I wish I had not gotten you into trouble. My parents both smoke, so they will never notice the smell on me. Do you think your father might speak to them about this?"

"I don't know."

Carmen took the ashtray from Patti, she went around the room and very meticulously took the evidence from all the others and dumping the contents in her purse that she had hung over her shoulder, like this would erase all that had taken place in the last few moments.

Patti looked at her friends, "It's not your fault, I didn't think. I doubt that Dad noticed any of you. I don't think he saw anyone but me. After all, I would be in just as much trouble for letting you smoke as smoking myself."

"Patti, I want you to know we would never have thought of smoking here except we thought we were alone." Carmen, feeling their misfortune passed out mints to all the girls. She offered Patti one. She shook her head, no to the mint. Mary Margaret took one before she called her mom. They all followed suit with the telephone. They left the sinking ship with only the captain to do the honorable thing and go down alone with her vessel. After all, Patti didn't need a mint; she was already busted. Sure, she could taste the bitterness, but what was the point. She saw the hurt in her father's face, and she felt she could never face him again. She walked all the girls to the front of the house and waited as one by one all rides came for each girl. Hugs and encouraging words were offered to Patti, and every departing girl thought this might be Patti's last goodbye. As the last car left the drive, Patti made the long journey to her bedroom. It took enormous effort to walk up the stairs to her room. Because of the strange quiet in the house, she could hear every step as she made her way down the hall. Patti brushed her teeth and then gargled. She felt dirty, and a bath might help her feelings.

Patti knew that somehow she could make it up to her father, but first she had to make things right. Her dirty clothes only reminded her of the afternoon failure, and the scent made her queasy. She bathed, dressed and deposited the dirty clothes in the hamper. She thought I hope Mom doesn't smell this odor. Perhaps it was the meeting she had to make that caused her discomfort.

As Patti walked down the hall to her father's study, she could hear voices coming from the kitchen. This meant her mother and sisters were home. Would her father ever believe this was her first time? That really wouldn't matter. Would he ever trust her again, and that did matter. She was sure of one thing, her father was fair. After all, whatever the punishment would be, she knew she deserved it. That thought of fairness almost made her feel better. With her hands shaking, she knocked on the door. She was going to be brave and strong, admit her guilt, and ask for forgiveness.

"Come in, Patti." Patrick called from inside the study.

Oh, no! She thought. He's been waiting for me. How did he know who would be at the door? She turned the knob slowly, and just as slowly opened the door. Her father was standing, looking out of the window. With most of the room's light coming from the outside, her father's frame appeared as a silhouette. There was a lamp on his desk giving off only a shadow of light. Patti felt like she was in an interrogation room with a detective.

"Sit down, Patti." Her father said in his usual calm voice.

This large room had always been Patti's favorite one in their home. The wall behind her father's massive desk was covered with books. There were two dark brown leather wing chairs facing the desk, a table with a lamp sitting next to a huge black leather chair and ottoman by the window where Patrick stood. On the wall next to the entrance was a collage of old family pictures. Under the group of pictures, a family portrait was resting on an antique bachelor's chest surrounded by some old toy trucks and cars from her father's childhood. Patti remembered the day they sat for the portrait, a much happier time. She could not remember how many times she had played with the toy cars on the rug that centered the area in front of the desk. Patti took the chair that was the fartherest distance away from her father. She wanted to say the first word, but nothing would come out.

"First time?" Patrick asked.

"Yes, sir, how could you tell?"

"I don't know. You looked crude with your motion, and well, I guess I wanted to know. Do you plan to keep smoking?"

"No, sir, never again!"

"Good," was all Patrick said as he walked over to the chair beside Patti. He turned the chair around to face Patti and sat. Patti's small frame shook as if she were cold, but she felt warm and totally uncomfortable. She was embarrassed and looked in the direction of the books more than at her father; but she could see his face.

"Patti, I'm glad of that decision, but I want to ask for your forgiveness."

At this statement she turned quickly to face her father. "For what, Dad?" Patti asked with a quiver in her voice and tears in her eyes.

"I should have already had this talk with you. I seemed to enjoy your sisters going through all these stages. I felt like I was ready for all their escapades and they grew faster than I wanted, but you, Patti. Well, you've grown up too fast. You're thirteen, and I am treating you like a baby."

She just turned fourteen, but she didn't feel this was the time to correct her father.

"Maybe that's how I look at you, like a baby I mean. Patti, I want to tell you right now, right this very day, you need to decide what kind of person you will become. I feel you need to have a goal in every aspect of your life, and especially for life itself. What you want to be at the time of your death could affect the longevity of your life and the quality of your life. I could tell you to choose your friends better, but you will always have friends that are different than you are. Your life is not your friends'; it is yours. Always be sure when things come up, like smoking that it's something you want to do, and you are willing to accept the consequences. Not that I will allow it while you are in this house, but a person can find a way to do most anything he or she wants to do. I want you to realize that the choices you make are your choices no matter who entices you. This time it's a cigarette. Next time, it might be, let's see how fast a car will go. If you have your goals set, and your choices made in advance, then there is very little anyone can do to sway you into a decision you don't want to make." Patrick paused then asked, "Do you understand what I'm saying, Patti?"

"Yes, I think so. How do I set these goals, Dad?"

"I hope with the values your mother and I have shown you girls."

"Have I let you down, Dad?"

"No, Patti, you haven't let me down. I feel like smoking is wrong not only for you, but also for your friends. I would never permit you to smoke, and I wish you would always make the right decisions, but you don't think for a moment I haven't tried things in my life. For me, it was a cigar your Uncle Frank confiscated from our Uncle Joseph who was visiting at the time. Joseph was a traveler and when he came home, he always stayed with us. He never married although I know he lived with a woman for some time in Miami." Patrick stopped for a moment. He could not believe he made or admitted to his daughter that last statement. "Now, when I say traveler, I mean, he was on his way somewhere even when he came to visit us. I think he came home not only to visit, but also to reminisce with his family. Then he would be off again. Frank got the cigars somehow. Knowing Uncle Joseph, he might have given them to him just to try. Anyway we had them, and we couldn't wait to try them, so we went for a walk. Big old Cuban cigars, green and big around as a quarter, so big we had trouble lighting them. I would take big puffs in rapid succession, pulling the smoke into my mouth. When I got it burning good, I started taking slow long pulls on the thing, trying to blow a smoke ring. I must admit that as the smoke filled my mouth, the taste was kind of good. We were walking, smoking, talking, and having a real fine time. You know how much I love Frank, and I always wanted to be like him. He treated me like his equal even though there were four years difference in our age. I always felt he wanted me around. Just why he wanted to include me in this pleasure I can't say. Oh, well, anyway, I kept up with Frank, puff for puff. We were talking about Uncle Joseph as we walked down the trail behind our childhood home. Then in an instance, I was blind-sided. That old cigar hit me with a full load. I was as green as that old smoke. I went from the top of the world to the depths of hell itself, and I knew what caused the swing. I tossed that cigar down, and I started to breathe in the cool fresh air as fast as I could. Nothing I did seemed to help. I got so dizzy I had to lie down. Never had the cold ground felt so good. Funny just talking about it I can still feel that sick, nauseating feeling. My head felt as if it weighed fifty pounds, and my neck was made of rubber. Frank didn't laugh at me, but he did laugh at my predicament. I think he couldn't help being amused at my discomfort. I can hear him now, 'You'll get better at this.' Talking to me, he leaned back against a tree and continued to smoke his cigar. Frank stayed with me until I was able to walk again. He never told anyone or made fun of me, but I never wanted another cigar. Maybe that's why he gave it to me. He has always looked after my good. It was a long time before I could stay in a room with someone smoking one."

Patti laughed nervously at the thought of her father doing something like that. It was hard for her to imagine he was ever a child.

"Now, run along; it's time for dinner; and Patti, let's not mention this to your mother."

"Don't worry! I won't!" She gave Patrick what he called an ever-hug.

He watched as Patti closed the door. The door opened slowly, and she peeked back into the room. "I love you, Dad."

"I love you too, Sweetheart."

CHAPTER 8

John sat up in bed alarmed by the clock radio, which was set to a talk station. He glanced at the numbers shining 6:32. He switched off the radio and quickly showered. Hurriedly walking to the Jeep, John was still dressing as he closed the front door. He kept watching the speedometer as he drove toward the hotel. His eagerness to reach his destination kept his speed above normal. He pulled into a parking space across from the steps that led to the garden terrace where he hoped to meet his breakfast companion. He changed his brisk walk the last few steps into a more calm pace not wanting to look anxious. Before he went through the buffet line, John looked for Patti. She was not at their table. Disappointed, he got his breakfast, a paper, and sat at the new favorite table. He remembered Patti's day was to be one of leisure, so he reasoned she was probably sleeping. He started to eat as he looked through the paper. An article on a housing slowdown caught John's attention.

"Mind if I join you?"

John, surprised, looked up and stood to help Patti with her chair, John asked, "Would you like any breakfast?" She was wearing a short white hooded terry cloth cover-up, but she didn't have the hood over her head. She also wore huge white sunglasses with mirrored lenses. As cute as she was, John felt disappointed at missing the opportunity of looking into those big brown eyes.

"I knew you would be here, and yes, I would like some breakfast."

"Would you like to order or go through the buffet?"

"I'll go to the buffet. It's really too good to try anything else."

"My feelings exactly."

Patti walked to the end of the line ready to select her food. John watched as she inspected every morsel. She was so cute! At first John thought she wore a long skirt, but when she moved her long legs around the buffet line, John noticed she wore pants. She slipped around the table as she placed her food precisely on her plate. She turned to the table. Her smile brightened when she saw John was watching. It was no use trying; he couldn't hide his feelings. Patti was probably too preoccupied to notice or care, but he couldn't lie to himself any longer. The simple truth, John Reed was in love for the first time in his life. Returning to the table, she gasped as she settled in the chair with John's help.

"Oh my, did I ever die last night. We are still on for this weekend, aren't we? You haven't changed your mind since last night?"

"Yes! I mean no."

Patti puzzled, looked up at John.

"I mean, no, I haven't changed my mind, and yes, we are on for this weekend. I wouldn't miss it for the world."

"I want to thank you again, John. I just couldn't go without someone with me. I can handle guys like that in the office or on neutral territory. I wouldn't put myself in a situation like he proposed. I'm not sure there is a weekend function. What if I go to his island, and I was his only guest. When I told him my fiancé was with me, he didn't blink. He quickly said, 'Okay, bring him along. It's a family get together.' Then, I saw that look like he didn't believe me, and why should he? I'm a terrible liar. Anyway I'm sure he thought he would call my bluff."

John listened to Patti's confession and he could see she hated that she had lied to Jack Marshall. At the same time, he watched her eat and wondered how someone as small as Patti could eat as much as she did.

"I must admit he's different than he was in Chicago. At our first meeting, Marshall made several inappropriate advances toward me and that's why I'm on guard. Here, he is more, well, a perfect gentleman; yet I still think he is up to something. John, don't you want to take a day off and go to the beach?"

At this point, there was nothing John had rather do. He declined with an explanation. "I have to get numerous things lined up for next week and I'll have to get this done before Friday."

"By all means, then go. Can I help you in any way?"

"No, I have it under control, but you had better take the sun in moderation. The wind is cool, but the sun is hot."

"Don't worry," she held up a beach bag. "I have all kinds of oils with SPF's in this bag, and I intend to use all of them."

"Would you like to go out to dinner tonight?"

"I would love to. Can we make it early? I plan to eat a light lunch, so I'll be hungry."

"I don't see why not. What time would you like to eat?"

"Would five be too early?"

"That sounds fine. I'll pick you up here at five."

"Great! I'll be ready and in the lobby."

They finished breakfast, and John walked Patti to the spot where she would stake her claim for the day. The hotel had beach gear and towels for the guests. He carried a lounger for her, even though the hotel had a beach attendant. John arranged her chair so she would be comfortable. Patti removed her cover-up and started rubbing oil on her arms and legs. She stretched the lounger out flat.

"John? Would you think I was too forward if I asked you to rub some of the lotion on my back? I like to start and finish sunning on my back. It is more comfortable sitting or lounging the traditional way in a chair, and I tend to stay in that position too long, so this way I balance the time better."

John knew he looked surprised. Her light blue and white striped swimsuit was a one piece with a low cut back with a very modest leg cut.

Patti noticed John's face as she lay on the chair and asked, "Is there something wrong?"

"Oh, no! No, it's the suit. I was expecting something more revealing for a sunbather."

"I have a two piece suit, but I only wear it in private surroundings. You don't like my suit?"

"By all means, most definitely, I feel embarrassed for most of these girls out here." Nodding his head sideways to his left, as a couple of girls passed, "I can't see why anyone could feel comfortable in public in one of those swimsuits, you know why they wear the thongs or whatever they call them, don't you?"

"No. Why?"

"Marketing, some great advertiser has done one heck of a job selling those things. If you don't think so, wait until someone walks through wearing one that's not only skimpy, but is also too small. I always think, doesn't she have a mirror in her room? I feel they think they look like the girl on the billboard selling this lotion, or maybe that is why this lotion is so popular?"

Patti laughed, "You are wrong on the lotion." She took back the lotion from John. "This is great lotion. I never burn when I use it, and I love the smell. You are probably right though, with one correction. I think most girls see the girl on the billboard when they look in the mirror. My problem is I never like the statement my mirror makes."

John couldn't believe he was talking such nonsense. The smell of the lotion and the beach must have gone to his head. All of which was compelling him to stay. He thought about the guys that would be all over the waterfront, but his staying was not an option. Too many projects were ongoing and one task had to be completed before another could begin. John took the lotion from Patti. As he rubbed the lotion on her back, he noticed his hands were trembling. She was about five-foot-eight, slender; her suit fit her body like a glove. Making the swimsuit edition would never be a priority for Patti, but she was clearly the most attractive woman on the beach. John noticed a couple of young men talking and looking in their direction. They knew he was about to leave. Vultures waiting for the right time; John felt a bit jealous of the guys who had nothing to do but sit and gaze at her beauty. He placed the lotion by Patti, stood, and before he turned to leave, gave more parental-sounding advice.

"One more warning, watch this tropical sun. It's hotter than you think."

"Yes, Mother, I'll be careful."

John was careful not to get sand on her oiled body when he walked away. He mumbled to himself as he left, "Sand has always been the very thing I didn't like about the beach. Sand sticks like beggars lice on old blue jeans. You can't get it off." There was a shower for the beach goers, but a shower was out. John had to walk up several steps to the patio where they had breakfast. He kicked the sand from his shoes as soon as his foot touched the first step. He stomped on every step until he reached the top; from there, he turned to watch Patti for a moment before he left. She, knowing he would still be watching, looked toward John and waved goodbye. He waved, stomped his feet, and spoke aloud again.

"What's wrong with a little sand?" He then turned, walked across the patio, and then to the parking lot. As John drove to meet the carpenters, his thoughts were not on his sister's building project. No, his thoughts were back on the beach. He could see Patti trying to read and get some sun, and all the different men would be stopping to talk. This stayed on his mind so much he was compelled to return to the beach. What nonsense he thought. Feeling embarrassed, John leaned to his right, and in the rearview mirror, he could feel his own eyes speak to his subconscious as if the reflection in the mirror was using common sense, something he had forgotten in the last few days. You're acting like a ninth grader, trying to protect property that's not even yours, he reminded himself.

"She can't know my feelings?" He spoke aloud, "If she did, she would treat me like this Marshall putting me in a safe place. If she does know, then she would be toying with me? No, I think she enjoys my friendship."

He thought to himself, maybe she needs your friendship, John? I think she is so comfortable with me she becomes naïve.

He made a face to the mirror as he spoke, "That's awful. Nothing could be worse than her feeling comfortable with me! I know what's happening. I'm going through a mid-life crisis." He scolded himself as he adjusted the mirror parallel with the back glass so he couldn't see his eyes any longer. "It has to be I'm lonely. No, it is a mid-life crisis. It has to be. All I know is I wasn't having any type of crisis last week, but I do have to stop talking to myself."

Patti thought about John as she changed positions for more sun. He was a nice-looking and very pleasant person. He dresses nicely, maybe a little too traditional. She picked up a magazine and started flipping pages and looked for ads for men. I could help his wardrobe, she thought.

Chapter 9

The day went smoothly. Everything was lining up for completion of the kitchen. John scheduled two projects in the order he wanted for next week. The cabinets were to be on site Tuesday morning; the granite would be installed on Friday week. The flooring crew would come on Wednesday of the next week. The appliances were ready for delivery as soon as the flooring was complete. Only one thing was wrong. He was late. This upset him more each passing second. Taking off his shirt before he reached the front door, he entered the house. He omitted his normal progress check of the house but went straight to the bedroom. The machine had messages. Continuing to undress John ran by and started the machine as he picked out garments for the evening. The first message was from Susan.

"Where are you, John? I called Cheryl, our neighbor across the street from our house. She said that you have been keeping late hours. They hadn't seen you, but she assured me she would check on you. I'll call later, bye."

"Oh, great! I thought home was the only place in the world that people felt responsible to check on you."

He was walking into the bathroom when the next message stopped him dead in his tracks.

"John, this is Patti. When you get this, give me a call at the hotel room number 7158. I need to know how to dress, casual or dressy? Bye."

"I don't even know where I am taking her." John was in a panic.

"Think, John! What did you do with the address book Sis put together for a moment like this?" He started searching franticly in the desk drawers and then found the notebook in the nightstand. John sat on the bed turning to the section Susan left for restaurants. She had one circled Best

Cut with a note under the number that said, David Chappell, close friend, a great place to get a steak.

"Bless your heart, Sis; you're a sweetheart, always trying to make life easy for someone else." He dialed the number and waited for the answer.

"Hello, Best Cut. How can I help you?"

"Is David Chappell in?"

"May I ask who's calling?"

"Yes, this is John Reed. Tell him I'm Susan Thomas's brother."

"Sure, hold please."

David picked up the phone almost the same instance John was put on hold.

"Hello, David speaking, how may I help you?"

"Hi, David. This is Susan Thomas's brother, John Reed."

"How are Susan and Jeff doing? Aren't they in England?"

"They are fine, enjoying their stay. With the time difference, we seem to do a lot of phone tag with the answering machine as the go between for us."

"Wonderful gadgets aren't they? I can't imagine not having one."

"I know what you mean. David, I made a date for tonight and forgot to make any reservations. Susan left me a note to try your place."

"I'll be glad to take care of your reservation, John, what time?"

"Six."

"That won't be any problem. You can always get a table before seven."

"Great, now, where is your restaurant? I'll be coming from the Hilton that's located on Ocean Front Drive."

"John, you are in walking distance from the Hilton. You can come beachside, but I would suggest you go out the front of the hotel and walk to the right of the entrance. There you will notice a sidewalk that leads to a small park located between the hotel and an office building. Walk through the park, and you will come to a street, take the right. You'll be able to see us from there, and we are less than a block away. Look forward to meeting you."

"One last thing, how do we need to dress?"

"John, you are in a vacation spot. Dress casual, very casual, come anyway you want."

"Great! Thanks. See you around six." John immediately called the hotel.

"Room 7158 please."

"Hello."

"Hi, Patti. This is John."

"Hi, John. How was your day?"

"Busy. I might be running a bit late, but I should get there between five and five-thirty."

As much as he would like to talk, he quickly told her the dress for the evening. John hurriedly showered, shaved, and sprayed on cologne. He grabbed a white shirt and khaki pants.

"I forgot my deodorant!" he yelled and almost applied the deodorant to his shirt. "Calm down," he said in a more quiet voice as he jerked his shirttail out of the trousers. He placed his shirt neatly in again and reached into the closet for a favorite old sport jacket. When he turned on the main road, he looked at the face of the radio 5:12. His heart rate was above normal. He was sweating from the hot shower and the rush of dressing. Traffic was heavy all the way to the hotel. The news came on the radio as John turned into the parking lot in the back of the hotel. He ran up the familiar steps to the rear entrance of the hotel, still in a fast pace. He waited for the automatic sensor to open the glass doors. He hurried across the lobby to the elevators. He was ready to retrieve his ride, when the doors opened, and Patti placing her hands on both doors to hold the elevator in place stood in the entrance of the elevator.

"Going up anyone?"

"No, but if you are interested, I have a dinner reservation for two and need a date."

Patti stepped out of the elevator and looked at John with her chin pointing slightly down as she walked passed. His eyes were glued to her as he turned to see where she was going. Patti turned on her left foot and leaned back pulling her right foot in at the middle of the left and tilted her head back, just as if she were a high fashion model and she did look like one. Patti wore a black two-piece pants suit with a white-banded collar blouse. She held the bottom of the jacket and pulled each side back behind her. Even though a few people in the lobby took notice of the mini fashion show, Patti and John didn't notice anyone watching.

Patti spoke teasingly, "What luck. I had a date for five, and it looks like I've been stood up, and I'm famished."

"Well, too bad for that guy, but I'm available. What about you?" John asked as he walked toward her. He held out his arm, and Patti turned slightly as he approached. She took his arm in a fluid motion and walked with him out the front of the hotel. They walked through the park and to the restaurant. She never asked where they were going; she held his arm content to be led to their destination. John's tardiness was erased by the short distance to the restaurant. A friendly hostess escorted them to their table. The atmosphere was distinctly Southwestern. John helped Patti with her chair, and he took the seat opposite her.

John asked, "This is a bit unusual for the islands, don't you think?"

"Patti looked around, "I guess it is. I don't know. Why is it unusual?"

"I thought everyone's purpose in coming to the islands was to enjoy the island experience. This place could be in Texas."

Making conversation with Patti could not be easier. She never seemed to run out of questions. She wanted to know everything about Mississippi. It was hard to answer her questions because John wanted to listen to her talk.

"Tell me about your home, about Mississippi, John?"

"Walnut Grove is a neat little town. We're so small we don't even have a stop light."

Patti laughed, "Does this mean you never have to stop?"

"Well, no, I guess you don't, but you had better slow down because neither my mother nor any of her friends stop at any signs."

"I know it's hot in the south. I've made sales calls in many southern states. What's the weather like in Walnut Grove?"

"Well, it's hot and muggy all summer long, but dividends of fresh tomatoes, watermelons and vegetables make the sticky summer days bearable."

"Do you garden, John?"

"No. Not really. I have a couple of tomato plants outside my door that are cut out of an area of the landscaping. It works and doesn't look bad. Everyone does something like that back home. My mother and grandmother both have more gardens than our entire family needs. I find good things left in the refrigerator to cook when I get home from work. They are always cooking on the weekends and, of course, send me all the leftovers. I can't get enough vine-ripe tomatoes. I love a big thick steak with thick sliced tomatoes, and hot rolls; there's nothing better. I never eat a tomato unless it's in a salad or on a sandwich after the fresh ones are gone."

Patti agreed, "I love fresh tomatoes, but I don't think I have ever had one fresh from a garden. I'm sure Illinois has great vegetables, but I know

Chicago turns out a great steak. I'll bring the steak, and you bring the tomatoes, and we'll try that meal."

"Sounds great to me, but where do we meet?" John asked.

"Chicago, of course. It should be much easier to travel with a few tomatoes than to fly with fresh meat."

They continued their comparisons to their hometowns as they enjoyed their dinner. The owner came to their table to speak. They told David the meal was wonderful.

David said, "Our desserts are 5-Star, and I insist you try my two favorites."

"I love chocolate," Patti said, "Is chocolate one of your favorites?"

"Chocolate is always the top choice, and it is one of my choices. If you will let me I would like to provide the dessert?"

David left and the desserts came as promised. John and Patti both agreed the main course was wonderful, but the desserts were better. John had a pineapple supreme. It was a large bowl lined with a crust of sugar cookie, filled with vanilla ice cream, pineapple topping and a mound of whipped cream, and a cherry. Patti had chocolate brownie made in heaven. It was not as large a dish as John's, but each dessert could have fed both. Patti's dessert began with a brownie on a plate topped with coffee ice cream, drizzled with hot caramel and hot fudge, whipped cream, and toasted almonds on top. After sampling each dessert, they both decided that Patti's choice was the clear winner.

The restaurant had two entrances. John inquired about the second doorway when he paid their server and was told it opened to the beachside. John and Patti walked out the back door onto the deck. There were several tables for guests on the deck. A border of benches built in with the banister to enclose the porch, ideal for conversation and stargazing. The night was captivating. John and Patti sat for a moment on one of the benches and watched people stroll by. John pointed out that all the beach walkers appeared to be couples. They didn't see a single person or one group larger than two.

Patti commented, "We should have had our dessert out here."

"That would have been nice. Maybe we can come back, now that we know the layout. Would you like to walk up the beach?"

"Sure! Let's take our shoes off." Patti suggested as she kicked off her shoes and began rolling up her pant legs. John followed suit. They walked up the beach and talked about the moon.

"It just looks bigger here than it does at home," John pointing out his discovery.

"I agree. Do you know why?"

"No, I don't. Do you?"

"I know that when the moon is coming up, it looks larger because of the angle of the atmosphere, and it looks red because of dust in the atmosphere, but I don't know why it looks bigger when it's at its height now. I just know I have observed the moon more here than I ever have at home. When I do return home, I'm sure going to take notice. Look, John, we're at the hotel. I actually thought we were walking in the opposite direction."

"I must confess, I didn't even think about it. Do you think we should put our shoes on before we go into the lobby?" John asked as he pulled out a chair for Patti.

"I guess you're right, but I bet it wouldn't be the first time somebody walked through the lobby without shoes."

The inside of the hotel that is always hidden in the daylight behind the mirrored glass now revealed people walking around inside the hotel lobby and the dining room. Several other groups were sitting on the terrace, but they were engrossed in conversation and enjoying their drinks. They did not take time to notice the moon and his supporting cast.

"What time tomorrow do you want to leave?" Patti asked. "I'll be ready after lunch, so anytime is good for me."

"I'll pick you up say, two tomorrow. Does that sound okay?"

"Sounds great, I'll be ready, but don't be late tomorrow."

"I promise. I'll be here on time if not early."

John walked Patti to the elevator. They waited only a few moments for the door to open. Patti stepped halfway in and held the doors open.

"Good night, Patti, I had a good time tonight."

"I did, too. Thanks for dinner. You know, I'm looking forward to this weekend."

Releasing the doors, she took a step back. John stood motionless as he watched her disappear. He turned and walked to the parking lot. Slowly he pulled into the street. John drove past the cove where he and Patti stood watching the ocean and the view last night. He stopped, backed up, and parked at the same place where they had parked. He listened to the radio and thought how he might tell Patti how he felt. These feelings and the circumstances were very confusing. Otis Redding was singing a very appropriate song: "(Sittin' On) The Dock of The Bay." He listened as he sank deep into his seat. He made up his mind he was going to enjoy the weekend with Patti. He would tell her how he felt, but not this weekend. John wanted this weekend to be special; it could very well be the only weekend he would ever have with her, and he would make the most of it. As he sat there captivated by the view and the music, John thought of what his Uncle Andrew said to him when he was in love with his first sweetheart. John was in the seventh grade and came to his uncle for help. He needed to know how he could express his love for this girl who was in the eighth grade.

"John," Uncle Andrew explained. "Love is a very strange word in the English language. Look up love in the dictionary. Webster even had trouble explaining the word. You can use the word <u>love</u> anytime you want, and anyway you want if you are talking about cake, cars, your family, or your country. Use that word very carefully when you are talking to or about a girl. It's just a dangerous word to play with. Use it too often and in the wrong way and you might never really know the true meaning. When you are dealing with a girl and that warm fuzzy feeling comes over you, first thing you do is take a couple of aspirin. You might have a cold coming on."

John could see Uncle Andrew laugh. This made the moment feel a bit more lighthearted. Thinking still about his uncle's advice, John started home. Andrew was quite a philosopher, and he really prided himself in his direction of the young heart. Oddly, Andrew's advice turned out to be good sound advice. John's uncle would not avoid a subject because the nature of a question might be awkward. Maybe he just now understood what he was saying about love. John wanted to hold Patti. He wanted to tell her how he felt, and he didn't want to share her with anyone. His biggest problem was how would he tell her? Timing would definitely be important but how would he explain in a way she could understand. John felt good about one decision; he would not tell Patti until after the weekend.

CHAPTER 10

The phone had rung seven times, yet John was startled by the last ring and quickly picked up the receiver. "Hello!"

"John! Where have you been?" He immediately recognized the voice on the other end of the line.

"Hi, Sis, what time is it?" He looked at the clock, 6:00 a.m. John sat on the edge of the bed holding the receiver to his ear, with his elbow on his knee. More than awake at this point, but he was not clear-headed enough to side step any probe into his life.

"What has been going on over there?" Susan questioned with a sarcastic tone.

"Well, Sis, the house is going great. We are nearing the completion of the kitchen. In fact, it will look a lot different here next week."

Susan interrupted, "John the house is not what I mean. What's been going on with you? I've tried to call a dozen times. I've tried your cell, I sent an email, and I know the time difference, so I know when you are supposed to be home."

"Sis--" John paused placing a couple of pillows against the headboard so he could comfortably lie back and continue what could be a long talk.

"You know my cell just isn't working correctly here. In fact, it is so unreliable I've about quit checking it. I really don't know how to say this, but I met a girl."

Susan changing her voice to a devious whisper interrupted, "Who is it, John?"

"Just relax, Sis, you don't know her."

"That's okay, what's she like?"

"Oh, you will love her. Let me see. She is beautiful, smart, and has a personality you wouldn't believe. It's not like she takes my breath away; I'm just not sure I breathe when she's around."

Laughing loudly, Susan responded. "Oh my, baby brother, you are in love."

"I may be. I admit there is more than a simple physical attraction. There's one problem."

"And what's this problem?"

"She is already engaged."

"All right, you devil, going after another man's woman. Well, at least she's not married. We weren't raised that way," as Susan laughed again. "Now listen to me. Let the house go. I'm sure the carpenters can take care of the house. You should spend some time with this girl. I feel good about this one. I knew if I could get you to come to the island, then the island would work its magic on you."

"I thought you said no one but I could do this house. That no one else could be trusted to do the kind of work I do, and you wouldn't be able to leave and have faith in anyone to do this job but me. Oh, Sis, be sure your sins will find you out!"

"That too, I have to go now. I love you. Have fun. Oh, and check your email every now and then."

"I love you too, Sis. Bye."

John fluffed his pillows. He reclined in a comfortable position with his fingers interlocked, his hands behind his head, resting in a quiet dark room, and smiling as he thought of Patti Scanlon. John spoke in a whisper, "Island magic or not, I love Patti Scanlon."

John made his way to the kitchen and found a bowl and his raisin bran. He poured the milk over the cereal and couldn't find the sugar. He tried to eat a spoonful of his cereal and thought of the people at the Hilton. They must be getting the food ready. I need to eat this cereal and go for a run, he thought. He told Patti last night he wouldn't come in for breakfast today, because he needed to get some work done. He walked over to his makeshift table made of two sawhorses and a sheet of plywood. He placed his bowl on the table and took another spoonful, "This is awful." He walked outside to the trash dumped his cereal. Placed his bowl in the sink that was located on the patio, the closest thing to a kitchen sink John had. He then ran upstairs and before he could talk himself out of the trip to the Hilton he was dressed and on the road.

He walked up the steps and past the food and as soon as he saw their table he knew his trip was worth the effort. Patti was sitting reading a book. He sat on the top step and watched her. Somehow she looked up and when she saw John she smiled and that was his invitation.

Patti started talking before John pulled out his chair, "I thought you were not coming for breakfast today?"

"I didn't have anything to eat."

"Well, do you want me to get you something?"

"No, I'll get something in a minute." John thought I must look like an idiot staring at this girl, but I don't care. "Can I get you anything?"

Patti placed her book to the side of her plate, "No, I'm good."

Adam spotted John, "Hi, Mr. Reed. Do you want a Coke?"

"Sure, Adam."

Patti asked, "Are you packed?"

"No. I haven't started yet, but I can pack and be back here by two this afternoon."

"You better be. I'm packed, ready, and I have made arrangements for a bellman to be at my room at 1:45 p.m. on the dot. Have you got all your work done?"

"One more call, and I'll do that one as soon as I get back to the house."

A young lady came to the table holding a small frameless painting. "Excuse me. My name is Laura and I've been here on vacation this week. I am an art major and have been working on painting impressions while I've been on vacation. I watched you two each morning, and well I painted you sitting at this table each day. I am working on two other paintings, but this is my favorite." She turned the small canvas around and it was a couple sitting at a table and she continued, "I want you to have this one. I'm going to finish one of the others for a project I'm doing on impressions."

Patti reached out to take the painting, "Thank you. I love it."

Laura said, "It is my way to thank you for my inspiration." Laura excused herself.

"Wasn't that sweet?" Patti looking over the painting, "This is really good."

"I don't understand, why did she give the painting to you?"

"Because she knew I would take care of it." Patti sat with John as he finished his breakfast, but she reminded him many times he needed to go and pack.

John made his call, finished packing and after he placed his luggage in the Jeep, he still had a couple of hours. In an effort to pass the time, John started making a checklist for all the work assignments he would need for next week. Even this task was quickly done. He didn't want anything to eat and found himself walking around the house to pass time. He was ready to call Patti at noon, but he wouldn't let himself. John spent the last several minutes looking at his watch until the time they had agreed for his call. John arrived at the hotel at 1:57 p.m., and Patti was waiting with a bellboy. She had a large overnight bag, a small tote bag, one suitcase, and two hanging bags.

"Cutting it close," she said as John stopped the Jeep next to her luggage.

"Are you checking out of the hotel?" John asked as he opened his door.

"No, silly," she answered, "When I've never been to a place before, I don't know what I might need."

Patti looked stunning. John felt she had never looked prettier. She was wearing a blue chambray shirt, faded jeans, and old worn tennis shoes. John noticed that the label was taken off her jeans. Her flawless skin now had a sunbather's color. Patti was darker, with a hint of reddish hues and almost white around her eyes thanks to her giant sunglasses she now had on top of her head. She was so intent on loading her stuff. John stepped back and watched her work with the bellboy. She must have been engrossed in her task because when the gate to the Jeep was closed, she walked around and got in on the driver's side of the SUV. John gave the bellboy a nice tip for all his trouble and walked up to the door as Patti turned and smiled.

"Am I anxious or what?"

She timidly retreated from the driver position and walked to the passenger's door, which a doorman opened for her.

John, thinking if Patti was anxious, what could he call his feeling? He pulled away from the hotel.

"I don't know why I did that. I don't drive much at all. Most of the time I'm in and out of cabs."

"Then you do drive?"

"Yes, I drive. Why would you think I wouldn't know how to drive? I even own a car."

"What kind do you have?"

"Mercedes CLK 320 Convertible. It's Diamond Silver Metallic with black interior and a black soft top. It's a neat car and fun to drive. It's only my second car. What kind of car do you drive, John? Where you live, I mean."

"I basically drive a GMC pickup everyday. It's a crew cab; you know it has four doors, but it's a two-wheel drive. The black exterior is the only thing I dislike about it. I can honestly say it will be the last black vehicle I will own. In addition to being the absolute hardest color to keep clean, I use it for everything. I go to construction sites, and these sites are always one of two conditions: dusty or muddy. You can guess the condition the exterior of my truck stays. Most of the time, there's not a shade in sight, so I leave it parked with the windows down in the summer. When I return, I can barely hold on to the steering wheel. I go back and forth from home to work in it daily and there are not many days I don't go by the car wash. We have a company car that everyone uses on a first come basis, thank heaven it's white. We also have a white Suburban at work, but I seldom drive it, and I only drive the car if necessary. I prefer my hot pickup. Now, on the weekends, I drive a 1965 notch back Mustang, candy apple red. It's my pride and joy. If you can love a car, then I love this one. I've kept it original in detail except the paint job. The original color was a pale blue."

Patti leaned forward to look directly at John. "I would love to see the Mustang. Would you let me drive your beloved car if I came to Wall-Nut Grove?"

"Sure, you could. When you come, but its just Walnut Grove. Like the tree or the nut, Walnut, not Wall Nut. When do you think you can come for a visit?"

"As soon as you finish with your sister's house and I get through with Marshall, we will make a date." There was a brief silence.

"John."

"Yes."

"You say it."

"Say what?"

"Wall-Nut Grove."

"I do not!"

"You do, listen to yourself the next time you say the name."

John said it several times in a row to prove his point.

"Nope. I don't say Wall-Nut Grove."

Patti said as she laughed, "Bad phonics and stubborn too. Are there many walnut groves in Walnut Grove?"

"None. I don't know if the town ever had any groves. I do think the trees were plentiful at one time. The ladies that belong to the Thursday

Club are planting walnut trees in and around town for a project. I don't know why someone hasn't done it before now. I've been told they aren't the easiest things to grow nor the friendliest tree to have in a yard. I've planted several, and I can't get them to live."

"Why would they be an unfriendly tree?"

"I don't know unless it's because of the walnuts."

John and Patti had to go through a security checkpoint before entering the parking lot. This official airport that served small aircraft was located on the opposite side of the island from the International Airport and for good reason. Although small, this airstrip was a busy place. This is where all the island site-seeing tours and commuters to the outer islands were made. They arrived early, and to their surprise, the plane was already waiting to take them to the island. Marshall Industries painted on both sides of the four-passenger plane made it easy to spot, and John parked close to a gate that was part of a fence that separated the airstrip from the parking lot. The pilot had the plane positioned in the same proximity for the same reason. John emerged from the Jeep and walked over to the pilot who was busy checking the plane.

"Excuse me, I'm John Reed."

"Hi, John," as the pilot took off a grimy leather glove on his right hand, so he could take John's hand for a firm handshake, "I'm Terry Brown. How can I help you?"

John continued his explanation as he shook Terry's hand. "I am with Patti Scanlon, and we are early, but…"

Terry interrupted letting go of John's grip. "You're at the right place. In fact, I thought you could be the Scanlon party. Mr. Marshall said she was a beautiful girl, and I am to take you to the Marshall Estate as soon as possible."

John hadn't noticed Patti was standing behind him at the gate until he realized Terry talking and looking over his shoulder at the beautiful girl.

"John, all we need is to load your things and I'm ready."

"I'll get the luggage. Where do I need to place it?"

Terry helped with John and Patti's luggage. John locked the Jeep and as he was walking through the gate, his eyes locked on the small craft. Terry was helping Patti into the door of the plane and placing her in the co-pilot seat. John, a little jealous, thought it wasn't so much she would be sitting next to Terry. John would want Patti to have the best seat, but he also wanted her seated next to him. Terry also helped John into the fuselage. Then he closed and secured the door. Terry asked that they buckle up. He started the engine while asking for permission to taxi. They were in the air almost immediately. Terry explained he had been busy transporting others to the Marshall Estate.

"Mr. Marshall told me to take you on a tour if you would like to see some of the sites from the air."

"Sure, go ahead we would love to," Patti replied. John didn't feel like taking part in the conversation, so he remained quiet on the tour. He listened as Patti asked the pilot about the islands and about the Marshall Estate. John could not help but feel left out. The very idea he thought, Marshall describing to the pilot how Patti looked. John couldn't help feeling a bit embarrassed about the jealous feeling still there in his heart. Patti was a beautiful girl why should he be jealous of someone else noticing that? Terry flew around the main island tilting the plane's wing to Patti's side giving her a better view at these interesting sites. Terry and Patti were immersed in conversation about the region's detailed history. John could not take his eyes off the two in the front of the cabin to look outside. The guided tour ended as Terry changed course and leveled off to a steady position. Terry changed the dialogue from sightseeing to informing. He did his best to give a heads up on the way Marshall provided for his guests on this special weekend.

"Tonight there will be a party around the pool. You can swim, dance, or do whatever you like."

"Informal? Patti asked."

"Yes, it's a traditional luau. I think they do this every year on the first night of the weekend festivities. Some of the people have been here all week. Others come in for the weekend that is the main entertainment, so the luau gives people a chance to unwind from a day of travel. I think you will enjoy being at the Marshall estate. One thing I've noticed over the years I've been working for him is he really takes pleasure in catering to his guests. Look over to your right, and you can see the estate. There is where you will be staying."

John's feelings of jealousy changed with the tilt of the plane. As he looked out the window, it was replaced with a deep pain he now felt in the pit of his stomach.

"Is that where we are staying?" Patti asked.

"Yeah, big isn't it? Rumor has it that he spent something like fifty million on the main house alone, built it for his wife."

"Then he is married?" Patti asked somewhat surprised.

"No, not anymore, she ran off with someone they had painting for them."

It was massive from the air and looked like a large house, but not only a house. It looked like there was a mini hotel behind and away from the mansion. They could see people on the grounds and much activity all around as the plane drew closer.

Patti asked, "Does Mr. Marshall own this island?"

The pilot laughed. "No, not all of it, but he probably does own the majority. He seems to call all the shots, but then he is always doing things for the other families here. When I say things, I mean conveniences that he provides. There are three other estates on the island and a small military base fenced off to itself on the west side of the island. That is why we approach the island from this direction. People that work here also live here. I live here on the island. There is even a small school for children to attend. I don't have any children, so I don't know how that works."

John felt out of place, and why shouldn't he? He was on a weekend getaway with a girl he hardly knew who happened to be engaged to a guy back in Chicago for whom he was masquerading. Clearly he was in a place he did not belong. They landed at a small airfield with a large metal building.

"Is that the hanger?" John asked.

Terry answered, "Yelp, we have five airplanes, Mr. Marshall's Lear Jet and one chopper that we keep here, and there's about a half dozen more that belong to other people that live on the island. You can't drive to work if you live here."

The pilot's answer was polite, but it hit John wrong. It was only a few minutes before a driver picked up all three in a mini van. Terry and the driver transferred all the baggage to the van. John and Patti walked over to the hanger to look inside. It was empty.

Taking John's left hand, Patti smiled, "They must all be gone to the movies."

This helped John, at least she noticed the comment the pilot made. They walked over to the van and were carried to the Marshall estate.

CHAPTER 11

The drive to the Marshall estate was a short one with picturesque scenery. Estate was indeed the correct term for Jack Marshall's home. It was a very large mansion, built surprisingly on a Georgian architecture style. It looked more the size of a resort inn than a house, and the building set away from the house in the back was even larger than the main house. The grounds were immaculate. Both Patti and John were expecting something out of the ordinary, however nothing on this grand scale. They were dropped at the left front end of the mansion where they were greeted by one of Mr. Marshall's employees, who explained that their luggage would be carried to their room. He asked John and Patti to follow him and promptly escorted them to the courtyard. John heard the party before he and Patti had the courtyard in their view. They joined the welcome reception along with a large portion of Marshall's guests. Men dressed in business suits and women all in dresses. John guessed forty maybe fifty people were walking around tables set up with all kinds of hors d'oeuvres, cheese, and wine.

John whispered to Patti, "I think we are underdressed even for an afternoon tea."

Patti not fazed by the difference in dress, "It's okay, John. Remember this is a vacation, and we just got off a plane.

Mr. Marshall's personal secretary greeted them. "Hi, I'm Evelyn Tanner." She held her hand out to John.

John introduced himself as he took her hand.

"Good to see you again, Miss Scanlon, did you enjoy your flight to the island?" Evelyn asked, reaching for Patti's hand.

"Yes, we did; the pilot gave us a special tour. This is a beautiful place."

Evelyn still holding on to Patti's hand said, "Come; let me introduce you to some of the other guests. Most of the people here arrived this morning. Relax, they won't be this dressed up the rest of the weekend."

John's thoughts were again; "She thinks we are underdressed."

Patti reading his mind, whispered to John, "See I told you we are dressed okay."

Introducing them to many of the guests, Evelyn stayed with them as they mingled. One of the many staff members, seeing to everyone's needs, told John not to rush, but their room was prepared and to get his attention when ready to go to their room. As soon as John turned, he was introduced to a man Patti knew, Phillip Stegall. Patti and Phillip talked about a past meeting.

Walking away she said, "That's my competition."

"Who?"

"Phillip."

"Oh, I could tell you knew him. I thought he worked for Mr. Marshall."

"That doesn't feel right. Marshall is playing games with me. Are you ready to go to our rooms, John?"

"Sure, whenever you are."

John picked out the young man he had spoken to earlier and made eye contact with him. He came over at once, and John told him they were ready to go.

"Right away, sir, I'll get someone to show you the way."

It was a couple of minutes before someone came to escort them through the main house to an upstairs room. John looked the house over as they walked through-- very impressive for an elaborate house, and it was in what John considered very good taste. It was decorated very expensively but not gaudy. The details and décor were as Southern and Georgian inside as the exterior but with an occasional surprise. They walked into the back of the house, past the kitchen. Patti stopped to take a peek.

"Come look, John."

John was surprised at the men and women in the large, fully equipped commercial kitchen.

"For how many are they cooking?" Patti asked.

The gentleman answered, "This is only one of the kitchens. The larger one is in the lodging to the rear of the house. I believe everyone here would be preparing desserts and appetizers. To answer your question, a good guess, probably 200. This weekend is for Mr. Marshall's executives."

"Wow!" Patti stepped away from the door. They walked away from the kitchen, down a hall; emerging from under the stairs that led to the second floor, John and Patti were surprised to see a rotunda. The very nucleus of this house, the circumference of the marble floor, had to be fifty feet as least; six massive columns appeared to be supporting the second floor as well as the dome ceiling. John guessed the height at forty feet was painted a blue sky, with clouds. All that was missing were a couple of cherubs floating among the clouds. Patti left John and the attendant standing at the bottom of the stairs as she walked toward the front doors across the rotunda to a grand hall that led on to the front doorway. This entrance had to be forty feet long. There was at least thirty feet between the two rooms on each side of the hall that made up the entrance. Patti stood under a chandelier that would have been at home in Buckingham Palace. The chandelier gave the hallway a purpose. It was empty, but the light filled the room with a special beauty. The stairway opposite the entrance was in the middle of the great hall but a good distance from the center dome and was fifteen to twenty feet across the bottom steps. Each step up the stairs was shorter in width than the one before. The fan shape gave the illusion of a larger and longer stairway. Patti walked to the room on the left and then to the right.

"Come look, John."

John walked to the cased opening that housed a pair of massive pocket doors. The attendant walked with them.

"Is it alright to look around?" Patti asked.

The attendant nodded his approval, "Mr. Marshall is most happy when people are enjoying his home."

They stepped inside the large library. Opposite the doorway where they stood was the focal point of the room. A large fireplace centered a massive wall of wood. The paneling was rich in color and detail. Only a portrait of a woman in a green dress centered above the fireplace gave any contrast to the wall of wood. Oddly, she was standing by the fireplace in this very room, with the painting above the fireplace in the portrait. It was like looking into a mirror with a mirror behind them. To the right of the door was a wall of books, which covered the entire wall from floor to ceiling. Two ladders fastened to the bookshelves at different heights ran on brass rails with rollers at the base allowing mobility and access to the books out of reach. Patti left John standing in the doorway as she entered the room. She walked over to a large leather chair and ottoman that sat between two windows that extended from floor to just below the crown molding. She felt the leather of the chair with her open hand. The dark green velvet drapes adorned the windows and were similar to the lady's dress in the portrait. The drapes were pulled back and held opened with gold ropes and bold tassels proportionally sized for the drapes and a valance hung trimmed in smaller tassels of gold. Next to the leather chair was a table with a simple lamp on top. Two writing tables back to back each with a chair sat in the middle of the room centered atop a silk rug.

"What kind of wood is this?" Patti asked as she walked to the mantle.

The attendant reported, "There are over fifteen different varieties of wood used in this room walnut, oak, and many rare varieties of wood that I cannot name. I do know that the pine flooring was taken from an office building that was being destroyed in downtown Atlanta. Mr. Marshall had it refinished and brought here. You will notice the same floors in many of the rooms throughout the house."

Patti, crossing the hall to the adjacent room, walked past John and the attendant. Looking at the room and décor, she stood in the doorway. A grand piano sat with the keyboard opened. More pine floors and another chandelier, smaller to fit, but much like the one in the hall decorated the room. The room was festooned with beautiful paintings of the Old South. Recessed lighting washed down light on each portrait. Different seating groups nestled against the walls and left plenty of open floor space. The largest painting in the room was a beautiful lady dressed in antebellum clothing and holding her hat. Her hair and the ribbon that was part of the hat were pushed apparently in the same direction by the wind. She was standing in front of a Southern mansion. The lady stood out very colorful and distinct, but the backdrop was grayish and old. The mansion in the portrait was very similar to the front of the Marshall home. The only difference in the two homes was the portrait of the lady's house was old and run down, yet her mansion had stately oak trees with Spanish moss dangling from the branches, something the Marshall house did not have.

"Look at the size of this room, this is beautiful isn't it, John?"

John taking a bow using a deep Southern dialect said, "Why, thank you, Miss Patti. It makes my head swell with pride just knowing you appreciate my work. The design I mean, madam."

Patti walked back to John and the attendant; she was smiling at John's performance. She chuckled as she spoke, "I think I've drooled enough on Mr. Marshall's floor."

The attendant said, "If you will follow me, I'll show you to your room."

They walked up the stairs where they found more of the same décor. John could not help but notice the architectural design, as well as the furnishings. The walls upstairs were painted to look like vines interwoven next to the crown molding. They walked along following the vines to the end of the corridor. To the left of their door in the corner of the long hall was the trunk of the tree that seemed to be the origin. Patti was amazed with all the painted expressions as the gentleman opened the door to a large, beautiful decorated room. The walls again were hand painted. A bedroom sat in an English garden, trimmed with lavender, rose, and lace.

John turned and asked the attendant, "Whose room is this?"

"This room is for you; I mean both of you." The defensive attendant continued with his explanation. "I was told to make this room available for Ms. Scanlon and her guest. Is there a problem? Is there a need for another room?" Perplexed and defensive, he repeated the statement. "I was told to prepare this room for Ms. Scanlon and her companion."

Before John could discuss it any further, Patti took his hand and said, "Everything is fine. The room is beautiful."

"May I show you the room?"

"Please do," Patti said.

"Well, Ms. Scanlon, if you need anything at anytime of the day or night pick up the phone, and someone will answer." Very uncomfortable, the attendant walked to the bathroom door pointing and continuing, "This door leads to the bathroom. We put the lady's clothes in the closet." Walking and talking as fast as he could, the attendant opened the door to show and confirm. Walking past on his way out of the room, he touched the armoire. "We felt that your clothes, sir, would fit in the armoire." Looking over at John, "It was apparent that Ms. Scanlon needed more space."

His tour ended, and he was now standing at the door, which led into the hall. He pointed to the phone, "Just call if you need anything. I hope you will find everything to your satisfaction. Now, if there is nothing else?" He paused for a moment.

John reached in his pocket for a tip.

The attendant spoke as he held up his hand, like he was pushing air in John's direction. "I'm sorry, sir, I didn't mean to imply. This is not a hotel; I meant if there is nothing more for me to do, then I will leave you two to get settled."

Patti said, "I can't think of anything. Everything looks great."

The attendant, closing the door, dismissed himself.

Patti's mind turned as she spoke. "Marshall is pulling something. I don't know what it could be, but I feel better with you here. I hope this hasn't put you in an awkward position?"

That's all she had to say as she started walking around the room. John rationalized his purpose for being on this weekend excursion was only to be with Patti. Even though this set up could be tricky, he would certainly be spending more time with her.

"It's okay with me Patti, I'm sure we can arrange a dressing and sleeping plan that can work around this suite. Why the closet is as big as most hotel rooms; I'll sleep in there."

Patti walked around the room as John talked, but she was not really listening. "Look at this room, John. Isn't it wonderful? I think I've used more adjectives today than in the past year."

The furnishings in the sitting area across from the bed were antique, with a Victorian sofa, mahogany tables, one coffee table and two end tables. They were different in design, but all had the same type marble top. The gent's and lady's chairs were different, but the lavish detail and upholstery were the same. Between the two chairs that sat to the right of the sofa was a smoking table that needed a marble top. Years of abuse to the wooden top told the owner smoked carelessly. Burns branded the top along with one corner that not only looked bleached out, but also the raised grain in the wood showed where sweating glasses had been. The opposite side of this bedroom kingdom from the entry door had a painted wall of stone around French doors; on each side of the double doors stood a painted square stone column with the image of an iron archway over the top. A stone wall continued on to the corner of the room but gradually changed texture with the changing wall which looked like stucco. This plaster crumbled in places and left moss as the only remnant to the bare stone. The doors, enthralled by the painted stone and iron, opened out to a small balcony, which overlooked the pool and garden vicinity. Although the scenery was paint, it was clearly the thoughts of a talented artist with a detailed imagination. John, watching Patti inspect the room and all the details, took a seat on the sofa.

"Look at this room. Have you ever seen anything so beautiful? The sofa where you are sitting could be sitting in the garden."

Patti asked, "John, have you ever seen this type of decoration?"

"Hand painting, yes, however, nothing on this scale, Mr. Marshall must know Debbie Travis,"

"Who is she?" Patti asked.

John stood and turned to the wall behind the sofa. "Look at the definition of the wall. Stones lying on stones, with a flat cap stone header on top of the wall, it has a 3-D effect, don't you think?"

Patti touched the wall lightly with her fingertips. "Would you look at the fine strokes? I shouldn't touch," pulling her hand away from the wall. "Look, the courtyard brings you to the window behind the sofa. Would this be a central point? No, in a way the paintings have a way of taking you from one point in the room to another. Notice the trim around the doors and molding. It's marbleized. Look at the clay pots painted on each side of the doors. Notice the vines are growing from the pots, up the trellis, and around the wall." Patti touched a switch that turned on two recessed lights in the ceiling.

"Look, John, look how the lights shine on the wall." She switched them off, then on again. A framed portrait of the same woman hung over a table and to each side of this portrait two columns protruded from the wall with a half round bowl on each top. These 3-D columns added a different effect to the room. Patti switched the lights off, then on again.

"See, John. The light appears to be coming from the top of the columns shining up from the bowl. What kind of light is that? You see them in the funeral parlors. Aren't they called torch lamps? So these are lamps instead of columns?"

"I see what you are saying, but I'm not sure of the lamp's name." Inspecting the lights, John made a discovery. "Look, Patti, the plinth, the capital and the column are pilasters and the globes are glass, but they don't have lights in them. The top of the each capital has a mirror facing upward to make the light shine against the wall like it does."

"What is a pilaster?"

"A pilaster is a half column that projects from a wall for design and usually not support, most of the time used to add detail and I guess something like this decoration."

Patti turned now looking for other hidden treasures.

"Look over here, John."

Patti intrigued with something again. John didn't speak but stayed with Patti. The massive, tall bed had four large posts with a flat canopy over the top of the bed. The painted vines that completely encircled the room turned into a silk vine that draped over the headboard and ran down the post of the bed.

"It's a bit much, don't you think?" John asked.

"Oh, no, I like it. I can't imagine the time and work it took to do something like this. The definition of all the painting and the furnishings intertwined to make the room look, well, beautiful. I feel like I'm in a story book."

Turning back to the portrait, Patti asked, "Who do you think she is?"

"I haven't a clue maybe Marshall's daughter?"

"Did you notice that everywhere we go there is a painting of her, but she's not Marshall's daughter? He doesn't seem like the type that would let his daughter dress like that; not to mention, he doesn't have any children. I bet that is his ex-wife. I think she's pretty. Don't you, John?"

"Yes, she is very pretty."

"Is she wearing anything under the sheet she has pulled up around her?" Patti moved close to the portrait. She inspected it from different angles like she might see under the sheet.

"Nope, I don't think so."

The picture was of a woman in a field of flowers. In this portrait, the lady sat slightly down the side of a hill, but higher than the artist. With a background of wild flowers, tall grass, and blue sky, her reddish hair was blown a bit, and she was holding one of the tiny flowers close to her mouth. She had a timid expression on her face, with a faint smile. Her eyes were intent on the subject that was before her, or so one would imagine.

John walked over to the sofa, "I've slept on a sofa many a night. I bet this will be the best one to date. This thing is actually comfortable."

"John, I'll sleep on the sofa."

"No way, I'm on the sofa. That's all I intend to say. I usually sleep some part of the night on my sofa at home, unintentionally, of course. Besides, I don't think I could sleep in that bed with all those vines hanging around the post anyway. Where I come from, you would look for a snake in vines like that. Plus, that's a girl bed if I've ever seen one."

"Thanks, John, that's sweet of you. I could have done without the snake part. I had better choose something to wear."

Patti and John's clothes were already unpacked and put away. Patti opened the door to the closet and rummaged through her things. Patti selected a brown tee and dark brown leopard print wrap skirt. She added deep bronze thong sandals with metallic beads.

"What do you think, John? Do the sandals work? I have a pair that matches the skirt, but I must have left them."

"I think they look fine."

"Well, they will have to do. I want to wear this, and I don't seem to have the other sandals."

Patti continued to search in the closet. John thought she had not given up on the sandals. Looking concerned, she walked to the phone, picked up the receiver, and paused for a moment as she waited for an answer.

"Excuse me. This is Patti Scanlon. May I ask where my personal things might be?" Another moment of silence, "Okay, thanks," was all she said picking up the clothes she had displayed on the bed and retreated to the bathroom closing the door behind her. Then it opened again. Patti looked around the door and asked, "John, do you mind if I take the bathroom first?"

"No, not at all."

John wondered what the master bath could be like. He thought how attractive, but strange some of the décor was in this magnificent house. This bedroom was very feminine. Maybe this room was the private room of Marshall's ex-wife. That made sense, of course. Probably the reasons for the divorce were separate lifestyles and separate rooms. John couldn't help but notice the woman in the painting. Her features were different, but there was something that reminded John of Patti. She had blue eyes and strawberry blond hair. It was her smile. She looked innocent, but alive. Maybe it was her soft schoolgirl face. John noticed the signature on the painting, J. Marshall. The phone rang. John answered. "Hello, John Reed speaking."

"Hi, John, this is Patti. This is a really neat bathroom. I'm in the tub enjoying a whirlpool bubble bath. The bubbles were about to cover me, so I turned the whirlpool off for a moment and thought I'd give you a call."

"I can hear the whirlpool."

"No, that's some kind of fan that is blowing warm air down on the tub. I love this bath and dressing area. The shower has two showerheads, a waterfall over the bench, and jets that spray in every direction. I think the shower is also a sauna."

"I thought you were in the tub."

"I had to do something while this thing filled up," Patti giggled. "This is a beautiful house. This room is extraordinary. It has the same basic look of the bedroom. I have never in my life seen anything like this. How long do you need in the bathroom?" she asked.

"You take as long as you need. I had a shower before we left. A few minuets to shave, wash my face, and change shirts, and I'm good to go. They did say luau, right?"

"Yes, they did."

"Don't you think what I am wearing will be fine?"

"Sure, you'll be fine. I'll be out in a few minutes. Someone placed all my makeup and toiletries on the vanity. Marshall surely knows how to treat his guests. Bye, John."

"Bye, Patti."

CHAPTER 12

A few minutes to bath and change turned into more than several minutes. In fact, it was more like an hour. As John changed his shirt, he could hear the faint sound of music from the outside. He opened the balcony doors to look over the courtyard. The party had begun. He stood for a moment, and then he returned to sit impatiently on the sofa. The bathroom door opened, and Patti entered the bedroom.

"How do I look?"

John couldn't believe her garments were the same ones that were displayed on the bed earlier. Patti looked like an islander. Her skin was a golden color that blended with all the bronze and brown that she now wore.

"Patti, you are beautiful."

She blushed slightly, "Did you give up on me?"

"No, but I did change my shirt. I'll splash on some after shave." John walked into the bathroom and opened the cabinetry. He splashed his cologne on his face. "The only work I've done today was to help with your luggage." He walked back into the bedroom. "If you can stand me, then I guess everybody else will have to."

"Do you think we need to call first or should we just go to the party?"

"I think it will be alright to show up."

"Okay, then I'm ready if you are?"

They could hear people talking downstairs as soon as they opened their room door. Patti thought, what kind of event am I going too? Without thinking she took John's hand. This surprised John, but he liked it. Was she needing support, or leading him to the first floor? Downstairs people were stirring all over the bottom floor.

"Why don't we go out the front door? I'm sure we can find all the festivities," John suggested. When they joined the party, it was in full swing. The area where they arrived that afternoon was transformed from a patio setting into the luau. A stage was set at the edge of the courtyard, and a band played island music. The music stimulated this family of professionals to dance. The talking and laughing were almost as loud as the music, and plenty of excitement filled the air. All over the courtyard were tables loaded with all kinds of food. At one table a man was carving a baked pig complete with a red apple in its mouth while another man helped serve the guests.

John spoke in a loud voice to be heard over the crowd and music, "This sort of reminds me of a cruise I went on a few years ago. Ice sculptures really jazz up a party. There's a bunch of folks here, but they'll never eat all this food."

John and Patti walked around munching on appetizers, watching, and listening to the merriment of the crowd.

John asked, "Is this what one calls grazing? Do you want to sit?"

"Sure."

Patti took John's dish and gave it to a young man who was retrieving glasses and plates from the guests. John found a table as far away from the buzzing crowd as he could. He placed their napkins on the back of two chairs and placed their drinks on the table. He caught Patti as she pondered over the main course options. She handed a plate of baked pig to John, and they found some food to complement the pork. They were happy to eat and talk all alone with the music and laughter in the background. John, looking at Patti, pushed back from the table.

She turned and said, "Let's dance, John."

"I don't dance."

Patti burst out laughing, "What?" Standing, she took his hand and pulled him to the action. "Come on, it will be fun."

John baulked with each step, "You don't understand, I don't, I never have. I mean, I don't know how."

Patti continued to pull. She nudged her head backwards and referred to the people who were out in the courtyard dancing and asked, "Do they look as if they care if you can dance or not? Anyone can dance to this kind of music."

Before John could say another word, she pulled him in the direction of the band. People were dancing and carrying on in all parts of the courtyard with many sitting around tables and others were standing and talking in groups. Patti wanted to be in front of the music. John was doing a good job of stand dancing. He watched Patti's every move. As he watched her, he forgot about feeling self-conscious. Watching Patti was a pleasure, even if it meant making a fool of himself. After all, who knew him, anyway? Every few moments she would push him or nudge him so he didn't look stiff or intentional. Finally, the music stopped for a moment.

"I want to get something to drink," he stated quickly. "Would you like something?"

"Sure, dancing for both of us has made me thirsty."

There were two fountains: one fruit punch and the other mostly rum mixed with fruit juice and small bits of fruit. The fruit drink was delicious. John selected the fruit drink for both of them and walked back toward Patti. She was talking to a very handsome man.

"John, I would like to introduce you to our host, Jack Marshall. Mr. Marshall, my fiancé, John Reed."

John's heart raced at the announcement. He was now headfirst into his part as fiancé, and he couldn't help thinking, he wished it were true. John handed Patti her drink, trying to recover before he shook Marshall's hand. "Thanks for inviting us to your home." John thought, that wasn't so hard, now keep your mouth shut and let Marshall and Patti do the talking.

Jack Marshall with a bewildered expression, studied John over a firm and long handshake, "I'm glad you two could alter your plans to join us. I know you must have hated to share Patti with the rest of us?" Marshall, releasing John's hand, continued after a brief pause. "This is a company get away. A few guests arrived early in the week, some yesterday, and some today. I find it's the best way to boost morale. Just act like you both are part of the group."

They chatted for a few minutes longer. John, as he planned, let Patti and Marshall do the talking.

Taking John by surprise, Marshall turned and asked, "What kind of work are you in, John?"

"I'm an architect."

"I noticed an accent, John. Where are you from?"

"Mississippi." John felt pressure and wanted to stay away from any personal chitchat. John added, "I'm in awe of your home and would love to see all of it."

"Thank you, I must give you and Patti a tour. My former wife was a Southerner and wanted to feel at home. As a native of Georgia, she wanted this to look like the mansions of her home state. She has very good taste and likes the best of everything. This house was her project, and I gave her full rein. I must admit she did a great job, that is, until she met a bum of a painter. He was doing some of the artwork on the walls of the house. You will see some of his work throughout the house. He did some portraits also. In fact, he was in the process of doing one of her portraits." Then he paused.

What luck John thought to himself. Now, he's on a subject that is uncomfortable for him.

"Well that's a boring story." Marshall turned to Patti, "I am relieved that you're not with that arrogant, high and mighty date you had with you the last night we were in Chicago." As Marshall turned away he looked at John, "You know I'm trying to steal Patti away from you, don't you. I hope you both have a good evening."

Marshall smiled like he had won the play on words as he turned to speak to someone and walked away. What he said could not have pleased John more. Patti was embarrassed; her face was flushed, but not from the sun.

"Did I say something wrong, Patti?"

"No!" She answered short, "He has a way that always gets under my skin. I can't put my finger on it, but he's different, charming, and always thinking through his conversation. You know what's strange? I would really enjoy liking him. Do you want to sit and listen to the band for a while?"

The suggestion to listen to the band suited John, but the part that she would enjoy liking Marshall did not.

"Sure, let's go by the dessert table. I think I'm ready for something sweet now," John suggested.

"Fine with me."

They both scanned the dessert table. John had a chocolate cake with a chewy fudge center with white chocolate and milk chocolate swirls to decorate the plate. Patti had shortcake with fresh strawberries and whipped cream. They returned to their table and a strange quiet loomed in the courtyard as the music stopped. It took only seconds before the noise level picked up again, as people started new conversations.

Patti looked at John, "Is the party over?"

"No, I don't think so. Everybody looks like they are going back for food. What timing, look at the dessert table now."

Patti pointed to the stage, "Something is happening; they are changing instruments on the platform."

Men were shifting the instruments, from the rear of the stage to the front and center where the other band had played. Other instruments were already on each side of the stage. John and Patti kept eating their dessert and watching the crowd converge on the table of foods.

"Mr. Marshall sure looks a bit different than I thought he would. How old do you think he is, Patti?"

"I don't know, probably about 45, maybe 50. I haven't thought about it. Why?"

"I just wondered. I thought he might be in his early 40's. He is certainly younger than I had pictured."

A young man in a tuxedo sat behind the drums. He began placing the drums where he wanted. He tapped the different parts of the drums, much like a four year old would do, making minor adjustments and almost unnoticed by the crowd. He toyed with them, and then he started a little roll. He was alone on stage. The drummer played with more intensity and picked up the tempo as he played. He continued his solo for several minutes. It wasn't long until his long hair was wet with sweat, even though it was a cool night. The drummer looked neat in his tux, even with the sweat slinging from his head as he shook it over and over.

Patti spoke, "I never thought a single drummer could do all that by himself. He's very entertaining, isn't he?"

"Yes, he is. I'm somewhat puzzled at what's happening."

"Look, John!" Patti nudged him on the shoulder like he wasn't already looking. The drummer, carrying on and motioning to the crowd to clap with the beat of the bass drums stood for a moment. He kept a constant rhythm with the base drum. He began removing his jacket to the cheers of the crowd. He tossed it aside and took off his tie. Patti elbowed John this time. The drummer was surely capturing Patti's attention.

"What is this, some kind of adult entertainment? John, do you think he's a stripper?"

The drummer was waiting for the crowd to encourage him as he unbuttoned his shirt and pulled it from the waist of his trousers. He returned to the drums with chants for more and started showing off his ability. The crowd's attention now focused on this performance. The drummer was a nice looking young man with maybe an ounce of body fat. It was apparent that the drums weren't the only things with which he worked. When he removed his shirt, he wiped his face, twirled the sweaty shirt, and threw it in the air. The audience went wild. His muscular torso, tight and defined, rippled when he moved the sticks with his hands and arms across the skins of the drums. He then changed the beat to a fast exhibition of his skills. Six other members were now at their instruments, but they watched the drummer as well. Then all at once he stopped. Everyone clapped. The other men, wearing tuxes, began to move into position on the stage. He paused behind the drums with his head bowed as the crowd slowly returned to quiet. All eyes were on the drummer, and then he jerked his head up, and tapped his sticks together in sequence with the base drum four times. All band members kicked in at the same time on the fifth beat with a familiar tune. An eighth member wearing a tuxedo jacket, shirt, bow tie, and cut off blue jean shorts, ran out to the microphone. He was barefooted and wearing a straw hat. Patti jumped to her feet clapping with the rest of the audience.

She nudged John saying, "This is your kind of music."

Everyone was going wild.

The singer started, "Get your motor running, head out on the highway, looking for adventure, and whatever comes our way."

Patti grabbed John's arm pulling him toward the stage, "Let's dance. This is real rock and roll."

The music was loud and very good. In all John's years in high school and college no one had ever gotten him in front of others to dance. John, hardly moving, had his eyes fixed on Patti. She would smile and move so smoothly to the music. The band played the best songs and all the old rock favorites. Many would make the all time best rock and roll hit list. The bands performance was unbelievable. Each song sounded as good as the original group could if they were performing on an outdoor stage. It was uncanny how the singer's voice matched each original singer; he was great and the band fantastic. They played nonstop for over an hour and moved from one song to another. Very few people were sitting, even the older couples were dancing and letting loose. Most were dancing as close to the stage as they could get and others were around the pool. Couples were dancing and singing along.

"Patti, do you think we would look ridiculous if we sat and listened to the band a little while?"

"No, John, I don't think anybody is noticing us now. They are great, don't you think?"

"I don't think I have heard any better, ever."

A large portion of the group, possibly Parrot heads, brought the entire crowd to a sing-a-long as the band played a Buffet song "Come Monday." The audience seemed to take over the song, so the singer backed from the mic and listened. After the music stopped, the lead singer paused to let the crowd express their gratitude. Everyone in the courtyard was standing and applauding for the magnificent performance. After the ovation, he returned to the mic. "We are going to take a twenty minute break and will be back to do a few more songs." All the band members left the stage, and the crowd gave another prolonged applause.

Patti looked at John placed her right hand on top of his left hand. "Don't you think the entertainment was worth the trip over here?"

"By all means. The band was great. I can't wait to hear what else they have for us."

"I know. My ears are ringing. I love the music, but I wouldn't care if they turned it down a little.

"I know what you mean, mine are too. Would you like anything to drink while we wait?"

"Sure, I would like more of the fruit punch. If you will get that for me, I will find the ladies' room."

John immediately joined the punch line. It was moving quickly. John looked back to see Patti talking to the lead singer of the band. John reached for the glasses and filled them. He turned to find Patti gone, and he returned to their table. Patti was gone for several minutes; he had finished his drink before she returned. "No wonder she was gone so long," he thought. She had changed into a mid-length, long sleeve, black knit dress.

"I was wondering if I had lost you. You change clothes!"

Patti smiled, "I stood in line for the rest room, and I realized I could go to the room quicker, so I did. I changed because I was cool and thought this would be more comfortable. One thing my mother taught me when I travel was to always pack something warm even if I am going to a warm climate, and also something light if traveling to a cool climate. She would said, 'A lady is always prepared.' You know, John, my mother is a smart woman."

"I would love to meet her."

"Do men ever have to stand in line at a restroom?"

"I can't think of many times. I do remember one time at a movie theater. I guess the only reason I remember that day was a funny scene with a very tall man and a child's urinal, but I won't go into that. You would have to have been there to see the point of the humor."

John was thankful for the band's return. He didn't feel comfortable talking bathroom talk. The crowd applauded their return, and a couple of requests sounded from different people in the audience.

The lead singer took the mic, "Thank you. We might get to some special requests after while, but right now I would like to say how glad we are to be here again with the Marshall team. We sing here often with convention groups from all over the world, but your group is always the most energetic."

He was interrupted with shouts of excitement.

"But this is home for you guys. We are going to play and sing for your enjoyment and if you want to dance or sing along with us, feel free to join in. If you want to listen, then sit back and enjoy."

The first song was a Boston great: "More Than a Feeling."

"Patti, would you like to move away from the music?"

"No, this is okay. Would you like something else to eat, or drink? I am going to see what might be good to nibble on."

"Sure, I would like another drink if you can bring both."

"I think I can handle it."

John watched her as she made her way across the courtyard, and he wasn't the only one watching. The lead singer, at the conclusion of his first song, turned and said something to all the band members. They played "Long Cool Woman (in a Black Dress)." Was everyone looking at Patti? She, choosing her snack, moved along the tables then back to John. Patti, swinging her leg with the music, sat with one leg crossed over the other, while she sipped her drink.

John leaned over speaking into her ear, "He's singing to you, Patti."

She smiled, "I know. He's cute."

John, taken back by her statement, was glad she wasn't looking his way because he felt his face flush and was not sure why. Could he be jealous? Sure he was. He tried not to think about it. John and Patti sat listening and talking very little mainly because of the volume of the music. John noticed Patti holding her arms close to her body.

"Are you cold?"

"Yes, a little. I love the music, but do you mind if we go inside?"

"It's fine with me," he answered.

The night was very pleasant. He thought her slight overtime in the sun might have something to do with her being cool. They walked around the house to the front entrance. The music from the courtyard sounded distant as John opened the door. There was also a party inside the house. Two men mixed drinks in the rotunda, where small bistro tables and chairs were full of people enjoying conversation with a drink. Many people were moving in and out of the foyer and in the library, but the room with the most activity was the piano room. A gentleman, playing the piano, was singing softly and purposely omitting a lyric occasionally. John liked his singing, but he thought his playing was the better mood setter. He was playing and singing "Smoke Gets in Your Eyes." John and Patti sat next to the keyboard. A cute blonde took a seat by the musician and started to sing with him as he played. She sang well but was also a bit tipsy. They would complete a song, and she would ask for requests. The instrumentalist was annoyed, but he indulged in her antics and played as directed. The musician asked if he might take a break, and the beautiful blonde gave him permission to go.

"I'll play while you are gone."

She didn't ask permission but informed. She started playing softly and smoothly. She looked Patti and John over making eye contact with John. She asked John a question mocking his accent.

"Where're you from, cowboy?"

Patti nudged John, "I think she is talking to you."

"I'm sorry," John replied. "I'm from Mississippi. I was concentrating on your song. That is "Rhapsody in Blue" isn't it?"

"Yes, it is. I love Gershwin." She blinked her eyes and kept playing as she continued the conversation and briefly held up her thumb and little finger. "I'm a Texican from Austin. Why my third husband is a Mississippian."

John thought to himself she looked extremely young to have had more than one husband. Did she mean she was now married to her third or fourth? A nice looking young man setting a drink she did not need on the piano joined her on the piano bench.

Patti thinking along the same line as John asked her, "You've been married three times?"

The young man answered, "No, just twice. I'm number two. We were married two weeks ago, and, well, I guess we are still on our honeymoon."

She smiled and winked at John as she continued to play.

Patti asked, "John, are you ready to go to the room? You look beat."

"Yeah, I guess I am. It's been a long day."

They left the party unnoticed. They walked up the stairs and down the hall to their room. As John opened the door for Patti, she stopped short like she had a revelation.

"She was making a pass at you."

"I don't think she was making a pass at me. I got the feeling she was making fun of me. She might have thought I looked out of place."

"No, she wasn't making fun. I can tell. That girl was flirting with you; she is on her honeymoon and making a pass at another man. No wonder she is on the second husband; she's already looking for number three."

CHAPTER 13

John flopped back hard on the sofa. Patti, taking her place on the opposite end, joined him.

John spoke, "I have a feeling we'll know when the party is over."

"You mean the music?" Patti asked.

"Yeah, I don't see how they can go on much longer."

They could hear the music from the courtyard even though it was faint.

"I had a great time!"

"I did too. It was entertaining,"

"I was briefly talking to a lady downstairs, and she told me that Mr. Marshall has several different things that are available for his guests tomorrow. She told me everything was on a first come kind of arrangement. I don't remember all the activities, but she did point out he has a very nice stable. She mentioned we could go horseback riding if we wanted. Do you ride, John?"

"Yes, I do. I love to ride. I'm certainly not a pro, but I do ride occasionally with friends of mind. Jim and Carol Ann Bush have several Quarter Horses. Carol Ann is the horse enthusiast, and I must admit when I ride, it's to be with them more than to ride for the pure fun of it."

"I love to ride although I seldom get the chance."

They began to talk about some of their horse experiences. The music from outside stopped, but now a faint sound of celebration coming from inside the house was apparent. Patti explained to John how she inherited a pony from her older sister who long neglected the small animal.

Patti explained, "Samson wasn't a Shetland. I'm not sure if he was anything but a small horse. He managed to frighten my older sister who was his original owner. I loved him so much he didn't have the heart to be bad to me. I took care of him long after I was too big to ride him. We had to stable Samson several miles away, and I didn't get to see him like I wanted, but the caretaker at the stable took good care of him. He lived to be 25 years old. I actually had a childhood dream that one day I would own a ranch. I don't even want that dream anymore. In fact, as much as I travel, caring for any animal is out of the question, but I do enjoy riding when I get the chance."

John spoke, "Well, I wanted a horse, and we had a place to keep one. My father didn't mind having one, but he didn't want the job of caring for a horse. He kept putting me off by explaining, 'Son, this is not something I want to add to my daily list of things to do. Feeding and caring for an animal takes commitment.' Plus my mother never wanted me to have a horse. She was afraid of horses and wanted me to be. Well, I came home one day from school and my dad said, 'Son, I have some good news for you. I traded a washer for a horse.' My dad had never laid eyes on the animal before we got to the man's house. The guy heard through a friend of mine that we-- let me rephrase-- that I was looking for a horse. He approached Dad with his deal and sold him on the idea that the gear that came with the horse was worth the price of the washer. That day, my dad officially became a horse trader. He and I delivered the washer that afternoon, and I got the pleasure of riding the little filly home. All the way to Standing Pine and to that man's house I daydreamed how we would gallop all the way home. She was a strawberry roam with a blonde mane and tail. She had four white stocking feet and a blaze face. I'm not sure if a horseman would describe her that way, but she was a beautiful horse. She always got the attention among people because of her color and markings. My mother even said she was beautiful. There was one problem: she was young but old enough to ride. In fact, she had been ridden only enough to be familiar to a saddle and rider. She wasn't trained to say the least. In fact she didn't obey any standard rider commands. Like neck rein, nudging her flank or giddy up horse," John chuckled. "She was more of a pet that didn't mind my riding her. We saddled her, and I started in the direction of home. My dad knew I was ready to ride. So he finished the washer hookup, and I got a head start. I would guess Standing Pine is about eight miles from my home. She didn't want to leave her home. I had to keep nudging her while she kept trying to turn around and go back home. Oh, I forgot, she did know one command. She would stop when I pulled back on the reins. More than a couple of times she got the idea that we were headed to her stable. She would turn and I would stop her, dismount, turn her in the right direction, and lead her for a while before mounting to start the process again. She had a good bit of spirit, but she was greener than I was at the time. I was leading her when my father passed us in his delivery truck. I was a little sad at my good fortune, but she would follow me perfectly as I led. Of the distance we covered, I guess, I walked about ninety percent of the way. I heard an automobile approaching in the distance, and it was my father pulling my Uncle Andrew's cattle trailer. We loaded her on the trailer and carried her to my Uncle Andrew's barn. She would stay there until she got familiar with his place and me. The funny thing when we got her home, the feeling of ownership washed over me. I fed her and brushed her daily, not caring if I had a pet or a horse. She became both. In fact, she learned faster than I did, which was strange because I was her only trainer, and I didn't know how to train a horse.

"She had one bad habit, and she kept it all her life. I could be riding her, and all of a sudden, she would want to go exploring. This was something with which I learned the hard way. My first experience taught me to be on guard. One day when we were both better at our riding skills, we were with a group of my friends one Sunday afternoon. This was good for both of us. She helped us both learn by following the other horses. My friends kept asking me could she run. I really hadn't tried anything but walking and neck reining at the time. Best I can remember there were at least seven guys riding. Someone hollered, 'Last one to the top of the hill is a rotten egg.' He took off before the last word was out of his mouth. Frosty, her name before I got her, took out after the others like a bat out of, ah, well, like the devil was chasing her. I was surprised when she passed them all. I was so proud as I looked back at the others who had some pretty good horses. That is what I was doing, looking back smiling, when she came to a trail, which led to a wooded area. She took the trail, not missing a step, but a rider. On the other hand, I continued in the same direction, and I hit the ground hard! I was lucky in a way. The road we were on was being prepared to pave within a few days and it had been scrapped and it was mostly red dirt. I could have landed in gravel. I didn't lose any teeth, but my mouth was bleeding, and my teeth felt sore for days. My hands, my arms, and my face were bleeding. I was skint or should I say skinned from head to knees. Since it was a warm dusty day; I was sweaty, so most of the dirt I landed in stuck. I had plenty dirt and blood on me. The guys got there about the time I came to a complete stop. I must have looked awful because they all thought I was hurt. I was. My pride was shot. My blue jeans were in rags, and my hands had tiny shreds of skin hanging from both palms. I sat numb until Frosty was brought back. I dusted myself off as best as I could and walked all the way home."

"How badly were you hurt?" Patti asked.

"I wasn't hurt. My mother, who never wanted me to have Frosty, nearly had a heart attack when she saw me. All the guys admitted they thought I was critically injured. You know I wished someone had taken a picture. If you have to be hurt in some kind of accident you ought to have proof. Anyway, when Mom cleaned my wounds, all I had to show for the pain were the scrapes on my hand and knees and a few bruises. I never again let Frosty run without paying close attention to where she was going."

"What happened to your horse?"

"Well, I don't know. She was around two and a half years old when I got her. I had her for seven years, which is not old for a horse. She was fat as a pig and looked healthy, but one night she got sick and before the vet could get to my uncle's farm, she died. The vet said it could be a number of things, but he never gave a diagnosis.

"John, I'm so sorry." Patti yawned and said, "I'm going to change into my P J's, if that's all right?"

"Sure, go ahead. I'll sit here and unwind."

Patti stayed in the bathroom a few minutes. When she returned, she was wearing a Cubs baseball shirt and shorts with fuzzy house shoes. She didn't pause but jumped right into bed. John washed his face and brushed his teeth with his turn in the bathroom. Then he realized a fact that he hadn't thought about. He didn't have any P J's. He had not owned any pajamas since he was a young boy. A pair of briefs was all he had needed for years. He tiptoed to the armoire. Luckily, he had packed some gym shorts. He returned to the bathroom. He reappeared to find a bed made on the sofa. Patti had taken the bedspread from her bed and placed it on the sofa and had a pillow on the opposite end of the sofa arm. The spread was resting across the back of the sofa. John glanced at the makeshift bed and then back at Patti curled up in a ball, probably fast asleep. John quietly turned off the light in the bathroom and made his way across the room to his bed. He quietly pulled the cover across his body and lay on the sofa.

"Good night, John." Patti said in a whisper.

"Good night, Patti"

Lazily, she asked, "What is Mississippi like? Tell me about Mississippi."

"Tonight?"

"Please."

"Well, let me think. What could I tell you about Mississippi? I'll start with the weather. Mississippi is hot and muggy in the summer. We have long falls and short springs. The winter is pleasant most of the time. Every now and then we have a hard winter, but even then it rarely snows. Most of my Christmas days were spent in short sleeves."

"Tell me about your work," yawning through her suggestion.

"I work as an architect."

"No," she interrupted, "I know what you do. Tell me about your work."

"I mostly do family homes. That is my specialty. On a custom built home, I like to get to know the people, and I try to understand what they want then work with the builder to make sure he understands what they want. It's always on the blueprints, but I stay involved with the project to build the type of home I desire to build. I have to be there to see and feel the house as it's constructed. Building a house can be fun or dismal. There are times during every building that the client wants to make changes. Sometimes I suggest changes myself as I see a house taking on its own character. Only when I am involved can I make sure the changes are architecturally correct. Watching concrete, wood, brick, mortar and work turn into a house and home is satisfying. That is why I do homes. Office buildings are not fun for me. It seems like I'm the only one at my firm who likes to work on houses. Everyone else seems to like commercial buildings best. Each of us has our on specialty, and at times, we are involved in each other's work. Are you awake?"

No answer came, nothing but quiet, no more noise outside or downstairs. John could see a motionless form under her cover. As tired as John felt, he couldn't keep from looking at Patti. He thought back to the day he asked his Uncle Andrew why he was not married.

He was sitting next to his uncle on the bench in front of the bank. All of their friends were having a wife discussion. It seemed like Andrew was being left out of the wife conversation. Gus and Lec were also sitting on the bench. Max, leaning against the wall of the bank between the door and the bench, was in his usual position. He wanted to be in on the morning conversation, but he was ready to head to a phone if needed. Martin was sitting on the hood of his pickup with his feet on the bumper, and J. W., sitting on the concrete sidewalk that was less than a foot higher than the street, his bony white legs showed with his pants pulled above his socks as he cleaned his fingernails. He had his back to everyone yet very much in the conversation. Most of the time whoever started the best tale of the day was challenged by a larger fabrication from one of the others. John's question caused the group to pause and listen as in a state of reverence. Uncle Andrew started by telling John he had been married one time. He usually joked about things in a serious kind of way. Somehow he was different about this answer. The other guys listened as he talked not interrupting as usual. Because they knew this was a tough subject for Andrew, and it was a question that needed a serious answer.

"John," he said, "I married a young girl Katie when I finished high school. We lived here in the same town and grew up together. She was the prettiest thing I ever laid my eyes on. We dated, if you could call it that in those days, all throughout our school years. About the only place to go was to church, ball games, and an occasional school function. It was only a few weeks after we finished school that I asked her to marry me. We were married for almost four years. I was happy and thought she was too until I came home one day, and she had left. I felt she would come back. Because she left on her own, I felt she would come back on her own if she wanted to. I was stubborn, I guess. She must have been too."

Andrew paused in deep thought. Maybe he wanted to share more. No one spoke for several seconds until Lec who most always occupied a space on that bench broke the silence by adding a narrative of his.

"One time my wife started crying for no reason." Lec was smoking a pipe. Holding the pipe in his right hand, his right hand lying in his left, he leaned over with his elbows on both knees. The smoke from the pipe was rising around his face. He looked at John and twisted his body so he could see Andrew at the same time. He shifted his eyes back and forth to hold both their attention.

"She went to our bedroom and took an old suitcase out of the closet. My wife said she was leaving and started packing her clothes," he paused for a draw on his pipe before continuing. "She was crying, shouting, and stuffing that old suitcase with everything she could put in it." He paused momentarily waiting for a response.

Uncle Andrew taking the bait asked, "What did you do, Lec?"

Lec explained, "I got a nap sack and started packing my things too. She asked me, 'Where are you going?' I told her I was going wherever she was going." He paused again taking another draw of his pipe.

Andrew a little impatient asked, "What happened then?"

"Well, she thought that was the sweetest thing to say. She thought I had been ignoring her."

Andrew, a bit frustrated, "What then?"

Lec leaned back on the bench and took a long draw on this pipe and said, "Well, neither one of us went anywhere that night." He looked at John and winked. John smiled because he didn't have a clue what Lec was talking about that day. The men, taking his comical anecdote in stride, teased him. They all stopped talking as John Henry Calhoun approached the bank. J.W. moved from the curb and gave John Henry a place to park his pickup. They could see something across his nose under his glasses as he parked. He slowly got out of the pickup. Both of his eyes were black, and his nose was larger than usual.

J.W. asked immediately, "John Henry, what the devil has happened to you?"

John Henry never said a word until there was room for him on the end of the bench next to his truck. He sat down, got fixed just right, took a deep breath and blew all the air he had in his lungs as he sat there a moment in silence. He looked at everyone with the most exasperated expression. He gave out another breath and big blow and looked away.

"Well, boys, I darn near killed myself last night."

He paused blowing hard again. John could remember thinking John Henry must have had a wreck. It must have been in Ms. Martha's Cadillac. Ms. Martha always had a new Cadillac. She would keep one about two years before she would trade it in for a new one. John Henry blew again, the air almost whistling and even John knew he was having trouble telling his friends his story. Fearing the news John Henry was about to share, John's heart raced.

"I've been home this morning trying to think of a lie you would all believe. I thought of several, but I was afraid Martha would tell the story, and I had rather you hear it from me, so here it is." All eyes were on John Henry. "Well." He paused and blew hard this time. "Let me start at the beginning." He took a deep breath, but didn't exhale. "Well, Martha." He stopped and started in another direction. "You all know how she is when the kids are coming home. She gets in the biggest panic. She cooks for days; then she cleans. The whole time they are here she cooks and cleans. Why she can't enjoy their visit for trying to keep them full of something."

He was looking away in the direction of the grocery store where at the same moment of his story Ms. Martha was parking. In almost a cry he continues, "Just look at her buying more food. She's got enough cooked to feed the town." Pausing or being distracted by Martha, he was doing the best he could to delay.

"Well, anyway the kids are coming in today sometime. Last night she was cleaning and straightening up, while she had a cake baking. You know just busy, so I was tired and went to bed. I never knew when she retired. Well, over in the night, I got up to go to the bathroom. I didn't want to wake her so I made my way across the floor into our bathroom without turning on a light. Y'all might not remember where our bath is located in relation to our bedroom, but it's on my side of the bed. Inside the door, there is a lavatory, and the toilet is next on the same wall to the left as you go inside, then the bath tub at the end of the room. It's a small room, so there is nothing on the adjacent wall except a towel bar just to the outside of the tub and in front of the toilet. Well..." He blew hard one more time. "Martha cleaned up our bathroom the last thing before she went to bed. She washed the toilet with a toilet brush, and then she placed the toilet brush to dry with the handle between the seat and the base of the toilet bowl. She does this all the time. She just can't put up a wet brush."

Feeling of his nose with his fore finger and thumb, he paused one more time and pushed up his glasses with his right hand. Sliding his hand over his mouth, he continued. "Well, anyway I sat down on that toilet seat, and when that brush hit my butt, I lunged forward and the first thing that hit was my nose and the towel bar. The doc says my nose is broken, and I need this extra gauze just to wear my glasses."

J.W. said, "John Henry, you didn't have to go to the doctor. I could've told you your nose was broke."

John Henry's voice changed from a passive to a gruff sarcastic tone. "That's just it, you idiot, the doctor was there when I came to."

Thinking back at the moment, John laughed to himself at how all the men laughed that day at John Henry's expense. They laughed until they had tears in their eyes. John Henry, never saying another word that morning sat there. He knew the worst was over, but he also knew it would haunt him the rest of his life. He sat on that bench and let them laugh at his misfortune. After everyone regained their composure, Martin, a hard-nosed man and sometimes hard to get along with sort of guy, took over the floor with his wife story. Maybe Martin was trying in some way to help John Henry's feelings. He was chewing on an unlit, half eaten cigar when he slid off the hood of the pickup on to the sidewalk.

"Well, let me tell you something, boys. There are some good women in this world, and mine is one of the best. All women are wanters: they want this, and they want that. You can never please them no matter what. For instance, when the Misses and I got married, she wanted to buy the Murphy place, where we live now. I wanted to build a new house, but, no, we bought the Murphy place. It didn't have indoor plumbing. The first thing my wife wanted was indoor plumbing, so I got it for her. We built a bathroom, and then there was the plumbing for the rest of the house. It took nearly two months to get everything working. Then we moved in." He was making faces, prancing, holding his hands like he was drying his fingernails stood as if he were mad at everyone. "Guess what?"

No one said a word. There was a several second pause. Every eye on Martin, and he would have stood there frozen in that position forever until Max challenged him, "Martin, would you just spit it out."

Martin changed his voice, like making fun or mocking someone, "It's been forty years, and we got bathrooms all over that house. To this day, she complains if I leave the toilet seat up. Well, what am I to do, piss on the seat." Shaking his head back and forth as he counted out every word, he shook his finger at the men and said in his regular angry voice, "I don't see why it's anymore trouble for a woman to check the seat to see if it's up than it is for a man to put the seat down when he's finished." Martin, by this time, was furious. "It is just as easy to let a seat down as it is to lift one." He walked over to his old pickup, got in, slammed the door, and left in a huff. There was a pause in the conversation until Martin was out of sight.

John didn't understand every accusation the men were making that day, but he did understand enough to announce, "I'm never getting married."

Andrew, trying to end the morning meeting spoke. "John, one day you will see a girl, and you won't know what hit you. It happened to all us old codgers"

There were several amens from the guys.

"As I was trying to say, be careful with a girl's feelings. Never tell a girl that you love her just to make her happy. Never use the word love until you find the right one; then you tell her you love her every day. Tell her how much she means to you and how precious she is. Do something special for her every now and then. Never let her go unnoticed."

John asked, "How will I know the right girl, Uncle Andrew?"

As serious as he could speak, Andrew finished, "You will have to trust me with what I'm about to tell you. Listen to me closely, John. If you question the fact that you love a woman, then you don't. You can feel all warm inside and plum silly, but that doesn't mean squat. When it's right, there will be no doubt about it. Take Martin for an example. He talks tough, and he was and still is a tough man. You are thinking he is going straight home and tear up that whole bathroom over a toilet seat. He is mad right now, probably been eating at him for years over that toilet seat. John Henry's experience," Andrew chuckled, "just reminded Martin of his training. More than likely I would say the reason it makes Martin so angry is he forgets to let the seat down for

Maggie. By the time he gets home, he'll be over any bad feelings he has over the seat thing. Probably did him good to get it out."

J.W. interrupted, "Yeah, I bet he ain't had that on his mind but about ten times a day for the last forty years."

"J.W., please, I'm trying to make a point."

"Uncle Andrew, I'm confused. I don't like girls at all. I don't see how I will know the right one?"

The men laughed at John's admission. Even John Henry smiled.

"Well, Johnny, you will just have to trust me on that. Be patient and listen because you will change your mind about girls."

CHAPTER 14

John was awake at his usual time and not because he got enough sleep. He didn't know what time he dropped off to sleep the night before, but he knew it couldn't have been much. He thought he might catch another nap, so he remained curled up on his makeshift bed. He stayed there as long as he could, but he decided this would be the best time to get into the bathroom and get out of the way before Patti awoke. He looked over at the bed, and Patti appeared to be in the same spot she was the night before. Fast asleep, she had not moved. John quietly walked to the chest and got his clothes. He glanced at Patti before he closed the door to the bathroom. John shaved, took a shower, and dressed before eight. He opened the door ever so slowly, but before he could step out into the hall, there was movement in the bed.

Patti sleepily spoke, "John, what time is it?"

He whispered, "It's a few minutes before eight."

She sat up quickly in bed and said excitedly, "Do you still want to go riding today?"

John, standing with the door slightly opened, whispered, "Sure, I'm game. That is if we can. I'll go downstairs and see what's happening today. I'll check if we will be able to ride."

Patti threw back the cover. "Great, I'll be down in about thirty minutes," and she jumped from the bed. "See about breakfast. With all I had to eat last night, I'm hungry."

At that moment, music came from the radio beside the bed. John looked at Patti; never saying a word, he gave her a fake grin and shrugged his shoulders. He turned, closed the door, and walked quietly down the stairs to the main part of the house. He decided he was up too early. There were no sounds of life in the main house. He was thinking about going back to the bedroom when someone walked out from the piano room. "Did you sleep well, Sir?"

"Yes, I did."

"Would you like breakfast? We have coffee and tea ready on the courtyard and breakfast will be ready soon."

"I would love breakfast."

"Please follow me, Sir."

John was escorted again to poolside where he found tables being prepared with breakfast foods. He was the first of the guests to emerge. The breakfast foods consisted of everything a man could want. There on different tables were pastries, fruit and then Virginia ham, link sausages and sausage patties. John walked by the warming trays and could smell the food. The aroma made him want everything, and it was certainly building his appetite.

A chef was standing over a burner spoke to John, "Sir, we have eggs any way you would like them. I can make an omelet, and we also have eggs benedict. There are several different casseroles, and a beautiful frittata."

"I'm going to think about what I want. I'm waiting on someone to join me."

The chef smiled and nodded, "Sure thing. Just let me know when you're ready."

Since John was the only one up, he selected a poolside table. Different waiters accommodated him. One brought a paper and orange juice, and another asked his choice of coffee, espresso, or cappuccino. For some reason, John asked for black coffee. One waiter explained the set up while two others attended his table.

"It's a very simple setup," the waiter pointed out. "Help yourself or let any of us know what we can get you. If you don't see something you want, please ask."

John said, "This will do for now; I am waiting on someone."

John did not drink coffee that often and before he could really think about his choices he said, "Black." It was poured, and the waiters were gone. John was reading the paper when a server came with another tall glass of orange juice, and freshen his coffee. He stopped him by covering the cup with his hand.

"I don't drink coffee that often, thanks." Before the waiter left, John asked, "We were told last night that Mr. Marshall has horses here. What are the chances of riding?"

"I'm not sure, but I'll be glad to find out for you, if you like?"

"Please, I'm here with Patti Scanlon, if that matters?"

"No, Sir, everyone here this weekend is Mr. Marshall's guest, and it's our responsibility to make each person feel at home."

John was taking the sections of the paper apart when a very nice looking young lady approached his table. Holding out her hand to John, she said, "Hi, I'm Janet Pierce, Mr. Marshall's personal secretary."

John stood. "Nice to meet you," he said as he took her hand. He laid his paper aside. "I'm John Reed. I'm here with Patti Scanlon. Would you care to join me?"

"Sure."

John, pulled out her chair, and a waiter returned to their table.

"Would you care for breakfast, Ms. Pierce?" He asked.

She thought briefly, "I would like some coffee, please with cream and sugar."

"We are glad to have you and Ms. Scanlon with our family. I try to get around to all our guests during the weekend. I was told you two might want to ride today."

"Yes, we would if it's possible, but I have a question. I thought Ms. Tanner was Mr. Marshall's secretary?"

"You are correct. She is. Believe me he needs two. I head the operation on the estate. Evelyn is his personal secretary, and she works in the corporate office. She also has to travel with him at times. We talk quite often, but we seldom see each other. The reason she is here now is because this weekend is our entire organizations week to vacation here. She is on vacation, but I can assure you I'm not," with a bit of frustration in her voice.

"This is the most difficult week of the year for me. I enjoy my work, but when I am hosting the family so to speak, well, I want everything to be perfect. Mr. Marshall always wants his guests treated as royalty, but this group is special to him."

"You mean he has all this for his people?"

"The entire week of festivities, yes, not necessarily the estate. Before his divorce, he did this a couple of times for different branches of his corporation. Mr. Marshall, thinking it worked so well in boosting morale, later built more rooms to accommodate his guests. Everyone can now be here at the same time. Continuity within the network of offices, everyone gets to know each other on a personal basis. I'm sure you noticed the mini hotel in the rear of the complex. If you haven't seen the rooms, you wouldn't believe the expense he encountered to make his guests feel special."

"If those rooms are anything like our room, I would believe you."

"Well, your room is a bit different," she continued. "You and Ms. Scanlon are in Mrs. Marshall's room. It was neglected completely after their divorce. In fact, you are the first to stay in the room, and at Mr. Marshall's request, I might add." Janet took a sip of her coffee, "I'll get back to my story. The operation here was started that way. He now keeps this place booked all the time, or all that he wants, to other corporations. This is my job. I'm in charge this weekend. My workers and I may not be included in this weekend, but Mr. Marshall does make it up to us. He is very good to all his employees. We go to a destination each year of my choice. A perk I enjoy." She giggled, "I do plan a great trip, and no one has ever complained. I know he knows everyone that works on the estate by their name and much about their families. I wouldn't be surprised if he didn't know everyone here this weekend on a personal basis. Now back to the horseback ride, I'll call the stables for you. Do you ride often?"

"Yes. We both do."

"Would you like to have a guide?"

"Do we need one?"

"It's not mandatory if you are comfortable with the horses. You might not be able to get back to the stables, but you can't get lost on this island. When do you prefer to go? If I could make a suggestion, I would go this morning. This is a beautiful place with some unique sights. I can't imagine anyone wanting to see it on horseback but to each his own."

"I'm sure Patti would like to go as soon as possible."

"Fine, then I'll arrange the ride ASAP."

"Thanks, Ms. Pierce, is that right?"

"Yes, Miss is correct, but please call me Janet."

She stood and confiscated her cup of coffee. John watched her leave and then returned to his paper. John was catching up on the sports when Patti arrived. Wearing denim jeans, denim jacket, with a white oxford cloth shirt and boots, she jetted out of the house.

"No wonder you had all that luggage; you came prepared."

Wide-eyed and enthusiastic, she sat in her chair, arms folded on the table, leaning forward. "I don't have a hat; can we ride?"

"A nice young lady is planning our ride as we speak. Do you want to eat while we wait?"

"Definitely!"

John and Patti walked over to the tables of food at the same time. John looked at the various foods but decided he wanted an omelet. Patti served her plate as John called out the ingredients to the chef. They returned to the table, and a waiter brought Patti an orange juice and asked what else she would like to drink. She selected café mocha.

"A young lady came to the table. Ms. Pierce, I believe was her name. She said she was Mr. Marshall's secretary," John explained.

"Ms. Tanner is Mr. Marshall's secretary," Patti corrected.

John, knowing something Patti did not, smiled. "Well, I do believe that is the title she gave me. She did say she was the head of all operations here on the island. I told her we wanted to ride. Then she asked morning or afternoon. I told her as soon as possible, and she said she would take care of everything."

John and Patti enjoyed the early morning feasting on fabulous foods. Others slowly began to fill the courtyard. The young waiter returned to see if Patti or John wanted anything. He informed them someone would carry them to the stables when they were finished with breakfast.

Patti looked at John and said quickly, "Let's get going; the clock is ticking."

The waiter had a towel draped over his left arm. Patti touched his arm to get his attention. "We want to go as soon as we get through. Okay with you, John?"

"Sure."

The waiter never looked at Patti, and he finished pouring the juice. "Then I'll tell Ms. Pierce you are ready."

Patti reminded John of a child in her acceleration to go. He was still eating, and she was ready to go. The waiter brought sandwiches and soft drinks in a soft nylon mesh bag when he returned.

"Ms. Pierce told me to pack a snack for the ride, and the car to take you is ready when you are."

"Thanks, I'll be right back," Patti informed them as she left the table. Momentarily, she returned and they walked through the garden to the awaiting van.

CHAPTER 15

Patti and John were driven a couple of miles to the stables. The stable was well designed. The front was a two-story red brick structure and looked much like a house, except for the two large doors that were open in the front. Behind, but connected to the two-story front, was a long wooden structure painted white with a red metal roof. The building had many split doors that opened to outside fenced enclosures. The corrals were sectioned with steel rail fencing. One of the corrals had a horse walker, used for training in the middle. Only a few tops of the split doors were opened and fastened back to the outside wall. A black horse stuck its head out nosily to see the visitors. The driver pulled the vehicle to the front of the stable, within a few feet of the double doors. The day was bright and sunny, perfect for riding horses. They could only see a few feet inside the hallway of the barn from the van. John opened the side door of the van and stepped out; Patti followed. The barn was clean, neat, and very modern.

Someone in the back of the hallway yelled, "Come on in."

They walked a few more feet into the hall before their eyes adjusted to the light, and they could see two men placing saddles on the horses Patti and John would be riding for their excursion.

John did the introductions, "We are Patti Scanlon and John Reed." John held out his hand as one man stopped what he was doing with the horses. He took John's hand and then politely tipped his hat to Patti.

"Nice to meet you two, I'm Barry, and this is Doug."

"Hi, we don't have many riders this early," Doug, looking in their direction as he finished tightening the girth of the saddle, nodded.

Patti asked, "We haven't put you to any trouble, have we?"

Doug spoke up, "No ma'am, it ain't any trouble. We're here anyway; it's just most folks sleep in out here. They don't get up this early, and most don't ride anyway."

"Do I detect a Southern accent?" John asked.

"Yes, Sir. I'm from a small town in west central Alabama."

"Where, Doug?" questioned John.

"Now, don't laugh." Thinking a joke would soon follow, he paused for a moment, and said, "Cuba."

Feeling as though he was with someone from home, John excitedly stated, "I know where Cuba is. I'm a native Mississippian. It's about an hour from Meridian."

"That's pretty close. More like forty minutes."

John and Doug took a brief visit home; Patti stepped away from their conversation and remarked to Barry, "This is a beautiful place. I have seen some nice barns if I might call it that, but I do believe this is the most up-to-date barn I've ever experienced."

Barry said, "This is a barn and a replica of one that is on a farm outside Louisville, Kentucky. They do have a statement to make with the farms you find in Louisville, and the stables are a part of that statement."

"It sounds like you are familiar with the area." Patti stated.

"Lived and worked on a farm all my life. My wife and I decided this would be a great place to live and an opportunity of a lifetime." Doug turned with the reins in hand to face Patti. "Doug and my family live here also."

"Where?" Patti asked.

"The front complex of the barn has two apartments, one on each side. They both have three bedrooms, kitchen, and living areas. Our apartment has three bathrooms, Doug's has only two."

Doug joined the conversation, "Yeah, I'm the single guy, so I have to rough it," and laughed.

Patti asked, "You said family. A wife? Children?"

Barry nodded, "Yes, one wife, and two girls one eight and the other nine months."

"If you and your family live here, where does your little girl go to school?" Patti questioned.

"My wife home schools our daughter, but there are also other children on the island. Mr. Marshall has three different people that school several children." Barry stopped momentarily, "Ms. Pierce called ahead to tell us you both were avid riders. We took the liberty and picked out horses for you both." Barry and Doug led the two horses from the barn. They all walked together until they were in the sunlight in front of the stable. Barry suggested, "Why don't you put your things in the saddle bags?"

Doug offered to take the lunch packs, so Patti handed the drinks and sandwiches to Doug, and he placed them in the proper place.

"What are the horses' names?" Patti asked.

Doug handed John the reins to a tall jet black gelding with the exception of the white star on his forehead, "This old boy's name is Widow Maker."

"Barry, tell Ms. Patti her horse's name." Patti put her left foot in the stirrup, bounced upward, and before she could sit firmly in the saddle, her horse twisted his back legs in a motion to move away from her mounting. He shook his head a few times as Patti rubbed his big thick neck. John watched along with Barry and Doug as Patti, unshaken, settled the horse.

Barry spoke light-hearted, "Now, don't worry, Ms. Patti. This big boy got his name when he was a youngster -- Flipper."

"Should I take warning?" Patti asked.

"No, ma'am, I can't remember the last time he's thrown someone."

Patti and John knew both horses were spirited animals, but they also knew they were well trained. They were given the layout of the land and were told they could go in any direction. The two sightseers decided to go behind the stables in the direction of the beach. Doug opened a gate for the explorers to exit.

He said as they passed through the gate, "One last thing, if you get lost let the horses have a free rein in a walk, and they will bring you back here. This fenced in area doesn't go very far in any direction. It's mainly here to keep the horses away from the front of the barn if we let them out to run free." Doug pointed to the rolled blankets fastened behind the saddle. "We put those for you in case you might want to rest or picnic."

As they walked away, Barry recommended a general direction to start the scenic route. He walked through the gate and pointed to the back of the stable. He said, "If you would like to see the beach, keep to the left from here. Have a good day, and we'll see you when you get back."

John was riding close but slightly behind Patti. As they moved out of hearing distance he said, "They were having some fun with us. They might have been saying part of that to see if it would affect our actions."

"You mean the horses' names?" Patti asked.

"Sure, before they let us go, they wanted to watch us with the horses. Doug did a little something to your horse when you mounted him.

Nothing to hurt you, but, I think, it was to see if you could handle your horse. Another horse was also saddled a couple of stalls from where we met them in the barn. I bet one of the two would have come along with us if you hadn't passed the test."

"I'm hurt. Why didn't they test your horse instead of mine?"

"Probably, because they were told to take care of Ms. Patti, they don't care what happens to a tag-a-long. I bet there's not a stable in the world that doesn't have a Widow Maker. Plus, you know that horse's name isn't Flipper."

When John said the name Flipper, Patti's horse shook his head and snorted. They both laughed.

"Well, what do I know about anything? I could be wrong."

The main island was a beautiful place, but commercial, nothing like what they were seeing.

Patti asked, "Do you think this place has ever looked different than it does now?"

"Take away the houses and roads, and I bet the landscape hasn't changed in hundreds of years."

John's mind focused on the beauty of nature for a change. No signs of life other than John, Patti, and the horses. The smells of leather, the fresh air, the aroma of the vegetation, the sea, and the horses as they worked up a heat were all completely therapeutic.

John caught up with Patti and settled in at the same pace, "You know, I've always liked the smell of horses as they heat up. I've never been to Europe, but last year some friends of mine spent several weeks. They said the first week they crammed in all the usual sights, but the next week, they rented a car and got away from all the tourists. They stayed away from the beaten path and enjoyed the countryside. They felt they found the charm of the old world. In fact, they want to go again and do the same. They even stayed in hostels while they were there and loved it. I hadn't realized how commercial the other island is. I don't just mean hotels and restaurants. I mean the whole island is in tune as an industry, but this is a true paradise."

Patti, taking in what John said, remained quiet for several minutes. Then she said, "Can you believe all the flowers and foliage? Look at all the wild fern everywhere." Patti spoke, but it really was an observation. She remained quiet, and John thought she did not really want to talk. They rode and enjoyed the countryside. The green grass and the undergrowth of all different colors had large patches of flowers everywhere. John jumped down from the saddle and picked a hand-full of flowers. He could smell them as he broke the stems away. They were as sweet as honeysuckle. John gave Patti his loot. Smiling at John, she never said a word, as she smelled the bouquet. This sign of approval was good enough for John. They came to an open pasture; and after a quiet ride across the open land, they traveled up a rolling hill. As they neared the peak, they could hear the sound of the ocean.

Patti suggested, "Let's look for a place to let the horses rest, and we can have our lunch and enjoy this view."

He followed as Patti found a perfect place for a picnic. It had a view of the ocean, with shade, and tall soft grass to place the quilts. John made sure he tied the horses to a sturdy tree.

"I'll tie the horses away from our picnic. Doug said they could find their way back, and I feel I could too. I just don't want to on foot." John loosened the saddles to let the horses breathe and relax. He removed the blankets from the back of the saddles and gave them both to Patti. She spread the blankets on the ground. Supported by the tall thick grass, the blankets seemed to float. John returned to the horses and took the sandwiches and drinks from the saddlebags. They sat on the blankets and inspected the lunch goodies. John leaned on a little palm tree where they sat. He ate his sandwich as Patti nibbled on hers. She was eating, but she seemed more interested in the container that held the soft drinks. It was made from nylon and had a solid but flexible interior. They wrapped snuggly around the soft drinks and were attached with Velcro. A one-inch nylon strap held a cup-like top and bottom. The cups slipped over the top and bottom of the canned drink and looked like small camera lens cases. All pieces felt like they were filled with something flexible most likely insulation. The drinks were ice cold.

Patti asked, "John, can you believe how cold these drinks are?"

"They are good, aren't they? My guess is they freeze the drinks and then put them in these containers. The container covered in this nylon, is filled with some kind of foam insulation."

"Then you are familiar with this little gadget?" Patti asked.

"No, just a guess really, it's too thin and light to have much insulation value so I thought the drinks were frozen. One thing is strange."

"What's that?"

"See how the drinks are sweating. The interior is not wet from any defrosting, see."

John held the can up to show Patti the water forming on the outside of the can that was now out of the insulator. She continued to eat and then removed her boots and rolled up her jeans. She moved next to John, but instead of sitting, she laid beside him in partial shade. Her legs remained in the sun.

"One thing I must say about Mr. Marshall," as she looked up at John. "He and his staff really know how to treat their guests. Don't you agree?"

John, sitting very comfortably back against the palm, answered, "Uh huh."

Patti asked, "Why do you live in a small town so far from your work?"

John lethargically answered, "Mainly because it's home. Walnut Grove is a great place to live. It's where I've lived all my life. After all, my office is only 53 miles from my house. How long does it take you to get to work?"

"When I'm at the home office and not on the road, I guess it would take me about 45 minutes to an hour, Patti answered."

"So the time of our commute is about the same."

"Tell me what's it like to live in a small town."

"It might seem strange to you, but in a small town everyone knows everyone else. I mean they know what everyone is doing and who everyone is seeing. Why, I expect the news of my trip is going around the triangle right now."

Patti, propping up on her left elbow, turned to look at him, "Triangle?"

"That's something else about Walnut Grove I like. The town is built around a triangle with a beautiful white gazebo in the center. When I was a kid we played inside the triangle. There's not any room to play now, but people enjoy the area in a different way. More like a park. The past few years, there has been a revitalizing project to landscape the triangle. The folks back home probably know I'm sitting under this tree with a beautiful young girl right now."

"If you are serious, does that bother you?" she asked.

"Not one bit. Have you ever known anyone who might have been running around with someone's husband or wife thinking and feeling that no one knew?"

Patti reclined on the blanket, "You mean an affair? Yes, I have."

113

"Well, that is what I'm talking about. You knew, didn't you? Someone told you or you saw the evidence for yourself, yet you didn't act like you knew, especially to the adulterous couple anyway? The couple felt invisible to everyone. Yet, people knew, and people will talk. Are you ashamed of any of your accomplishments?"

"No, of course not."

"If you are doing something your mother would be proud of, then that would be moving around too. You know it's funny. The people of Walnut Grove, even if they are a little jealous of someone, still have pride in any success of a member of the community. At least, they show pride if they are talking to a stranger or someone from Carthage. The best thing about a small town is the way people treat each other. Now we have feuds that go on too, but they will lay aside any differences, in time of need."

Patti butted in with a laugh, "Feuds, is that really a word you use?"

John, smiled, "Yes, what would you use?"

"I'm not sure, altercation or dispute maybe. I don't know really. I guess where I live if someone gets huffed, yes, that's the word I would use. If you get huffed up at someone, you stay away from him or her at parties; otherwise, you probably wouldn't go out of your way to see them."

"Altercation, conflict, uproar, or huffed—well, it's more like war in the South when you are at odds with someone. If you don't like someone, your family is not supposed to like them either. Back to my point, if someone has a family member that dies, for instance, then everybody in town grieves with that family. They take food and stay with the family until after the funeral.

"For example, my mother makes an enormous hamburger casserole and takes it to any bereaved family as soon as she knows of death. I know Mother keeps egg noodles and the fixins just in case someone goes suddenly. Her casserole is so common the very sight of Mother buying the goods has prompted people to call the funeral home to see who has died.

"My uncle Will was sick and in the hospital for weeks. When he came home, he started stirring around the house and yard. Well, his wife was worried he might walk too far away from the house and fall dead, and she might not be there to see it. What good it would have done for her to be there isn't clear, but she, giving him strict orders not to leave the house finally had to go to town for something one day. Now where was I, oh yeah-- Their children lived away and were coming for the weekend. While Aunt Mary was gone, Mother cooked the casserole to help out. My mom left the casserole on the table with a note under it. In the mean time, Uncle Will walked off from the house. Aunt Mary came back, saw Mother's casserole on the table, and screamed for Uncle Will, who wasn't there. When he didn't answer, she fell on the floor crying and wringing her hands calling his name. Uncle Will came in a few minutes later and found her that way."

Patti with a worried look asked, "John, you can't mean that really happened."

John chuckled, "No, it didn't happen, but that's how common this dish is to everyone. My Uncle Will tells that story on Mother when he gets a chance. We all call her dish the "Death Casserole." She makes it for many different occasions, but times of bereavement are included without exception. She says she cooks the dish mainly because it feeds so many, it's easy to make, and people like it. Have you ever lived anywhere besides Chicago?"

"Yes, I lived away during my college years. In fact, that was the smallest town in which I've ever lived. I would like to visit your hometown one day."

"You would be welcome to come anytime, but you would never want to live anywhere else. Our town is really like a large family."

"What do you do for entertainment in Walnut Grove?"

"There's always something going on. It's really a busy place. My friends and I go to the movies often in Philadelphia. We all get together to cook or go out to eat nearly every weekend."

"I love to go to movies. What kind of movies do you like?" Patti asked.

"All my friends are married, so the majority of the time we go to see movies the girls like. Sometimes the guys go to one movie and the ladies go to another. Then the movie is most always an action movie."

"Do you cry at sad movies?"

"Well, I've never revealed this to anyone, but I have this right eye that's weak. It gets carried away in some settings. I don't think it reflects my true personality."

"What kind of movies do you cry over?" Patti asked.

"What kind of movies? Let me think, *Old Yeller, A Few Good Men, E.T., Casablanca,* and nearly all Hallmark commercials."

"How do you want to be remembered?"

"I don't know what you mean?"

"Like when you leave this earth, when you die. My father told me one time you must have a goal for yourself. Your goal for life and how you end your life are the most important of all."

"I guess I've never really thought of it that way before, Patti. What do you mean by remembered? Maybe, what do I want as my epithet, my headstone, that sort of thing?"

"Okay, yes, I guess so. What do you want on your headstone? If that could relay what kind of person you are, or who you were in life, what would it say?"

"I can't think of anything I would require prior to my demise. I don't care if I'm remembered when I'm dead. Why should I?"

"John, you don't mean that. Everyone wants to be remembered. Why do you feel that way?"

"I don't know. I guess it goes back to what an uncle said to me one time. He said a man couldn't decide for himself if he's a conservative or a liberal, good or bad. A person might want to be one or the other and strive for what he desires. I feel most people like for people to think of them as good. People who know you and are around you are the ones that label you. You can't say you're something you're not just because you want to be that person." There was a slight change in his voice, like he might have had a special idea. "Now that I think of it, maybe Uncle Andrew was saying basically the same thing as your father. Maybe I've been wrong all this time about what my uncle said. I can remember clearly the day as if it were yesterday. I walked across the triangle from our store to the grocery store. The grocery was located off the northwest end of the triangle. Odd because it was in the morning, close to lunch, I would say eleven. The conversation was in full swing when I got there. Uncle Andrew was sitting on one end of the bench in front of the store with a bag of groceries. I walked up and stood by him. I leaned over and asked quietly what he was doing in town? He changed arms with his sack of goodies and placed his hand on my right shoulder to pull me close, sort of a hug and told me he needed some sugar and jar flats to make some fig preserves. He must have been intrigued by the topic, or he would have never stopped from his mission. The men of our town liked to sit in front of the store and talk. Several men including my uncle were there, and a discussion was in progress. He was watching and listening to one of his best friends talk. Then we both turned our attention to Martin who was talking about something. It was a Saturday the second week in August. School had started."

Patti looked at him for a moment. She wanted to ask why school had started so early, but she didn't stop John's story. His speech had become lighthearted and calm. Unaware, John started playing with Patti's hair. She closed her eyes and relaxed with the story and the attention.

"I remember because Uncle Andrew had taken me and several friends to the Neshoba County Fair the week before. He had just bought a brand new pickup. First one he had ever owned with an automatic transmission and air conditioning. I don't think I ever remember him using the air. I rode in the front with Uncle Andrew, and the other boys rode in the back. We did this every year as an end of summer treat. A week or two before the fair, we would save our money. Then we would go with Uncle Andrew and walk through the exhibits and the stock barns. When the midway was in full swing, he would dismiss us to squander our savings on the rides and great food of the carnival. Uncle Andrew would go to the pavilion to hear some blow hard politician talk, or he would go to the racetrack and watch the horse races. These races were for trophies, fun, and pride. Betting wasn't allowed, but there was plenty of friendly sideline bets. I know it went on. Uncle Andrew ran into us between one of our blitz runs on the rides. He was folding up his money and put it in his front pocket. He made the statement, 'I just left a man that had a few too many drinks. The man had a big mouth, poor judgment, and his money was of no value to him.' He said the man was bragging on a beautiful, spirited animal, but my Uncle knew the horse wasn't ready to run. Now, I've heard him say so many times, 'Son, never bet. I wouldn't bet on an ant eating a bale of hay if he was on his last straw.' Now he never told me he won a bet, but he asked if we were ready to eat. We hadn't officially eaten yet, so he offered to buy. We accepted his invitation, and he treated us to the greasy foods of the fairway. I got a sausage dog with onions and peppers and the biggest lemonade I could get. We left the fair at dusk, we were tired, and we had the scars of the red clay hills of Neshoba County on our clothes to prove it. The ride home was quiet, and there was little stirring in the back of the pickup. Uncle Andrew carried us to our homes, and at each stop, he would stay long enough to inform what a great time we all had. Unlike most times with my buddies who asked to be the last one home, there wasn't an argument. In fact, it was a relief to be the first to get a bath and wash the beads of dirt and sweat and that slimy feel we got for being in a place like that." Patti's eyes closed somewhat hypnotized by the story, she wanted to hear about John's life and wanted to drift off to sleep at the same time.

"I'll get back to my original story. Uncle Andrew had picked two gallons of figs early that morning. He needed jar flats and more sugar. This was the urgent need for a mid-morning trip to town. He was a self-sufficient man. He did his own cooking and most of the cleaning. He had blooming plants all over his yard, and time and again he said how much he liked color around his house. He had very few shrubs, and they were only in the very front of the house. He always had a rose garden, and the oddest thing he would only have one color. It had to be red. He would say, 'Red, is a rose; any other color is just a flower.' He felt red was perfect," John chuckled, "There was probably a story behind the red roses, but I never knew it. He did all his gardening and never allowed any help or advice, but he had a lady that helped him clean. She came in to clean twice a week, but for the most part, he did everything himself. I asked him why he used her, and the only explanation was, 'A woman can see dirt a man can't.' I think she needed the work more than he needed the help. I would say there was not a neater farm in the county. His house, yard, barn, even his pastures were immaculate. I guess I'm rambling."

Patti opened her eyes, and John was looking at her. "Please, go on, I'm enjoying this."

"Well, Uncle Andrew was wearing a white shirt and khaki pants. Clean-shaven, he smelled of Old Spice. The conversation was about this ole codger that lived in town. He wasn't much of a provider for his family when his kids were growing up. He would leave his family for weeks at the time. There was only one thing worse, and that was when he was home. At least when he was gone, his family didn't have to feed and cater to his wants. He was mean, or at least, he was always mean to the kids around town. I know I always stayed out of his way. He was hard on his children and wife. I don't guess he beat them, but I know from what I saw in him he was cruel to them. I don't remember anyone ever saying a kind word about him, but he did mellow in his last years. When he finally died, I think everyone in town thought it a blessing on the family, although it was never spoken.

"Martin had been to the graveyard to clean around his relatives' tombstones. This was a good trait in Martin. He was probably out there cleaning around this man's grave to help his family. People do that where we live; we don't have caretakers at our cemeteries. My Uncle told me one time that Martin was a person that did for others the way a man should do for others. He helped so many people in our town, but he did it in secret. Martin told everyone what the new headstone stated: 'I guess you know what they put on his headstone: Loving Father and Husband. Now tell me does that make sense?'

"Uncle Andrew spoke, 'No it doesn't. What makes less sense is why they put up with him all these years? Maybe that's what his family saw in him and probably loved him unconditionally. I feel like that could have been the only way they could have stood him. Might be they were afraid to put anything else. If you are paying the bill, you can put anything on a headstone you want. It doesn't have to be the truth. When I die, it's not important that I'm remembered. It's less important what is on my headstone. What is important to me is if I am remembered by anyone, I can only hope I've done something they remember as good. Anyway, it's their call. It will be their memory of this ole codger and how they saw me live. If you're not famous, twenty years is probably tops on anyone ever thinking about you, anyway. Unless some family member picks up the old family Bible in an effort to trace their roots, or stomps around in the graveyard looking for their ancestors and find some old fart like me in the middle of the family plot that comes to the end of a branch'."

"What did he mean by the family Bible?" Patti interrupted.

"When my Uncle Andrew was born, he was my great uncle, my mother's uncle. They kept up with the births and deaths in the family Bible. He was making a reference to tracing family history.

"Anyway Uncle Andrew continued, 'Why does it matter. In a few years, none of us will be here to remember what the ole S-O-B was like. No need in the grandchildren knowing the truth. Plus, every one of his kids turned out all right, in some ways turned out better than most kids around here.' He got up, went to his pickup, not the new one, the old pickup. He shut the door and leaned his head out of the window and smiled. 'I got a good mind to buy a headstone and put something like if there are two dates with a dash in the middle of this stone, THEN I'M DEAD.' He started the truck and drove off. It's just strange how things work. How could I have happened to hear those words?"

Patti noticed John's voice change. It became slower, more precise. She looked at him again. He was looking across the field toward the ocean. His eyes were wide and filled with water; he was reliving the scene as he shared it with her. He was caught in some kind of time travel. He was no longer with her on the island. No, now John was in Walnut Grove, year unknown. Patti listened as he spoke, her eyes glued to his face as she watched his emotions. She was anxious and moved by the intensity in his voice.

"About three that afternoon, I was helping my father load a washer and dryer when my mother came to the truck. Mom was crying. We both stopped what we were doing to listen to her. Her message was bad, 'Uncle Andrew is dead'."

The emotion in John's voice brought tears to Patti's eyes as she felt his hurt.

"My father called the people to whom the delivery was for and gave them an explanation. He locked the store and drove my mother and me to my uncle's house. It was about a mile and a half to his white house on the edge of town. The yard was full of friends and neighbors. I remember noticing his new truck was in the garage and feeling like Uncle Andrew was somehow cheated because he didn't get to enjoy his new truck. Maybe he used the old one out of habit, maybe he was saving the new one, I don't know. His old pickup, the one he had been driving that day was in the front yard near the front door. I always wondered if he felt sick which would have given him a reason to park that close to the porch. I don't remember him ever parking in his yard. Our minister met us as we approached Uncle Andrew's house. He touched the top of my head as I passed by. I waited on the porch for my dad before I would go in. I could see Uncle Andrew on the sofa inside the door.

"My dad and I walked into the house together. It wasn't a large room. It was a ten by twelve room; there were several chairs, one end table with a lamp, and a coffee table in front of his sofa. It was a simple room to sit and talk with company. The sofa was against the wall just inside the front door between the front and kitchen doors. The table lamp gave more heat than light. Uncle Andrew's head was on the end farthest from the front door next to the end table and the kitchen. He often took naps facing the front yard and road so he could see any cars that might come in his drive. His head was on a pillow and lying on his chest was his opened Bible. It appeared that he had been reading. Maybe he needed to rest his eyes so he laid his Bible on his chest to mark his place and his left hand rested on the Bible; the other arm had fallen to his side with his right hand on the floor. Gently and quietly, death had come to a good man. I can see him now. The cleaning lady found him. There was to be a coroner's inquest. I walked to him and was surprised that I could smell the Old Spice he always used. How could he still look the same, smell the same, and not be the same. I never touched him because I was afraid. Even to this day, I can't understand why I was afraid. He was my best friend, and he thought the world of me. I looked at him for what seemed like minutes and then walked slowly into the kitchen. I sat at the kitchen table where I always sat when I came to visit. I guess sort of numb. I could see Uncle Andrew; I could hear the bustle of friends talking in admiration of him. There were plenty tears. When I looked outside I saw Lester, crying and wiping away tears with his handkerchief. That didn't seem to bother me.

"Then I heard my grandmother's voice when she came on the porch. She spoke louder than usual. 'Where is Andy?' she asked with a nervous and impatient voice. 'He's just inside the door on the couch, Mary Sue,' was the reply someone gave. I heard the screen door creak open and slam shut. I heard my grandmother speak to someone. I didn't see her enter the door, but I heard her. Her heart broke at the sight of her only brother, and grief overtook her. She cried in a way that brought tears to my eyes." John's voice broke slightly as he gasped and swallowed then continued, "I had attended many funerals for a young boy, but never had I been in the presence of someone sobbing like Grandmother did that day. She broke my heart. I knew there was nothing anyone could say or do to help her. When she had a good cry, she started to talk to him. 'Oh, Andy,' she said softly as she cried. She lifted the Bible off his chest; it was turned to the twenty-third Psalms. She started to read. 'The LORD is my shepherd; I shall not want. He maketh me to lie down in green pastures; He leadeth me beside the still waters. He restoreth my soul; He leadeth me in the paths of righteousness for His name's sake.' When she got to the next verse, she paused for a moment. She struggled as she read each word. It was hard, but she continued. 'Yea, though, I walk, through the valley, of, the, shadow, of death, I will fear no evil…' There was another long pause. She could go no further and wept unashamed. I was trembling, and the tears were coming from everywhere and not because of Uncle Andrew, but for my grandmother. I didn't want to let anyone see me cry, so trying to regain my composure I walked to get a glass of water. Uncle Andrew had a dish rack with a rubber mat under the rack next to the sink. He washed his dishes and placed them in the rack for drying. I reached for the one glass that was in the rack, and I couldn't help but notice there was one dish, a knife, a fork, one-cup and saucer. All had been washed and left to dry. That sight made me realize how lonely he was. Then the tears hit me again, and I ran out the back door, walked around the yard, and waited for what I'm not sure. I sat under the massive oak tree in the front yard and waited. The moment came when they carried him from the house and placed him in the funeral home's van. My mother, grandmother, and grandfather followed behind the van. My father and I stayed until everyone left. He and I locked Uncle Andrew's house and tended to the animals. I remember leaving; it was still daylight, but I could tell there was no sign of life in his house. It sounded different and looked different than ever before. Many times I had been in his house alone, but that day I felt alone, even though I was with my dad. As my father and I left that evening, I couldn't take my eyes off the farm until it was out of sight. This was the first time I had lost someone close to me.

"Weeks passed, and I overheard my mother and grandmother talking about his headstone. I told them what he said that he wanted on his headstone.

Grandmother laughed and said, 'That sounds just like Andy. I don't think we should use the words he wanted, but I think we can come up with something he might have accepted.'

"Then when the tombstone was delivered, I rode my bike to the graveyard to look at the new piece of granite. Ms. Maggie, the lady who found Uncle Andrew was there, and we stood and looked at the headstone together. It was perfect. Etched in the stone was. John Andrew Jones, born, February 26, 1920, a dash, and August 10, 1985, and underneath "A Farmer." Maggie placed her arm around me and said one of the nicest things about my uncle. 'John, what made Mr. Andrew different from most people was he had a heart the color of a rainbow. He didn't see people in red, black or white. He just saw people'."

There was a brief pause, and then Patti said, "John, that's nice. Are you sad?"

"No, not really there're good memories of a sad day, and they should never make you cry."

Nothing was said for several minutes. John nodded making him think he could nap for a brief moment.

John said, "Okay, now it's your turn to tell me about Chicago."

Feeling the quiet and needing the rest, Patti complained. "Oh, John, I'm enjoying your stories."

John pleaded once again.

Patti began, "Chicago is a great city. Have you ever been there?"

"One time, I went with several guys on a train to Chicago to watch the Cubs play at Wrigley Field. We stayed downtown, ate at a deep-dish pizzeria, went to the top of the Sears building, rode the L-train to the stadium and back, and had a hot dog from a street vendor. I wanted to see some of Frank Lloyd Wright's work, but I realized I was the only one interested."

"Well, how did you like what you did get to see?"

"I loved it. It is an exceptional city." John confessed what he saw he liked better than any other big city he had visited.

"I live in an apartment in midtown, but I grew up north of the city. My dad loves sports, but my sisters didn't get into sports like Dad and I. I don't know if I told you, but I have two older sisters."

John said, "I don't remember you saying anything about your family."

"Well, my dad and I really lived from one baseball season to the next. I try to make opening day with him each year. We both enjoy our little tradition. I don't make as many games as I once did, but I grew up going to see the Bears play football, the Bulls play basketball, and the Cubs play baseball."

John interrupted, "Do you ever go to a Sox game?"

"Who?"

"The White Sox."

"Don't know them. Where do they play?"

John acknowledged her question, "I get it. Go on with your story."

"We love the Cubs, win or lose. Outside of sports, there is so much to do. If you could come and stay for a few days, I would love to show you Chicago. Even if you don't buy anything, every one needs to see the Magnificent Mile, the grandest shopping experience in the world. Then there is Lincoln Park, Lincoln Park Zoo, and the Art Institute. One of my favorite places to go is the Art Institute; the two bronze lions in front of the Institute alone are worth the trip to Chicago. For me, these places are home. We could go to Oak Park and see some of Wright's work. You said you have been to Wrigley Field, but we would have to go again if you visit during the baseball season. I could go on and on, but I guess you can tell Chicago is my kind of town." Laughing, Patti looked at John. "Do you catch the pun?"

"Yes, I caught that, Sinatra?"

"You got it. You might want to stay in Chicago after you get to see it with a native. I have lived there all my life and feel like I have only scratched the surface. Ronald and I have talked about living close to our old neighborhood when we are married. He and I lived in the same neighborhood as children." Patti kept talking about Chicago, but John didn't hear her. He didn't go deaf. Oh! He heard her speaking. He just couldn't hear what she was saying. When she said the name *Ronald* his heart sank.

He looked at her hands lying on her stomach. She was playing with her ring. John had been suspended in time, he and Patti completely alone. Now, of all people, Patti jump-started the clock. John wasn't thinking about Patti being engaged. He had forgotten that for the moment until she said the name *Ronald*. Now Ronald was here in her mind and John's. Ronald barged right in on what could be one of John's only days with Patti. Not only had he joined them, but now John also felt like he was doing something wrong. Until now, it was just a ring on her finger; it wasn't personal.

Patti asked, "John, John, are you listening to me?"

"Yes, I was trying to imagine where you live."

She explained their plans, "We have kicked around the idea either to buy a flat in the city or an old home in our neighborhood. Now that I know a world-class architect, I might want you to design our home. What kind of home would you design for us?"

John's thoughts weren't as clear as they had been a few moments earlier. He avoided the question by stating he would have to see the neighborhood to get ideas.

"Oh, I guess I understand." Patti asked, "John, you would design my home, wouldn't you?"

"Sure, Patti, I would love to design you anything you want."

"I don't understand. You said you would have to see the neighborhood, and then you say anything I want."

John had to compose himself. Maybe he wasn't making sense.

"Patti, let me put it like this. A good architect takes your ideas and makes them work in a setting that is pleasing to the surroundings and to your taste then creates an interior to your liking. The outside is built for the neighbors, and the inside is built for the owner."

"You sound like the man I want for the job."

He was the man for the job. He also thought he might have the perfect house already built for her.

"Are you ready to go back to the barn?" John asked.

"No, I'm not, but we had better go anyway." Helping her stand, John stood and took Patti's hand. John helped her fold and roll the blankets. He took the blankets and secured them to the saddles. He was tightening the saddles and getting them ready to ride when Patti walked over. Patti allowed John to assist her with Flipper.

Patti looked at John and said, "I've decided that I'm not going to pursue the account any further. I haven't given up, but I realize I've done all I can do. I don't have anymore to add to my presentation so after this weekend, I guess, I'm through. If there is anything I can do for the project, the suggestion will have to come from Marshall. Otherwise, I'll take a couple of days of my trip for vacation. This place has spoiled me."

John listened, moved to his horse, and took the reins. He put his left foot in the stirrup. About the time he got his right foot off the ground, Patti took off at full speed. John's horse bolted like he was let out of the gate on derby day. John, hanging on, finally managed to fill his saddle. Patti unaware of John's dilemma kept running her horse. John caught her, and they ran for several minutes then slowly came to a walk. They could tell the horses liked to run. John could feel Widow Maker's energy. Maybe all the emotions John was feeling could be released with a run. The short run excited both horses, and they knew they were on their way home. John felt they would be happy to run the entire distance. Neither John nor Patti had anything to say. As soon as the stable was in sight, they quietly walked the horses back to their home. Patti stayed a few steps ahead of John and sat perfectly in the saddle. He couldn't take his eyes off of her, but he wondered, after her announcement, if he would have more time with Patti or less. How soon would he be saying goodbye? Would his last look at her be walking away in the airport and going home to Ronald? The very thought made his stomach feel hollow.

Patti never looked back in his direction. There were deep thoughts running through her head. He rubbed the neck of the big black he was riding and began to talk in a low voice to his horse.

"Yeah, ole buddy, she will look me in the eye, tell me she wants to visit my little town, and she will be sure to write. I'll do the same. We'll talk until the last minute, until we hear the last call for her flight, oh yeah, that's right they don't call at the lobby anymore. Then she will turn and walk through security, and before she's out of sight, she'll turn, give me that big smile, and disappear. We will probably email occasionally and maybe call one another weekly at first. Then before we hang up, one will promise to visit. Oh, it will be after my next house is complete or after her next big sale. Then she'll call and ask if I could come to the wedding. Ronald wants to meet me, and they would both love to have me there." John felt rage as he continued to let his feelings out, and Widow Maker was the only one he could unload on. "Well, I won't go. Ronald is a liar if he said he would want me there or an idiot if he really did. I sure as hell wouldn't want him anywhere around." The horse's movements were increasingly impatient as they felt they were close to home.

John straightened Widow Maker's mane and said, "Tired of listening to my problems, big guy?"

Doug was walking a big gray mare when he saw the two wanderers approaching. He turned and walked over to the railing of a pen. He tied the oversized mare to one of the rails.

"I was beginning to wonder if we needed to come looking for you two. Did you have a good ride?"

Patti answered, "We surely did! I wish we could ride again!"

"Well, you can. Barry and I will be here; all you have to do is work it into your schedule."

Again, Patti spoke, "I'm sure we can't, but I still would like to ride again. I can't remember when I've felt so tranquil on a ride or anywhere."

Doug took hold of the reins and helped Patti dismount.

She softly asked, "Could you point me in the direction of the restroom?"

"Sure, Ms. Patti, it's just inside the main door, on your left."

Patti walked ahead of the two men.

"Can I do anything to help?" John asked.

"Sure, we will walk these guys back to the stable, and I'll call for you a ride back. This one over here is getting lazy." Doug pointed to the big gray mare, "She's due to foal any day now, and she doesn't even want to stand."

Doug called for their ride, and while they waited Patti brushed her new friend. She never said a word; it looked as though she were brushing her own cares away.

CHAPTER 16

The short trip back to the Marshall mansion was quiet. John looked at his watch; they would have to hurry to be ready on time for the party. They noticed people were gathering in the courtyard as they drove up to the front of the house. The lights were on, and the music was playing. They could hear the guests talking and laughter coming from the courtyard. John opened the door and took Patti's hand to help her from the van.

As they walked to the house, Patti broke her silence. "John, I have enjoyed your company over the last few days; you've made this trip fun. You are a real friend, maybe the best friend I have ever had."

John opened the door to the house as she entered. He thought that was the worst thing she could have said. John felt like he had just kissed his sister.

Walking into the room, Patti suggested, "Why don't you take the bathroom first and dress. I'm not sure what I want to wear. I don't really want to go." John swallowed and before he could say anything, Patti walked over to her closet. Patti, talking to herself more than to John, said, "That wouldn't be a nice thing to do to a host as kind as Mr. Marshall has been to us. The party is to be dressy but not formal." She added, "Plus, I've noticed it doesn't take you long to dress."

John retrieved his personal things from the chest along with a white shirt and pants. He went straight to the bathroom, jumped in the shower, shaved, and like Patti said, he was out in a matter of minutes.

"The bathroom is all yours, Patti. I just need to put on my tie and jacket."

Patti was wearing a fluffy white terry robe. Her clothes were lying on the bed, so she picked them up and disappeared to the bathroom. John was having trouble understanding Patti's changed disposition. How could she change so quickly? She was so talkative until they started back to the stable.

John picked up a magazine and tried to make a comfortable place to rest on the sofa. This was about the last bit of energy he had. Skimming the pictures, he turned a few pages. He thought of the afternoon, and how she had knocked the wind out of him with the mention of a name. He never thought of *Ronald* being such a powerful name. Ronald Reagan was a hero of John's. He could not help speaking aloud, "Best President we ever had. I don't know why Patti's boyfriend couldn't have a name like Bill or Bob."

His thoughts on names were interrupted by three quick knocks on the door. He opened the door. It was Jack Marshall.

"Come in, Mr. Marshall."

Jack Marshall stepped through the door, "Please, call me Jack. I dropped by to see if you two were enjoying your stay."

John said, "I've never had a more enjoyable day."

"I came by earlier this afternoon; I missed you and Patti at lunch. I inquired where you two might be and was surprised to hear you were on a riding exploration. Where did you go?"

"Well, I'm not really sure," John answered. "Patti loves to ride, and she is an excellent rider."

"Did you go through a gate or away from the barn by the road?"

"Through a gate and then sort of behind the stable."

"Well, you went toward the beach. The area behind the barn is fenced to keep the horses from roaming too far away, but it's not like they could go anywhere. We like to let them roam free some of the time. Do you mind if I sit, John?"

"Please do. Patti is getting ready for tonight. I would think any direction on an island would carry you to the beach." John pointed out.

Marshall chuckled, "I guess you're right, but that is the closest way to the beach."

Jack Marshall took a seat in the wing chair by the sofa. John sat on the sofa at the end opposite from Marshall.

"John, how did you meet Patti? I guess it's all right to ask?"

"Yes, sure, I saw her at breakfast one day. She was looking for a place to sit, and I offered her a seat at my table. We talked, and somehow everywhere I went the next couple of days we ran into each other."

He didn't try to make up anything. He knew the easiest way to keep up the charade would be to tell this story as close to the truth as he could.

John told him how he felt when he was with her. "She makes my heart rate go up just when I hear her voice." John didn't try to hide his feelings from Marshall.

He continued, "I feel sort of foolish sometimes, I'm not use to this kind of feeling. It's kind of a giddy feeling." Somehow John felt good to be able to tell someone how he felt. Marshall stood from his chair and started for the door. He stopped short of the door.

"Yes, I have felt like that before. My ex, we were married for fifteen years. She is beautiful, don't you think." He pointed to her portrait hanging over a console table at the opposite end of the room.

"Yes." John agreed, "She is a very beautiful woman."

"She loved this place, and I loved giving her everything she wanted. It is a strange thing. Love, I mean." Marshall opened the door but remained standing in the room. "When she left with the painter that..." Marshall paused in the middle of his sentence, and then he started another. "You know all she wanted in the divorce were all of her portraits. She didn't ask for one dime more than the settlement we offered." He grinned, "Of course, I wouldn't let her have them. Did you know I asked her to marry me? Patti, I mean." He chuckled, "I would take her away from you in a minute. That is if I could."

John asked in a sober voice, "Do you love her?"

"Patti? No, John, I still love my ex-wife, but I could learn to love Patti. I need a companion, and this time I'm going to pick the girl before I let myself love her. Patti is the type of girl I believe every man wants. Have you noticed the other men looking at her when she enters a room?"

"No, but I understand what you are saying. I can't take my eyes off of her long enough to notice what anyone else might be doing."

"Well, I noticed, and I like being seen with someone like Patti, sort of pulling from her strength. I've noticed one other thing and that's the way she looks at you. It's different. She does admire you, and by the way, don't let her do anything unwise. Be sure you tell her how you feel before it's too late."

"What do you mean?" John asked. Shocked and dumfounded, he stood for a moment. He didn't have a clue as to what Marshall meant.

Marshall explained, "Don't let her go back to Chicago. The guy she is engaged to is a real jerk."

Slightly flushed, John asked, "What did I say that gave me away?"

"Oh, don't worry. You didn't give your masquerade away, John. I can see you mean every word you say. I came to talk with both of you to see if you were for real or an excellent actor. I can see you are for real, and Patti's not that good of a pretender. One gift I possess is my ability to read people. It was Patti that made me question your setup. You might not remember, but yesterday when we met, I said I was glad she was not engaged to that idiot I met in Chicago. I noticed a speck of fire in her eyes and her face." He almost laughed as he stepped out of the room, but before he closed the door, he looked John in the eye and said, "You know, I brought her here to sweep her off her feet. Oh well, whatever happens, happens. Remember what I told you: I read people well. Tell her how you feel. The other thing I like about Patti is her commitment to someone. I can see it in her work. She is devoted to her company. That is why you need to let her know how you feel. Patti's the type of girl that would marry a guy because she said she would. She would never do to someone what my ex-wife did to me."

"Mr. Marshall, can I ask you a question?"

"Sure, John, go ahead."

"Where is your wife? I mean has she remarried?"

Marshall corrected John, "You mean my ex-wife. She left with the painter, but they didn't stay together. He lives in L. A., and she is, to my knowledge, back in Georgia."

"Well, why don't you go and get her? Forgive her. At least tell her what you told me. You might work things out." Marshall listened but never responded to John. "Mr. Marshall, I knew a man that had less to forgive than you do, but his pride wouldn't let him go after the only woman he ever loved. I'm not a marriage counselor, but it sounds like there is only one girl for you. Maybe she doesn't want to come back. Maybe she loves the artist. I'm going to tell Patti how I feel. I know I might not be successful, but I have to try. Mr. Marshall, if you go to your ex-wife and tell her how you feel what is the worst thing that could happen? You might find there's nothing there for either of you after you see her. You might be surprised at the outcome. I think I like your chances better than mine."

Marshall stood briefly before he spoke, "I don't know, John. I just don't know. I'll see you later this evening, I'm sure." Marshall closed the door, if for no other reason but to get away from a conversation he had not intended to have.

John returned to the sitting area. Bewildered, he sat first in a chair by the bed. Rubbing his face with his hands, he tried to get everything clear in his head. Maybe fatigue was setting in; anger was surely building. He wanted to kick something and maybe tear into someone. How could he vent his anger? He stood in front of his chair. He wanted to be angry with Marshall for knowing the truth.

Speaking aloud, "I can't be mad a Marshall! It seems he's on my side, or is he? After all, he at least gives good advice. Why should I be mad?" Walking around in a circle between the sofa and bed, John started listing the reasons for his confusion. "First, after thirty-five years, I am in love with someone who doesn't love me. At best, she thinks of me as her brother, or the best friend she's ever had. Not only that but she is also in love with someone else, some jerk in Chicago, named Ronald. Marshall even admits that. Second, we are here for a stupid reason: trying to fool Marshall, who is not fooled. Third, he wants her. He came right out and said it. He brought her here for that very purpose. Forth, he's rich, filthy rich." Again feeling mad at Marshall, he whispered under his breath, "I could sell everything I own and might be worth half of what he spent on the entrance to this house." He turned seeing the portrait of the ex Mrs. Jack Marshall and became mad at her. It was her fault; John kicked a throw pillow across the room that was on the floor. It hit high on the wall very close to the portrait, bounced off, and knocked over a vase of fresh flowers which was setting on the console table under the portrait. He ran across to pick up the vase. "Good, it didn't break."

The flowers that were in the vase protected it, didn't do the flowers much good, but the exchange brought his thoughts to the flowers. John arranged the flowers in the vase, and this calmed him somewhat. After all, it was no one's fault that he loved Patti. Then he thought of Marshall again. He knows we are not engaged. He might not be as nonchalant as he acts. He doesn't strike me as a person to do something on a whim. Maybe he was feeling me out. He might be able to use this to his advantage. John sat on the sofa with his hands over his eyes. Marshall definitely came to feel me out, but I know what we talked about was not planned. Marshall seemed real.

He whispered aloud, "Should I tell, Patti?" No, that would not work. She seems to have made up her mind concerning this work. Maybe she's thinking Marshall had something beside work in mind. Why, sure she does! Patti knows he's proposed. That is the reason she brought me along. She told me he was working her from a different angle than he did in their first meeting. He hasn't said anything about refusing Patti the contract, and he admitted he brought her here for different reasons than for business. No sense letting yourself get all paranoid, John.

John walked over to the chest where his ties were neatly hanging. He picked out his favorite one, lifted his collar, and proceeded to put on the tie. He made some adjustments to the knot before tightening it around his neck. He stood there and looked into the mirror. He was in deep thought of the past few days. He stood there, looked in the mirror, and held the knot of the tie in place. When he saw his reflection, he studied his own eyes almost hypnotized, and stuck in a daze.

Marshall was a good-looking, middle-aged man, fifty tops, probably mid-forties; and John was jealous of Marshall, jealous of Ronald and if he is a jerk, and if Marshall wants to marry her, then what about me? I have to tell her how I feel. She must be in love with Ronald, even if he is a jerk. People sometimes cannot help who they fall in love with. He certainly couldn't help loving Patti. John jumped slightly when Patti looked around his shoulder.

"Penny for your thoughts."

"Oh, no, my thoughts go for more than a penny."

He poked around on the knot he had made in the tie to smooth it out. Hoping he was not talking to himself when Patti entered the room he felt his face flush. John pulled the knot tight, straightened the tie one more time, and folded down his collar. If she only knew his thoughts, John turned his eyes on Patti. He stood there speechless and wanted to grab her, kiss her, and tell her how he felt. The worst that could happen was she could slap his face. No, the worst thing that could happen would be to end the charade and the friendship they had formed. The time isn't right. How dazzling she looked! He admired her from head to foot.

John finally spoke, "I wish I had a camera to take your picture. Would you mind standing there for a moment? I want to make a mental note of the way you look." She turned and posed shyly as John described what he was seeing. "The lady is wearing a black dress, with long sleeves, and the fabric is a smooth texture under lace. The dress hangs as if it was made just for her. Her pearl necklace and earrings are the perfect accent for an evening on the lawn of Mr. Jack Marshall. Wait! My phone has a camera. It doesn't work as a phone here, but I can take a picture."

To go along with the dress, Patti now had a beautiful island tan to accent her outfit. Her smile was sort of timid, amid the compliments. Her short brown hair turned under slightly. Not one hair was out of place. She smelled so good. The perfume she was wearing was not overpowering; it was like her, sweet with a hint of something tart. John started to ask her the name of the fragrance, but he did not.

"Ready to enjoy the evening?" John asked as he took his jacket from the chest, and slipped it on. He held out his arm. Patti paused for a second like she wanted to say something. She took John's arm only to walk a couple of steps. He opened the door for her; she walked through and waited in the hall for John to secure the room's door. She took his arm again, and they walked though the house. John wondered how he would tell Patti. He knew he did not know the words but that he did have to explain to her how he felt. Knowing he could never live with the outcome if he did not. Too many lives have been altered because someone was afraid to act on his or her emotions.

CHAPTER 17

The evening started much like the prior night outside in the courtyard. It was twilight, but gas torches lined the perimeter making a cozy enclosure to the garden. There was no stage, but an orchestra in the middle of the congregation played very tranquil, soft, even tunes. The music playing was as soothing as water running over smooth stones. All over the area were tables with enough room for dancing and movement between musicians and guests. There was no buffet tonight, but there would be a planned menu. Both John and Patti needed this evening to unwind and let someone wait on them. They took their seats as the waiters started bringing out the appetizers.

"Patti, I recognize the music. I believe most are theme songs."

She answered, "If my father were here, he could tell you all the names. It's déjà vu from the other night, isn't it?"

"Yeah, I guess it is. I must read more titles from now on."

John didn't know if Patti was tired or if she was a bit sarcastic. They were seated at a table with six other people; Patti was seated to John's left. They talked some, but most of the mealtime conversation was spent talking to the others seated at the table. The meal started with an array of appetizers, a salad with a very pungent dressing, then a champagne sorbet to cleanse the palette before the prime rib, and completed with the waiters carrying baked Alaska, marching out, as the orchestra played, "Auld Lang Syne." After the meal, people danced. Only a few at first, but after several minutes, nearly everyone was dancing.

Patti took John's hand. "John, let's dance."

He skipped the routine that he could not dance this time. John moved his chair and followed as Patti rewarded him with her bright little smile.

Instead of going to the forefront as she did the previous night, she led John off to the most spacious place in the courtyard, behind the torches that bordered the party. All to themselves unnoticed by the celebration, but alone like they had spent the day. John was pleased being alone with Patti. He did not mind swaying back and forth pretending to dance. He could only ask for one thing: that Patti could enjoy the moment as he was. He could tell she was burdened.

Patti complemented him. "John, you are showing much promise as a dancer."

"Why, thank you, Ms. Patti," with a soft Southern inflection in his answer.

"How did you go through your teen years and college and never learn to dance?"

"I just stayed away from dances. I was always afraid someone would bump me on the shoulder and want to cut in."

Patti looked John in the eye and asked, "Why would that matter? That is really kind of fun?"

"It might be for you, Patti, but what about the guy. Where would he go; what would he do? Does he go home? Does he stand there until the music is over? I would hate it if someone cut in on us."

Laying her head on John's chest, Patti blushed, smiled, and moved closer. Finally, a smile, what a rush; John felt better. They danced a little while longer, and then returned to their table to listen to the music and visit with the other couples. Unlike the unending party the night before, this night went like a shooting star. John and Patti left the party to return to the room. They said nothing as they walked away from the crowd. John had not noticed the noise Patti's dress made until they walked down the hallway to their chambers. The dress made a sanding sound as the two textures shifted against each other. John opened the door. As she walked into the room, she kicked off her shoes. She walked over and fell into a chair and cried. It was more like a whimper, but there were tears. John's throat swelled shut. He couldn't speak. He knelt beside her as any best friend would do, and Patti laid her head against his shoulder, much like she had while they were dancing. After she cried, she looked in John's eyes.

"I'm so mad! I looked over at the head table, and Marshall and I made eye contact. He held his glass up in a toasting motion to me. When he sat down, guess who was sitting by him?" John said nothing; he felt her left hand tremble as he held it. She continued, "Phillip, whatever his last name is." John didn't speak. He would have, but he didn't know what to say. John was not following her, he didn't know Phillip, but he knew she was upset.

"You know the other guy, my competition. I'm just mad! I put a great deal of time and energy into this project. I've researched to make sure everything was exactly what Marshall wanted not only with the quality, but also with my company to offer the price both parties could survive with. Well, I felt it coming, but I did not want to see him give it to some other company. I mean I'm sure what's his name worked as hard as I did, but I didn't want to be an eyewitness to the deal. Leaving with my last option on the table would have been hard enough to take. I planned how I was going to use my bonus; I wanted a new car. I had decided on everything even the color and wheels. Have you ever driven a Mercedes-Benz SL before?"

"No, I can't say that I have."

"Well, I love them. I think it's one of the sleekest, most luxurious cars on the road." She looked dejected and sighed, "That's what I get for spending the money ahead of time. It seems to make me work harder when I have a goal or a reward for myself, and I don't always buy what I've set my goal for."

John did not tell her of the conversation he and Marshall had early that evening. He may have been doing this to spite her, but somehow that did not seem like Marshall's style.

John tried to comfort her, "Patti, sometimes we can do everything we are asked, and then can we help it if our best is not enough? After it is all said and done, we have to be satisfied with our effort."

"Oh! I could have gotten the account," she said angrily, "Just one roll in the hay back in Ole Chicago, and I wouldn't have had to come this far."

"Are you second guessing your decision, Patti?"

Patti with a quick answer, "No, not at all! I would never do that; I'm not for sale. I am a professional but not that kind of professional." Pulling her hand away from John, she stood up hard and strong, as if John had made the statement. This motion ripped at John's heart. She turned and dragged herself into the bathroom.

What could he do? Never in his life had he felt so helpless. Patti was in a better state when she emerged from the bathroom. Without speaking, she went straight to bed.

"Patti, are you all right?" John asked.

Softly, she answered, "Oh, yes, I'm fine now. I have brushed my teeth and feel better. Brushing my teeth and washing my face always helps my feelings."

John left her to her method of healing. Indeed, if this could help one's feeling, he desired this magic. John took off his jacket, shirt, and tie and then searched for his brush for a moment in his travel bag. When he found his brush, he placed the toothpaste on liberally as he raised his hand to start the healing. He looked in the mirror and focused on the mirror's surface. Patti had brushed all right; the mirror was covered with specks of toothpaste. John laughed; he needed that. He rinsed a face cloth and washed the residue from the mirror. He dried the mirror with a towel.

He spoke aloud, "She must feel better." He took some soap and washed his face. He felt purged like he had been ridden hard and put up wet. John thought he would slip back into the bedroom to find something to sleep in. There, under the cover he used last night was curled a delicate form. The spread was covering all but a small portion of her face.

John spoke softly to himself, "She must have thought about my bed and got up to make it for me." John, placing his feet on the sofa next to Patti's, sat in the chair at her feet. After all, this is what he had wanted all night: to be alone with her. John could not sleep. He watched over Patti as she slept.

CHAPTER 18

Even before John opened his eyes, he felt the pain in his neck. He placed his hand on the right side of his neck as he squirmed in the chair where he had spent the night. He had to have been exhausted to sleep in a chair. Patti was still fast asleep and so was John's right foot. He placed it on the floor to let the blood flow and to bring the feeling back to normal. He, making sure he could move with his foot still tingling, stood and stretched. He went quietly to the chest and retrieved some clean clothes. He went to the bathroom for a hot shower and shave. John dressed and moved quietly out of the room. He looked back. Patti was still sleeping. She had a bad night; he hoped her day would be better. He closed the door. How he wished it were in his power to make her as happy as she was the first day he saw her. Knowing his way around the house, he turned and went out the back way. John's walk through the house made him feel better; the aroma that came from the kitchen excited his taste buds. He went to the patio where breakfast was waiting. He was handed a paper and a glass of orange juice.

The waiter asked, "You don't drink coffee, do you?"

"That's correct, but I would like a sweet roll. I had one yesterday, and it was great! It was drenched in cream cheese icing."

The young man seemed pleased that John asked for something. The morning was cool and bright and the air smelled sweet and clean.

John spoke to the waiter when he returned with the sweet roll, "It looks like I'm the first again this morning."

"Yes, Sir. Most of the guests sleep late, especially on the last day. A few people have already left, but none wanted breakfast. Most everyone is staying until tomorrow."

It was not long until others joined him. John read the paper, tried to relax, and worked out the crick in his neck. Patti came at last. She was in much better spirits. She wore a bright orange sundress. John could smell her perfume from across the table. John's waiter walked in their direction before he could ask if Patti wanted anything.

Patti spoke, "Just juice, and coffee please, thanks. John, do you want to go back to the main island today? We were invited to stay until Monday."

"Whatever you want. I'm in no rush at all," John answered. He told the truth; he would have been happy to stay. Staying meant he could be with Patti; however, leaving would somehow make him more comfortable. He could sleep in his own bed, but he might not be with her as much as he could be here.

Their waiter interrupted them, "Excuse me, Ms. Scanlon."

"Yes."

"Mr. Marshall asked that when you finish with your breakfast, would you mind speaking with him? He would like to see you in his study."

Patti looked at John with a puzzled look. The waiter, waiting for an answer remained at the table.

John responded, "I look at it like this. If I were going to a dentist, I would want to be there ready when the doctor got to the office. No matter what the outcome, it will all be behind you."

"You're right, John. I'm ready now," she turned to the waiter. She gave John a big grin, patted his left hand, and followed the waiter.

John, eating the last bite of his sweet roll, sat at the table. He thought of a conversation he had once with his uncle Andrew.

"Why did your wife leave you?" John questioned one day.

"Neglect on my part, was probably the main reason, I guess."

"Did she leave you for another man?"

"No, John, not really. You need to quit paying attention to those soap operas your mother watches. I'll tell you one day when you are older and can understand better. Back in those days, people didn't get divorced at the drop of a hat. Why, when I was your age, I didn't even know there was a divorce. I wouldn't doubt if we weren't the first in Leake County to divorce. I'll tell you this: she didn't leave with another man. She did marry again later. She moved to Louisville, and they had two or three girls. I see her every now and then, but it always makes me uncomfortable. I could never talk to her after-." John remembered his uncle stopping in mid-sentence.

"Did you ever think of getting married again?"

"*One time there was a young lady who moved here from the Midwest. She moved here and lived with her grandmother for a few years, her father's mother. She had never known her father. He died when she was very young, so she moved here to spend time with her grandmother. She told me one time it was to find a part of her life that had been taken from her. She found a job and actually stayed until her grandmother died. There were a few years difference in our age. Well, there were more than a few years, probably fifteen. Anyway she loved to fish, and you know I do too. She was a plain sort of girl but very beautiful in her own way. She never looked different if she was at church, at work, or at the pond. Of course, different clothes, but the same look, you know what I mean. She had a smile that would break my heart. I could have fallen hard for that girl, but one Saturday before Father's Day, she came by and asked me to lunch after church. I got there, and she had me a present. On the card, she wrote to the best dad anyone could have. What attracted me to her was a bit different than what attracted her to me. It hurt me a bit, but then I was able to love her as a father. You know that became a very special bond. I believe that there is one unique girl for every man. I let mine get away from me because of a mistake we both made.*"

"*Why didn't you go and get her?*"

"*I couldn't, Johnny. I just couldn't. I could never face her after she left. I believe she wanted me to come after her and that's why I wouldn't. I wished many times I had. That is the part you'll understand when you are older.*"

John wondered if he wanted one thing, and Patti wanted another. The thought of being her best friend did not seem to be a compromise he would accept. He looked at his watch; it was 10:35. "I wonder what's keeping her," he said to himself.

John started walking around the courtyard and felt he was in the way of the service people. They were getting ready to take away the breakfast foods and start with the next meal. He wandered away from the main house to a neat house across the road, approximately a couple hundred yards from the courtyard. The front was built on a cottage design and looked like a dwelling house. John walked around the road to the back of the house and found a long building attached to the house with three garage doors. Two of the garage doors were open, so John examined the set up. One of the vans that transported the guests around the estate was in the garage along with a Jeep Wrangler. John saw someone cleaning one of the vans, so he walked up to him.

"Could I help you, Sir?" the gentleman asked as he stood up from the van.

"Oh, no." John answered, "I was walking around looking the place over. Is it all right for me to be here?"

"Yes, of course. You just surprised me." The gentleman never gave his name but continued to talk. "We weren't expecting anyone to leave until tomorrow, but we've had some guests to leave this morning." John strolled around to the front of the van where he saw the young man with a white cloth and car wax. He had been cleaning and polishing the front of the van.

John said, "I don't know yet if we will be leaving today or tomorrow."

Another man who emerged from inside the house called out with urgency, "Robbie."

"Yes, Sir." Robbie answered.

"We got a VIP that needs to catch a plane. You know they are always doing something at the last minute." The gentleman noticed John. "Sorry, Sir, I didn't see you standing there."

"Oh, that's all right. I'm just looking around killing time," John replied.

"I'm on my way, Boss," Robbie answered.

The boss continued in an effort to rush Robbie. "It must be urgent, Ms. Tanner called. Bob is hurrying back from the main island and should be at the runway by the time you get there. It's a last minute thing. He's flying them straight to the international airport." Robbie threw the cloth and the polish over into a lawn chair outside the door of the house. Robbie, with one fluid motion, opened the door and slid into the driver's seat as he turned the key and backed out of the garage. John watched as he drove around the building.

"Was there something we could help you with, Sir?" The man asked moving toward John.

"Oh, no, I'm just one of the guests, not a VIP. I was looking around."

"That's fine, Sir, would you like to come in? We've been unusually busy this morning, but all the vans are gone for now, and I have some coffee inside, if you would like some."

"No, thank you. I'll walk back to the house. I don't want to be in the way."

"You're not in the way. My name is Eddie. I'm in charge of the taxi service we provide here on the island. Would you like to go somewhere, Sir? I'll have a driver back in about ten minutes."

"No, really I'm just killing time." John held out his hand as he made a couple of steps toward the middle-aged man who had moved toward John. "I'm John Reed."

"Nice to meet you, Mr. Reed. I would be glad to have you come in, if you would like."

John said, "I'm amazed at the way everything works around this place. I guess that's being nosey."

"It's really okay to look around; we all like to show the place off. It's home for all of us that work here and many times I wonder if the guests notice all this. If you would like to go sightseeing or something, ask anyone at the house to call, and I can arrange a van to take you anywhere you need to go."

"Thanks, Eddie," John reached back to shake his hand once more. "Everyone has been helpful. I have never been treated so royally. I do need to get back, nice to have met you." John walked back in the direction of the house. John watched the van from a distance, hurriedly being loaded. Then he saw someone running from the house and jumping into the van. John froze. Even from a distance, he could tell it was Patti. Robbie shut the side door of the van and ran around to the driver's side. He wasted no time getting behind the wheel and driving off. John's first instinct was to start running toward the house. He realized halfway there all that was said between Robbie and Eddie. Patti was leaving the island. What could possibly have happened? What could have happened so quickly that Patti would leave like this? John stopped. He could not catch her; he turned and ran back to the garage. He ran to the door and knocked frantically. Eddie came to the door and knew that something was wrong the way John had been knocking.

Out of breath John pleaded, "Please, quick, I need to go to where the other van is going. My friend is the VIP who was leaving just now!"

Eddie spoke, "I have a van on the way back from the airport now. He will be back here in about five minutes."

"I can't wait! You told Robbie how quickly she needed to leave," he was now frantic with his plea.

Eddie turned into the house, left the door opened, disappeared and reappeared with a set of keys. Eddie pushed a button high above the door which opened the last bay to the garage.

"Jump in!" Eddie said as he got behind the wheel of the Jeep. John jumped in easily with the open cab. Eddie started the Jeep, and John, already seated, looked back as the tires squealed on the smooth concrete of the garage. Eddie felt the urgency in John's voice and actions. Not coming to a complete stop, Eddie turned to the right, shifting into first gear, and then turned to the left spinning out as he popped the clutch in pursuit of the run away van. It was not a common site at the Marshall estate for an automobile to take off like a sports car. Fear ran through John's body as his thoughts were changing faster than Eddie's shifting. John's heart was pounding out of his chest, what could have happened to her? Could the news have been so bad she wanted to leave without saying goodbye. They were only a couple of miles away from the house when John and Eddie met one of the company vans. Eddie motioned to the other driver as they met.

Eddie almost yelled over the sound of the wind and tires. "Mr. Reed, we did use a 2-way radio system in the vans instead of phones, but with the new technology, we now have phones that have 2-way capabilities. I guess you know the other night the wind blew down our tower, and it hasn't been fixed. Otherwise, we could reach them on the phone. John nodded that he understood. He could not keep from looking at his watch. The ride from the small airport didn't seem this long two days ago. John saw another van coming. He sat up in his seat. It was the same dark green color as the van Robbie was driving. John looked at the driver, but he couldn't tell who was driving.

"That's not Robbie," Eddie shouted.

John sat back again.

Eddie was saying, "We are only about a mile from the airport," when they met the van that was carrying Patti.

"That was Robbie," was all Eddie said.

"I know, I noticed the look on his face when he saw us."

Eddie spoke again, "We are going to be pushing it, Mr. Reed. The way I understood Ms. Tanner she had to make International to catch a plane for the states."

"The states!" John thought what is she doing flying to the states.

They arrived at the airport to see a plane already moving down the runway. John jumped from the Jeep before it made a complete stop. He ran up to a chain link fence that separated the drive and parking lot from the small airfield. You could hear the small plane's engine screaming as it moved slowly at first and then quickly down the runway. John stood and watched as the plane at full throttle eased upward into the clear sky.

"John!"

The voice he heard made him turn his attention from the craft that was now airborne soon to disappear out of sight to another small aircraft at his left in front of the hanger.

"Patti!" was all he could say, as he ran to meet her as she walked away from the plane she was about to board.

"What happened?" John asked.

"Did you get the note I left you?" She asked.

"No! What note?"

Patti lifted her hand to signal the pilot to wait. The pilot slowed the plane's engine. "Patti, what happened?"

She said, "Mr. Marshall gave me the account. He had all the papers signed and ready for me. He said he was ready to get started." Even with the plane slowing his engine, they found themselves screaming so each could hear.

"Why then are you leaving? I thought you were going to stay longer. I love you, Patti. Please stay."

Patti grabbed both of John's hands and with tears in her eyes, "I'm coming back, John, I couldn't find you, so I left you a note with our waiter. The note will explain everything. He was to carry it to you. I have to take care of some business in Chicago that I couldn't do over the phone or by mail." She held up her left hand for John to see the ring that she had been wearing was gone. "Mr. Marshall, of all people, opened my eyes. He made me realize that I love you, John. I am going to tell Ronald, and then I'm coming back here, coming back to you."

"Wait and I'll go with you."

"No, I asked Mr. Marshall if he could get me on the next plane to the states, and I have to hurry, or I'll miss it. I have to go, and I feel I must go alone." She kissed John. It was not a long kiss. Not a sloppy kiss. It was just right to be a first kiss, perfect to seal a contract for life.

"I'll be waiting at the airport when you return. Go and come back as quickly as you can." John, receiving his second kiss for his effort, helped her into the plane. John backed away as Patti and the pilot buckled themselves in the plane. The pilot wasted no time. The engine was ear-piercing as he put the plane in motion and in the air. His last sight of Patti was a wave goodbye. John stood motionless with a lonely helpless feeling in the pit of his stomach, as the plane banked slowly to the left and faded out of sight. Not knowing what to do, John stood watching the sky.

"Mr. Reed, Mr. Reed," Eddie called out. This awakened John from his trance. "Are you ready to go back?"

John turned and walked toward the Jeep and said, "I guess so. I don't know anything else to do." John placed his hand on the frame of the Jeep and slid into his seat. Then he thought about what Patti said before she left. She left a note.

"Could you drop me off at the main house?"

"Sure thing, Mr. Reed."

Eddie started the Jeep. He backed in a wide semi-circle then shifted into first and the rest of the gears much slower than before. There was no conversation going back to the Marshall Estate. When they arrived, Eddie drove to the front of the house like any of the vans would. Before John got out of the Jeep, he turned to Eddie and held out his hand. Eddie responded by taking John's.

John spoke, "Thank you for doing this for me. I can't tell you what it meant for me to see her before she left."

"Mr. Reed, I was glad to be of service. After all, it's what I'm here for."

John moved slowly, lifted his legs from the Jeep, and then stood. "I don't know what's going on, Mr. Reed. Well, what I'm trying to say is, from what I gathered, from the events at the airport. Well, I think things are going your way."

This lifted John's spirits.

"I guess you're right, Eddie, thanks again."

Eddie shifted into first and eased up the drive. John walked straight to the courtyard. He didn't remember the waiter, but as soon as he started looking around, someone asked if they could help him.

"Sure, I would like a Coke, if you have one, and Ms. Scanlon left a note here for me, John Reed. If you could check on that, I would appreciate it."

"I'll get the Coke for you, Sir, and inquire about your message."

John, waiting impatiently for the return of the two things he hoped could make his morning better, sat at a table.

CHAPTER 19

John's mind turned in wonder over all that had happened in the past few minutes. He looked up at the sky and noticed the clouds rushing in. What had been a beautiful morning was quickly turning into stormy conditions. He felt worried about Patti, flying to the airport in a small aircraft. The waiter returned with his Coke, a glass of ice, and a cup of coffee.

"Your Coke, Sir." The waiter placed the tray on the table and poured the Coke over the ice. He left both the glass and the can of Coke for John. He placed the coffee across from John. "Ms. Pierce will be joining you. Is there anything more I can do for you?"

"No, thanks."

John hadn't taken his first drink before Janet Pierce came. John stood to greet her, and his heart pounded when he noticed the envelope in her hand.

"Good morning, Mr. Reed," and handed him the letter. "Mr. Marshall asked me to give you this, and also he asked to see if you would stop in his office at your convenience."

John looked at the sealed envelope and noticed his name hand-written on the envelope. John helped Janet with her chair.

"Sure, I would be glad too, Ms. Pierce."

"Janet, please, Mr. Reed."

"Okay, then it's John, Janet. Do you know what this is all about?" John asked while holding up the envelope.

John could see the puzzled look on her face and knew she did not know anything, "No, Mr., John, no, I don't. I was asked to give this to you." Sensing John's plight, Janet stood with her coffee and spoke politely and sympathetically. "I'll leave. Maybe, you will find what you need in your letter."

"Thanks, Janet. When would it be possible for me to leave?"

"Most anytime today, let me see what time I can get you and Mr. Marshall together, and I'll set your departure around your meeting, if that's okay?"

"Sure, sounds fine."

"You don't have to go home today, John. In fact, you can stay as long as you like."

"No, thank you. I do appreciate your thoughtfulness. I feel I need to get back home as soon as I can."

Janet walked away, and she knew that Patti had left in a rush. She also knew John was upset. She wanted to stay, but she needed to leave John with his note.

John took a sip of his drink. He looked at his letter and waited until he was alone. He took out his small pocketknife and tried to open the letter at the seal. Before giving up and sliding the sharp edge of the knife along the fold of the envelope, thinking he should have known Patti would seal a letter perfectly. He laid the knife on the table and carefully retrieved the letter. John looked at the page before reading. It was hand-written with one smudge at the bottom near the signature. It appeared a teardrop made the mark. He could almost hear Patti's voice as he read the letter.

Dear John,

Where are you? No one here seems to know. I don't have much time to tell you all that has happened in the last few minutes, but I got the contract. Mr. Marshall said he made up his mind weeks ago. He wants me to come with the deal. I mean he wants me to work for him on this project. I told him I would have to talk to you before I could give him an answer. They are here with the van to take me to the airfield and from there straight to International Airport. I do wish I could see you before I leave, but if I miss this flight; the next flight available is tomorrow. I'll call you tonight at your home.

I Love You

Patti

PS: By the way, this is the first Dear John letter I've ever written. I hope you like it.

John looked over the letter. He could not believe what he read and what all had transpired in the past few fleeting minutes. He folded the letter and put it back in the envelope, only to take it from the envelope and read it again. He was rereading the letter when Janet Pierce returned.

"Mr. Reed, Mr. Marshall is in a meeting right now. He can see you after lunch. If this is not convenient, and you need to go right away," she motioned with her hand palm up to the letter, "I can arrange a flight for you immediately if you need to go."

John folded the letter and put it away. "That's fine, Janet. I don't have anything else to do. I will pack and be ready whenever Mr. Marshall is free."

"Can I help with anything?"

"I don't guess you can. I feel like the rug has been pulled out from under me." He held the envelope. "Yet everything I could hope for is in this letter. All I need to do is be at home in time to answer a call from Chicago."

"If it's all right with you, John," Janet wanting to be useful, "I'll have housekeeping pack your things. You can relax here and maybe eat something. I'll have you ready to go right after your meeting with Mr. Marshall."

"Sure, that's fine, and thank you again, Janet." She smiled and left. John pushed back his chair and turned from the table so he could watch the labor of an efficient staff erect a tent. He laid his right arm on the table, and John's waiter returned bringing him a fresh Coke.

John asked, "Why are they erecting a tent? Is it because of the weather?"

"We are having a cookout tonight, and the forecast is for rain," replied the waiter. "We are running behind, but lunch will be ready in a few minutes. Can I get you anything while you wait?"

"No, I don't guess. I'll just sit and watch if that's all right? Do you serve every meal outside?"

"No, Sir, we have a large conference room in the guest facilities. Ms. Pierce likes everything set with a theme, and our guests do seem to love the courtyard meals."

The minutes past slowly while John waited to visit with Jack Marshall. People were eating lunch, and the laughter and conversation were louder. Friends were spending time with friends. For many in this group, it would be a year before they would see each other again, but one could tell they were already looking forward to next year.

Janet Pierce walked to John's table unnoticed. John flinched when she said, "Mr. Marshall is free to see you whenever you are ready, Mr. Reed."

"I'm ready." Picking up his knife and returning it to his pocket, John stood. He held the letter in his hand. John followed her as they entered the house from the back entrance.

Janet reported, "Your and Ms. Scanlon's bags have been sent to the plane. The plane is loaded and on stand by." She stopped at the door. "I'm calling the motor pool now. If I'm not here when you leave your meeting with Mr. Marshall, tell anyone you are ready to go." She held out her hand, and John took her hand. Somewhat surprisingly, she hugged him. "I do hope everything works out for you, Mr. Reed." She opened the door for John.

"Come in, John." Marshall stood and walked around his desk to meet John. He took John's hand and motioned for him to take one of the two chairs in front of his desk. John took the closest, and Marshall took the other.

Almost bubbly, Marshall continued, "John, it has been busy around here. Janet tells me she has you packed and ready to go. She senses there is something wrong. I have told her nothing. I love to see her in action. She is super and the most efficient person I've got at getting things done. She has a heart of gold and will make someone a special wife one day. Well, I know Patti didn't have time to tell you all we talked about in her letter, so if there is anything I can fill you in on?" Waiting on a response from John, he paused.

"Yes, I hope you can. It's, well, I don't know what to ask."

"John, I won't keep you, but to start, I would like to give you a brief background on our project. Patti most likely didn't tell you anything. The project we are working on is for NASA." Marshall handed John a familiar object, "Do you know what this is?"

"Yes, we used a couple of these yesterday. It is a soft drink insulator of some sort. Is this something NASA needs?"

"NASA probably doesn't need any of these, but you are right. It is an insulator. They do, on the other hand, need the insulation. I plan to make and market this little gadget and other products related to this." He handed John a circuit board that was standing in a wooden holder. "Do you know what this is?"

John answered, "A circuit board."

"Right again. If you will notice there is a coating over the board. Our project started out by trying to achieve a coating that could keep circuit boards like the one you are holding from aging or breaking down for use in the space shuttle or any other space craft. You know they are planning to scrap the shuttle. Now this is NASA's need: in certain areas of the space shuttle, there are extreme heat and cold. The changing conditions in temperature have created some performance break down in the circuit boards and probably other things as well. You can understand that NASA is always seeking to achieve a zero percent failure rate in any component. What we used before was doing a better job than the other companies who were involved in the project. I entered in this project to improve the old coating we were using on the chips. We have been in search of something better for years. Our old coating was a silicone-based product, but it aged too fast, meaning that these boards had to be replaced often. So I started with a silicone base and began putting different compounds with it to produce a more durable product. I had a concoction of silicone boiling on a burner. I added a mixture to the silicone that is something like molten sand. My thought was to make a glass-like substance that would coat the boards and be a hard seal and less flexible. In research and development on something like this, I use numerous ideas and keep a large wastebasket handy. When I mixed the two compounds, they started to firm, so I dipped that board and ten more before it became too firm to coat. I was going to reheat the mixture, but it was stable. That wasn't a total surprise." Marshall continued, "Many times compounds take on a different character when they go through a chemical change. I put that aside for the day and picked up where I left the next morning. I touched one of the boards that had a thicker coating, and it was still hot. Not warm, hot! This one had the smoothest and thinnest coating of all, and it was warm. I picked up the boiler and it burned my fingers. John, to get to an end, the mixture was more like a hard rubbery wax. We scraped some of the mixture in small chips to see how long it would take to cool. It took hours! We drilled a hole in the middle of the solid compound in the pan, and inserted a probe into the center, put sensors on the outside to monitor the temperature differences. When the outside cooled to room temperature, it stayed room temp. It took days for the center to cool. I thought the hot temperature was a reaction to the chemicals at first. Then we realized during the process of heating, when the mixture started to change, it became an insulation of the heat used in production. The mixture is easy to manage. It's flexible in sheets under one-inch thickness and relatively inexpensive to make. We got what we were looking for and more with this formula.

"The reason I tell you all of this is when Patti came in this morning, she appeared dejected and mad. Well, I surprised her twice. She was seated in the same seat where you are seated. I don't make a lot of small talk, especially in business, and I'm telling you all this so you will know something about the company since you will be helping Patti make her decision. The first surprise was on both of us. I told her I wanted her to come to work for me now that she was through with the details of our contract. By the way, her company makes the circuit boards for us. She asked me what I meant. I told her I had signed the contracts and put a clause she had to come with the deal, or no deal. The truth is Anderson and Company or OMC, the parent company, is the only company I ever considered. She acted angry saying, 'Well, it's nice you decided to ask.'

"I laughed. I guess her boldness is what attracted me to her in the first place. I explained that I didn't feel she would want to refuse my offer when she heard the package. I told her she could do the job I have in mind for her anywhere in the world. This would be a marketing job for the new product. I showed and explained to her basically what I've shown you. This wouldn't be working with OMC or against them in any way. I told her that you two might want to live here for a while. I handed her the paperwork she needed for OMC to start manufacturing the circuit boards. I repeated the offer again to her and presented a folder that explained her job description and a complete salary package with a sign-on bonus. She looked inside the folder at the salary package. The sign-on bonus is stock in Marshall Industries.

"Now, this is the job I offered her: to market a new product that has endless possibilities without any restrictions on where she needed to live. She was going over the figures, and they were very good, I might add. I told her I could have offered her the job in Chicago last month. I had my mind made up then on whom I would use. The reason I delayed was to have a reason to bring her here. I told her the basic story I told you yesterday, that I was going to sweep her off her feet. She didn't look very impressed.

She asked, 'You've made me a fantastic offer, and you say it really doesn't hinge on the contract, right?'

"I said that's correct. OMC is giving you their blessing. The contract signed, sealed, and in your hand, but they think it hangs with you taking the job I'm offering. She said, 'Let me talk it over with my fiancé. I do have to consider him in this matter.'

"I couldn't believe it. She was still going on with the charade or maybe she was thinking about the boy back home. I was quiet for a moment;

I really couldn't figure her out. I thought she might be protecting her company. She might be thinking of you. I said, Patti, I stopped by your room yesterday to talk to you and John about this deal."

Marshall walked around the desk and sat in his chair. "I told her about the conversation I had with you and that you explained she was getting ready for the evening, so we sat in the room and talked briefly. I told her that I understood why she was in the mood she was in this morning from the talk you and I had last night. You two must have thought she was not getting the contract, and I presumed she already knew.

"I brought her here for a couple of reasons. You already know of one; the other was to work with the research center. I told you I surprised her twice. Well, here is number two. I told her my plan to woo her changed because of the conversation you and I had yesterday. When I saw how much you loved her, I couldn't go on with my plan. At that statement, she almost dropped her fortune for which she came."

Marshall was speaking quieter now. "She was unaware. I mean I almost knocked her out of her chair. Then I said, Patti, listen to me. I know we are not friends yet, but I feel I need to give you some friendly advice. John isn't like me. He doesn't have a plan. I feel he's the type man that might not ever say a word about his feelings as long as you have that ring on your finger.

"She sat there for a moment, speechless. Then she stood and asked me if I could find out when the next flight to Chicago would be leaving the islands. She asked me if she could be excused because she needed to talk to you. Janet got busy finding a flight, and Patti went looking for you.

"Oh, by the way, John, I called my ex-wife last night. I couldn't sleep after our conversation." Marshall paused for a moment then looked away from John to a picture of her on his desk. "You know, I felt by her voice she had been expecting my call. There's more, but I hope we'll get a chance to talk again."

"Mr. Marshall, why did she leave in such a hurry?" John asked.

"I don't know, John, other than it was the only flight we could get booked for her, and you know how hard it is to get passed security now. I never thought I would interfere in anyone's business especially someone's love life. I never dreamed I would ever call Marianna, but I did. Now, I'm going to Georgia as soon as the last guests leave. I leave Monday night and plan an extended stay to visit and get to know her again. Thanks, John."

John stood, and Marshall followed. John held out his right hand to Marshall.

"Thanks again for your hospitality, Mr. Marshall. This adventure has been life changing for me. Maybe it will turn out to be life changing for you as well." John turned and walked to the door.

Jack Marshall said, "As soon as I return from my trip to Georgia, I'll call. Be sure to let Janet know where you can be reached."

John walked from Jack Marshall's office. No Janet Pierce in sight. He wasted no time looking for her and walked through the foyer on his way to the front door when he heard Janet's voice.

"Mr. Reed," she was running as she called out, "Your van is waiting on you outside." She was holding a note pad and pen. "Let me have your address and phone numbers."

John paused long enough to give her both. She gave John her card.

"Call me, John, if you need anything."

"I will and thanks. You all have been invaluable to me. This is a unique place, and I'll always remember my stay."

"Oh, I'm sure you will be here again. One thing about Mr. Marshall, his friends are always welcome." Janet opened the door and walked John to the van. The driver opened the door; then he and John drove away with Janet standing, watching, giving a last wave as the van turned onto the main road. The plane was ready when John arrived. He and the pilot boarded and were in the air in minutes. They flew over the estate on their way. He could see the tent now erected, and the open fields where he and Patti had ridden.

The trip to the main island was short. The landing was uneventful, and the pilot taxied the plane to the fence where the Jeep was parked. They had not come to a complete stop when it started to sprinkle rain. John and the pilot finally got all the luggage loaded in the Jeep. John was straightening the back of the Jeep when he heard the small engine of the plane start.

He had not thanked the pilot. John stepped around to the fence and waved. The pilot waved back to acknowledge. John returned to the Jeep and watched as the plane maneuvered into place, and then waited briefly before taking off. John wondered as the plane disappeared into the clouds about the weather conditions and the pilot's safety. The rain was steady as he traveled home.

Arriving at Susan's home, John unloaded the luggage. He put away his clothes and left Patti's things packed. John walked downstairs to the main room. He had not noticed the doors to the patio were in place. A note was taped to the door located in the middle of the wall. The note was in pencil and printed from the contractor.

John,

The door company tried to contact you Friday and could not find you. You had noted on the purchase order that I was the contractor. They called me, and I had them delivered. Nick came over, and we set them in place. They still need more shimmying, but they are steady and useable.

See you Monday,

Gus

The view was better than before. Now while waiting for Patti's call, he could watch it rain. John tried to occupy his mind, but he could not work. He thought of Patti's flight. He did not ask her departure time, but he felt it had to be near noon because of the rush in getting to International. She could have made a flight by noon but that might push it with security. When would she try to call? Leaving that late would put her in Chicago around two, maybe three in the morning Chicago time. John realized that he was in for a long wait. Hanging around a house with nothing to do was not John's idea of fun. The newly installed glass doors gave a view to the pool and patio. He stood and watched the rain drops hit the pool for a few moments. The steady drip from the roof and the sound of the rain brought a hollow feeling. It would be the longest day he had ever spent. How he hated to wait. He had to find something to do, but what. He did not want to watch TV, and he could not work. There was nothing to do, but wait.

CHAPTER 20

With a heavy heart and an empty stomach, John made a ham and cheese sandwich with bread that was a few days old. He placed the sandwich in the microwave for a few seconds to freshen the bread and melt the cheese. He retrieved the sandwich, and placed a splash of mustard and some dill pickles on top of the steaming hot meat. He took a bite and placed his snack on a paper plate. He returned the condiments to the refrigerator and grabbed a Coke. He took his snack to the bedroom where he thought he might watch TV to pass time. Walking into the bedroom, he noticed the answering machine blinking. How did he miss the messages when he brought in the luggage? He took a bite of the sandwich and listened to the messages as he looked for the remote.

"Mr. Reed, this is Tamara with R & W Windows and Doors. Your order is complete. Please call me at extension 456 to set a time for delivery. Thank you."

"That's taken care of." He deleted the message. The next message was from Susan.   "I knew you wouldn't be home from your vacation, but I can't wait to hear the details so call me anytime day or night, bye. I mean it. Call me."

The next message dazed John.

"John, I have a minute before boarding, and I will have a short stop in San Francisco. I doubt that I will have time to call from there. I would call from the plane, but I don't know when you will return home. I'm scheduled to arrive at O' Hare, 2:30 Chicago time. I'm so glad you followed me to the airstrip. It will make my trip seem shorter. Bye, I have to board now. I love you."

"I love you." John answered Patti talking to himself. "Let me think. If she gets to Chicago at 2:30, I don't know if she has a car or if she will take a cab. My guess is she will take a cab. Okay, it's probably an hour before she'll get to her apartment." John started worrying. "That's too late for her to be in a cab in a big city." He started to count the hours on his fingers. "So if she's home by 3:30, she can call me around 10:30." He looked at the clock on the nightstand: 6:38, "Four hours, I think I can make it."

John finished his sandwich and Coke. He decided to shower. He left the door open to the bathroom so he could hear the phone in case the portable decided not to work. A quick shower and John would be ready for the wait. He knew better than to work, so he pulled a club chair close to the end of the bed, found the remote control, and started scanning the channels. He found an old John Wayne western, "The Searchers." John placed the remote on the left arm of the chair. He held the portable phone in his right hand. He was set, and it was not long until the interest in the movie captivated his thoughts.

The phone rang. John jumped up and ran to the stationary phone on the nightstand not thinking about the portable in his right hand, an anxious, "Hello!"

"Hi, baby brother. How did everything go this weekend?" John looked at the clock 8:44.

"Great, Sissy, how are things over there?"

"Fine, just fine. Tell me about your weekend. I left a message for you to call when you got home. I knew you wouldn't, so I set my alarm to call at ten your time, but I couldn't wait because I felt you would be at home by now. Is something wrong?"

"Why do you ask?"

"Just a guess. The sound of your voice for one thing, and you haven't called me Sissy since you were ten."

"Well, Sis. I don't know how it went. I'm waiting on a call from Patti."

"Do you need to call me back later after you've talked to her?"

"No, it's still too early." There was a long pause.

"It sounds like something is going on?"

"Yes, there is. Patti's home is Chicago. She had to go back for a couple of days. Sis, I don't even know where to start telling you about all this, but I intend to marry this girl. I love her, and if, well... I guess that's all."

"John, have you asked her to marry you?"

"No, I didn't have time."

"What do you mean? You didn't have time."

"The night isn't long enough, and my head is not clear enough to tell you."

Susan, feeling the anxiousness of his answer, asked, "John, do you need me to come home?"

Susan's question was seriously offered on her part, but it made John laugh a little.

"No! Why do you ask that?"

Quietly she responded, "Because you sound like you need help."

"To put it bluntly, Sis, all I need is for Patti to say yes when she returns from Chicago."

"And if she says yes, John, what then?"

"We get married."

"When?"

"I don't know the answer to that question but the sooner the better for me."

"Okay, John, I'll let you go. It sounds like you need to get that call from Chicago. I'll call you back tomorrow, if that's all right?"

"Look, Sis, I'm sorry if I sounded angry, but the truth is I am on edge. Please call me any time after 12:00 my time here. I want to talk to Patti, and then I can make more sense."

"Let's set a time. How about ten in the morning your time; does that sound okay?"

"Ten will be a good. I'll be waiting for your call. Love you. Bye."

John felt many different emotions, too many for only one day. He could not remember the last time he was short with anyone, especially his sister. He walked to the lavatory and splashed some water on his face. He, with water dripping from his face onto his shirt, stood looking for a hand towel. He didn't see a towel and instead of walking to the linen closet for a new one, John used his shirttail to dry. He returned to the movie. Ethan was taking out his frustration with a six-gun, but then he was shooting at savages in the attempt to rescue Debbie. John had no enemies; he had no one to fight, but he wanted to rescue Patti. At last the phone was ringing.

"Where is the phone?" he cried out. He left the portable in the bathroom, so he grabbed the phone by the bed. "Hello!"

"Hello, John, this is Patti. I miss you."

"I miss you, Patti. When are you coming back?"

She laughed and said, "Believe it or not, I already have my flight. I'll be there Wednesday afternoon. ETA is 3:50 P.M. your time."

"How did you get a flight so soon?"

"I have my laptop, and if you got my message, I had a short layover which gave me enough time to schedule my flight. I am trying to tie some loose ends here. Then I will be free to stay as long as I need to stay with you. Mr. Marshall asked me to do some work there, and I want us to discuss that. I want to sit down with you and tell you what I want out of life."

John interrupted, "Patti, all I want is to spend the rest of my life with you. I don't know what we have to work out, but I know I'm willing to do what ever it takes."

She paused, and John's heart raced. It was beating 90 miles an hour and felt like it was in his throat.

"I need to get some sleep because I can't rest on a plane. I have to set my alarm to call my parents. I don't want my dad to leave for work before I have a chance to talk with them. I'll see you Wednesday. I love you, John, goodnight."

"Bye, Patti, I love you too."

John placed the receiver back on its base. He found the portable and placed it in the charger. He realized he waited all day for a call and did not even ask for her phone number. He tried *69, which didn't work.

He looked at the receiver. "I can't believe my sister doesn't have caller ID. Heavens, Sis, this is the 21st Century."

CHAPTER 21

With the radio playing and alarm buzzing, Patti looked around, not sure where she was for a moment, and sat up in bed. She stopped the alarm by switching to the radio and music. When her head cleared, she remembered the reason for her early rising. She grabbed the phone and placed the call to her parents' home.

The soft familiar voice of her mother, "Hello"

"Hi, Mom, this is Patti."

"I remember, Patti. How are you? Where are you?"

"My apartment."

"When did you get home?"

"Last night, late. Mom, has Dad gone to work?"

"No, dear, he hasn't. Do you need to talk to him? Hold on and I'll get him."

"No! Don't get him. See if he will stay until I can come over. I have news to tell both of you."

"I'm sure your dad can stay. What time should we expect you?"

"As soon as I can shower and dress. Mid-morning I would guess."

"If there is any reason he can't wait on you, I'll call you back."

"Okay, Mom. I'm getting in the shower now. I'll see you in a bit, bye."

Patti wanted to stay in bed but not today. She showered and washed her hair. As she was drying it, she heard her phone ring. She switched off the hairdryer to grab the phone when she heard her answering machine. Oh no, she thought, Dad won't be home.

"Patti, I guess, you are probably still in the shower. I thought I would call you and let you know your dad is staying home today, so there's no need to rush dear. Come when you can. We are both anxious to hear your news." Patti smiled at the news she had for her parents, and at the same time, felt a twinge in her abdomen at the thought of explaining to Ronald. She would leave the message signal flashing. She noticed she had messages last night when she arrived home, but all messages would have to wait. She styled her hair and applied her eye makeup. Patti hurried to her closet for a pair of old jeans and a sweatshirt. She brushed her teeth. Now, all she needed was her keys, and she was ready to go. The traffic was heavy as usual, but she was moving away from the heaviest flow. She had to meet with her parents before she could make her next meeting.

It was a beautiful morning and to see her old neighborhood was always special. Patti felt butterflies in her stomach as she turned in the drive. She parked the car by the front sidewalk. Patrick Scanlon watched for his daughter and met her halfway as she walk toward the front door.

"Come in," Patrick shouted. Patti put her arms around her father's neck and kissed his cheek. "What's the big news? I bet I can guess."

Patti grabbed his arm, and they walked inside the door.

"Where's Mom?"

"She's in the kitchen. She's making muffins, and we have coffee and juice."

"Well, let's join her." Walking through the living room, Patti held her Dad's arm. Her parents had remodeled the kitchen and added a spacious sunroom. The kitchen and adjoining sunroom were located on the south end of the house. The sunroom's half- octagonal shape opened the view of the Scanlon's grounds. The light from all the glass and the cheerful way it was decorated made this part of the house a fun room to enjoy food, company, or the view. A breakfast nook with a large round table and six upholstered chairs separated the large sitting area and kitchen. The table held three place settings, and the aroma of the bread baking and the coffee brought back good memories for Patti.

"Welcome home, dear." Patti releasing her dad's arm to give her mother a hug.

"Hmm, something smells good, Mom."

"You two have a seat. I'll give the muffins a few more minutes. Patti there's half and half in the refrigerator for your dad. Patrick, please pour the coffee."

Both Patti and her father moved to their assigned duties. Patrick poured the coffee into a carafe then walked to the table and filled each cup. Patti walked to the table with the half and half. "Is it all right to pour from the carton?"

"It's okay with me, what about it, Mother?" asked Patrick.

"Sure, you barbarians, go ahead."

"Okay, Mom, I'll get the glass creamer. Is that better?"

"Yes, dear, I'm proud of you."

"Other than snacks on the plane, my last meal was Saturday night," Patti admitted.

"Now when are we going to hear about this big sale of yours? Patrick asked.

"You know me too well, don't you, Dad?"

Elizabeth Scanlon joined the two with a basket of muffins wrapped in a linen cloth. Patti and Patrick waited until Elizabeth was seated.

Patrick began, "Thank you, Lord, for letting Patti have a safe trip. Thank you for this day and our food. Amen."

"Help yourself," Elizabeth urged. Patti broke a muffin in half as she placed it on her plate. She took her butter knife and cut a small piece of butter and placed it next to her muffin. She cut the butter into four sections and put one quarter on each half to melt into the muffin. She left the other two small pats of butter for another muffin.

"Well, I did make a big sale and with the sale came a job offer." Patti was taking her time and biting into her muffin. "This is delicious, Mom."

"Thank you, but what kind of job?"

"It would be with Marshall Industries, the company with whom I made the sale."

Patrick, with a serious tone stated, "I gathered that. Where would you work? Would it entail as much travel as you are doing now?"

"No, I don't think I would have to travel, but I really don't know what my job description would be at this point."

"You're thinking about a job, and you don't know what kind of job it is?"

"No, Sir, I don't know everything, but I know it's marketing a new product. Mr. Marshall offered me the job and said I could do this job anywhere in the world. I left in too big of a rush to have all the details. I had to catch a plane."

Elizabeth listened to the professionals talk business while they enjoyed their breakfast. She studied Patti's face as her father interrogated her.

"Where were you when you got this offer, at the airport?"

"No, Dad. I was in Jack Marshall's office on his private estate."

"Then why were you in such a rush to catch a plane?"

"I had to catch a plane on the main island in order to be here this morning. I didn't have time to pack or get all the details of his offer. He made the offer so I could be thinking about the job. It doesn't require an immediate answer."

Patrick asked questions about the job throughout the meal, and Patti answered as many questions as she could. Many times it was a guess to his question. Everyone had stopped eating, and almost unnoticed, Elizabeth cleared the dishes and food from the table. She left only the coffee.

"How much was the offer in a basic money package? They had - at least - to make an offer of money and benefits."

"Dad, it is a great package! He gave me a portfolio of the benefits. It's great; but even if I take the job, it could be for a short time. In fact, I feel I need to take the job, if for no other reason, to help merge the deal for both companies best interest."

"Now, I'm confused," Patrick admitted. "Is it a merger of the two companies?'

"Dad, I guess merge was a poor choice of words. I feel I would be an asset to both companies at this point." Elizabeth returned to her seat between her two loved ones; she placed her right hand on Patti's left hand and her left hand on Patrick's right.

"Patrick, I feel Patti has more to tell us than about the job offer. When has Patti asked us about a job? Doesn't she always inform you the minute she does something new?"

At her mother's perception, Patti closed her eyes and bowed her head for a moment. She smiled a girlish smile. With her face blushing and her heart racing, she was struggling with what to say.

"You're right, Mother, all I have told you is true, but there is more. I have met a man." Looking at both her parents, "I don't know where to start. I'm in love. His name is John Reed. I've come home to tell you and to give Ronald his ring back and try to explain to him. I felt this was something I had to do in person."

There was complete silence in the room.

"Then what's next, Patti?" Elizabeth nervously and upset asked breaking the silence, "What are your plans?"

"I have today and tomorrow to get everything done. I would like to wear your dress like I have already planned. That is if Marge can finish tomorrow."

"Tomorrow! This doesn't sound like you, Patti. This sounds like you are going back to be married."

"I guess it does, Mom."

"You have planned everything?"

"No, Mom. We haven't talked about marriage, but I know Mom and Dad. I know he is right for me."

Elizabeth, holding back tears, was interrogating Patti now, with Patrick watching, "How can you know? Is he a smooth talker? Has he brainwashed you? You've only been gone a week. When, Patti? When did you have time to fall in love in a week?"

"Now that the hard part is over, let me try and give you a brief recap of my past week. I met John the first day I was on the island. We shared a table during breakfast, and it seemed like I had known him forever. Mr. Marshall, later in the week, invited me to his estate for the weekend. He was having a corporate meeting at his home, and I had a bad feeling about going unescorted, so I asked John if he would accompany me to this estate. I guess I was afraid things might not be like Marshall described. After all, I didn't know him that well. Mr. Marshall I mean."

Elizabeth interrupted, "And you knew John well enough to escort you?"

"Yes, I did. John agreed to go, and we found the weekend to be more like a formal corporate picnic. Marshall has a wonderful home on an island, and all the amenities were at all the guests disposal. We went horseback riding one morning, and we stopped for a picnic lunch. We began to talk, so I asked John to tell me about his hometown. I listened to the way he described his home by its people and events in his life. I thought to myself, 'Why isn't a caring man like this married?'

"I thought of several of my friends that would like to meet a man like John. We started our ride back to the stables, and, in my mind, I would think of one girl after another, each time finding reasons they wouldn't be right for John. Then I thought of Janice Kellum, a colleague of mine. Yes, Janice would be perfect. She is beautiful, quiet, hardworking, loyal, and smart. She is in her early thirties and has said to me she would like to meet someone with character. There was only one reason not to introduce them: I didn't want John to be with anyone else. That's when I realized I was jealous of my thoughts of him with anyone but me. I even thought if only I had met John before Ronald. This gave me a hollow feeling in my stomach. I felt uneasy about Ronald and me since I was having thoughts like this. I wouldn't let myself think about John and another girl anymore.

"I decided I wouldn't continue pushing for the sale. As much fun as I was having, I was ready to cut my losses, get off that island, and return home to gather my thoughts. You know that's not like me. I was in agony; my every thought was about John and me. What could be or could have been possible if I had met him a few months ago. I decided to leave the Marshall estate the next day and come home as soon as I could arrange a flight.

"The next morning, which was yesterday morning, I think. It seems longer ago than yesterday, but I felt better, thinking somewhat more clearly. I was having a meeting with Mr. Marshall. He surprised me with this job offer. Anyway, we were going over this deal and job opportunity. When out of the blue Mr. Marshall said, 'Patti, don't make a mistake with John. This guy is crazy in love with you.'

"When he said that, a feeling went over me like I've never felt before. I couldn't think of anything but John; the sale, the money, the job opportunity, none of that mattered to me anymore. I wanted to find John and tell him how I felt and that I needed to come home and tell Ronald face to face what happened."

With a tear streaming down her right cheek, Patti smiled as she resumed, "Mother, you and Dad will love him. He is the most polite, sensitive man I have ever met, and Mom," Patti took her Mother's hand in both of hers, "the thing I love most is he looks at me the same way Dad looks at you."

Now tears were flowing from both Patti and Elizabeth while they embraced. Patrick, about one sob away from joining his wife and daughter, walked to the sink. He poured out his cold coffee, rinsed his cup, and left it in the sink. He stood there for a moment to regroup and gain his composure. He walked back to the table and placed his hands on each of his girls' shoulders.

"Patti, what can we do to help? Your mother and I will be your servants for the next couple of days."

Patti turned and put her arms around her father's waist and hugged him.

"You know, Patti, your mother and I never liked Ronald anyway."

"Yon didn't!" Patti said in amazement. Elizabeth, wiping away her tears, shook her head in agreement.

"I never knew that. Why didn't you tell me?"

"We didn't tell you, Patti, because we trusted your judgment, and we trust you now. We know you too well and love you too much to interfere.

It's not that we felt Ronald was wrong for you, but I didn't necessarily think he was right for you. We have prayed for many things in our lives, but your mother and I have always prayed that your sisters and you would find the right husband. You pray and trust God, and it's easy to trust, especially when none of your daughters bring home a rock star."

Patti, laughing through tears, wiped her face on one of her mother's linen napkins.

Patti asked, "May I be excused? I need to make a call."

"By all means, dear. Your father and I will clean the kitchen while you are gone. It sounds like I need to make a few calls also. I'll make my list."

As Patti was leaving the room, she asked her mother to call Marge right away. She wanted the dress to be finished if it were possible. Patti walked upstairs to her bedroom and made the call to Ronald's office. "Hi, Ronald, this is Patti."

"Well, hello, Gorgeous. I thought you weren't coming back for a couple of weeks. When did you get home?"

"Around three this morning. Can I see you tonight?"

"Sure, I planned to go to a game with Michael, Matt, and Drew tonight. Why don't you go with us? It's one of those great games: the Sox are playing the Yankees."

"No, thanks, you know I'm not much of a White Sox fan. Is there anyway you could meet me for lunch?"

"Sure, lunch will be fine. You name the place."

"Well, I'm at my parents' house. I can make it back to the city by one if that's good for you. What about the place across from your office you like so much?"

"Anthony's?"

"Yes, what about Anthony's?"

"Sounds great. I'll meet you there at one."

CHAPTER 22

Patti drove back to her apartment to dress for her last date with Ronald. Not wanting to overdress, she decided on a black two-piece pants suit with a gold sleeveless shell. Patti packed an overnight bag of things she would need to stay with her parents until Wednesday.

She arrived at Anthony's a few minutes before one. Ronald came in a few minutes later. He stepped to the side of the table and kissed Patti on her cheek, as she remained seated. He helped her with her chair to move closer to the table and sat across from her. Patti had both hands under the table with Ronald's ring in her right hand.

"Ronald, I have something to tell you, and I don't know how to start."

"This sounds serious. What is it, Patti?

She tucked her head sitting in silence for what seemed an eternity. Their waiter broke the spell handing them a menu. "Good afternoon. I'm Kevin, your server today. Can I get you anything to drink?'

Ronald feeling the intensity asked, "Could you bring us water for now and give us a few moments?"

"Sure." Kevin brought the water and disappeared.

With a quiver in her voice Patti started, "Ronald, I love you, but I don't want to marry you."

"What!"

"I don't know how to explain what has happened, but I met a man this past week… and I came to…What I want to say is I can't discuss my feelings with him until I've made things right by telling you." Patti held Ronald's engagement ring between her index finger and thumb giving it back to him. The moment was tense and both were silent. Patti looked at

Ronald, but Ronald could only look at the ring he was now holding in his hand. "I'm sorry, Ronald. I hope you can believe me when I tell you, I love you."

"Patti, you need to think this over. Do you know what this means?"

"Yes, Ronald, this means I can't marry you if I have any doubts about my feelings. I hate that this happened, but at the same time it has to be the best for both of us." Patti, hoping to spare his feelings, did not tell Ronald any more than he needed to know.

The news caught Ronald off guard, and he was angry. He stood and threw twenty dollars on the table, "Let me get the tip."

Ronald left, and Patti remained at her table. She took a drink of water.

"Excuse me." Kevin returned to her, "Miss, can I get you something?" Kevin noticed the exchange and thought *poor girl*. "Will you want to order?"

"No, I don't think I do. Will this cover your trouble?" Ronald's twenty was on the table and Patti handed the young man another twenty.

"Sure. Please come again; we serve excellent food." Kevin helped Patti with her chair. Patti knew this would be hard. She liked Ronald, but she now knew she never truly loved him.

Patti went to her parents' home. She let the top down and listened to an old song of Shania's blasting away. Patti could not remember feeling so relieved. She had to call John. Patti looked at her cell and decided she would wait until she got to her parents' house.

Patti returned to her parents' home precisely at three. No one was home. She ran to her room and called John. She dialed; the line was busy. She ran downstairs to the kitchen to find something to eat. She did not eat anything at lunch, but now she was ready for a snack since her troubles were behind her. Taking some cold cuts and cheese from the refrigerator, she wished she were on a plane for the islands this very minute. Ronald was the main reason she made the trip home, but he was not the only objective. She had one more chore to finish before she could return-- the dress. She dialed again from the kitchen. It was ringing. "Hello, John. This is Patti."

"Hi, Patti. When are you coming home?"

She giggled, "I like the sound of that. I told you I will be there on Wednesday, afternoon."

"Well if you won't come any sooner, will you do something for me?"

"Anything you want."

"Will you give me every number where I can reach you? I don't have even a cell number."

The next day was a busy day. Patti and her mother met Marge Fleming before her dress shop opened. Marge's hand-sewn creations had adorned the Scanlon girls to most of their special events. Marge's dresses were always Patti's favorites.

It did not take long for Marge to examine the dress when Patti stepped on the fitting platform. Marge was a magician. She did not like to rush, but for Elizabeth and Patti, she would do almost anything. Patti had her first fitting a few weeks prior to leaving for her island business trip. Marge pinned the dress in a couple of places and complained that Patti was to thin.

Wondering to herself at Patti's haste, Elizabeth was in tears for most of the fitting. Patti, in all her joy, thought her mother was caught up in the moment. She did not want to think of missing Patti's wedding and could not believe she was at this point in her life. After the fitting, Patti and Elizabeth made their way to another of Patti's favorite places to shop.

Lana Lorraine's was a unique dress shop that catered to the young and the young at heart. Patti assured her mother it was not necessary. Elizabeth said, "Some things are tradition." Tradition had been set with Patti's sisters, and it would not be broken at this point. There was not time to shop for everything Elizabeth wanted for Patti, but Lana Lorraine's was the place where they would find all the essentials for an adequate trousseau.

Late that evening, Patrick and Elizabeth were checking their list of jobs completed for Patti. Everything was in order. The wedding dress was the last item on the list, but not the least. Marge had the dress packed in a proper box for the flight. All the other clothes purchased that day were placed in the living room on display. Not only for Patrick to see, but also to make an inventory before placing them in Patrick's enormous suitcase which functioned as a trunk on wheels. They all thought this travel case was an albatross when he purchased it several years prior. Even if the airline charged more, it would handle Patti's wardrobe with ease. Patrick boasted of the capacity of this fine container; not to mention, its convenience and versatility. After the container was filled, Patrick pulled out the handle and rolled the suitcase to the garage. No need to put off loading the car because he and Patti would leave early the next morning. Patti pleaded with her father to let her take a cab, but he would not change his mind. He assured Patti he knew the best way to O'Hare. One thing Patrick hated about air travel was the rushed feeling he got on the way to the airport.

All three were standing at the foot of the stairway when the phone rang; Elizabeth searched for the phone. She was gone several minutes before she returned with the portable receiver, "It's for you, dear," handing Patti the phone.

"Hi, John, I'm about to go to bed." Patti walked into the living room and continued the conversation.

Elizabeth looked at her husband, "He sounds like a pleasant man, Patrick." Patrick sat on the stairs facing Elizabeth.

"Now, Elizabeth, you know he must be. Patti wouldn't be attracted to anyone who wouldn't be nice."

With arms folded, Elizabeth looked at her husband and asked, "Just where in the world is Walnut Grove, Mississippi?"

"I don't know, Baby, other than it's in the center of Mississippi. I found that much on the computer, but from the sound of her conversation, we will know more before long." Elizabeth joined her husband on the stairs, and Patrick placed his arm around his wife. "I didn't tell Patti, but John called me at my office. He told my secretary it was important. She has never given out my cell number to anyone before, but he convinced her it was life or death. He called to ask for my permission. I didn't know what to say, but for some reason I gave him permission. I guess I gave my blessing to Patti, so why not?" Elizabeth patted her husband's hand. They were trying not to listen to the conversation. Patrick whispered, "Listen to Patti's speech. She is happy; that's all that counts."

Elizabeth rested her head on Patrick's shoulder. "I must admit I do feel like I've been in a whirlwind the last 36 hours, but this has been the easiest wedding with which I've ever been associated. Patti and I talked about many things while we shopped. One thing I'll share with you that made me feel somewhat better. We were going over the cancel list." Elizabeth laughed nervously, "No one but Patti would make a cancel list of a wedding. She told me that she planned her wedding day and could see Ronald and her married, but never once dreamed of their life together. She went on to say she can't stop dreaming about her life with John. Listen she's not talking about a wedding. She's talking about life."

Patti was up before her alarm sounded. This was the day that she had to be on time. She would check baggage at O'Hare by nine, and her flight was scheduled to leave at 10:10 a.m. Chicago time. It was a nonstop flight, so it would be on time if not an early arrival. The day would be long, but she had to wait. She wanted to see John more with each passing minute. Patti went downstairs leaving her carry-on bag by the bottom of the stairs to eat breakfast. Coffee was ready and more muffins. Patti picked up a muffin and ate only a bite as she poured her coffee. She leaned against the cabinet, enjoying her coffee and ate her muffin by pinching off a bite at the time. Both parents entered ready to go.

"Are you both going?"

"Yes, I thought your dad could use some company on the trip back home."

"Not going in today, Dad?"

"No, some things come before work, Patti. I knew one day I would walk you down an aisle. I didn't have in mind a runway." Pointing to his watch, "Not trying to rush, but we are ready when you are, Sweetheart, and you have a plane to catch."

"I'm set. Let me brush my teeth. I'll meet you in the garage."

"I'll pull the car to the front and pick you and your mother up there."

"Okay, I'll meet you at the front," she called as she ran through the house.

Patti checked in and was given her boarding pass. She gave them both a hug and a kiss and said goodbye to her mom and dad. When she turned to walk away, Patrick and Elizabeth threw a sprinkle of rice on her. She could not help it, but she turned back and hugged them both at the same time.

"I hope you both know how much I love you."

With tears in all eyes, Patti walked through security. She, feeling a tug on her heart for her parents and the yearning for the adventure, waved bye one more time.

It would be a long flight, and Patti rarely flew first class. She never thought it was worth the price difference. Hoping she could rest, she reasoned to take advantage of the frequent flyer miles and upgrade this time. Her flight left on time, but late into the flight the pilot announced several times they were behind schedule. She looked at her watch. It was three, and John would surely be waiting at the airport. She grew more impatient by the minute. The plane had been descending for quite some time. They were more than 30 minutes late when the pilot announced they were cleared for landing.

Patti, looking for John, walked through her gate and rushed past security. She stood around in the waiting area and was surprised that John was not there. There was a crowd around the terminal station. She looked to make sure John was not standing out of her sight. She walked around several people then decided he might be at the baggage claim. She started to the escalator that would carry her to claim her luggage when she noticed people parting ahead of her. Some were going to the left, others to the right, veering away from their path and walking around something. Then John came into view! He stood in the middle of the passageway. Searching the crowd carefully, not to miss Patti. He stood there with his hands behind his back. He smiled when he saw Patti, and she picked up her pace. She stopped short of John when right in front of everyone he knelt down on one knee. Patti brushed her hair back with her hand as she looked into his eyes.

He took one hand from behind his back. It was a perfect red rose. He handed it to Patti, and she accepted the rose.

John took her left hand and said, "I didn't know what loneliness was until four days ago. I never want to spend another day without you. I wish I could write a song because if I could, then everyone would know how much I love you. One song should be in everyone. You are a magnificent jewel, the prize of a lifetime, and a rare gem I thought I would never find."

He moved his left arm from behind his back and presented a little black box. He let go of her hand long enough to open the box and remove a beautiful round solitaire diamond mounted in platinum. "Patti, I want you to be my wife." He slipped the ring on her finger. "Patti, will you marry me?"

With tears flowing, she looked into John's blue eyes, "Yes, John, I will marry you. I will be your wife forever."

A crowd, with only a few slipping by the scene, formed to watch the proposal. When John stood for a kiss and embraced Patti, the crowd applauded and cheered.

"Let's go get your luggage," John suggested. They held hands, visited, and walked through the halls of the airport. The luggage was late coming around the conveyor, but time was not a factor anymore. Patti was telling John all about her trip.

Patti's special package appeared first. "That package is mine, and there's my suitcase." Patti pointed at it as he waited for the conveyer.

John grabbed the suitcase, "It's one thing I know about you, you pack a mean suitcase." John pulled out the handle on the large bag and placed the parcel on top. They were driving away from the airport when John asked, "Where do you want to go?"

"To the hotel, I guess, why?"

"I thought we could go get our marriage license."

"What's the rush, John?"

John turned his head to face Patti, "I can't wait. I want to marry you as soon as we can find a preacher."

CHAPTER 23

Patti and John parked under the large portico at the Hilton. A bellboy helped with the bags and offered to carry them to Patti's room. John carried the parcel as he and Patti followed the bellboy.

John said, "Do you know this is the first time I've been past the first floor?" John tipped the bellboy and the door shut. John grabbed Patti and kissed her, and she kissed him back. She led John to the sofa where they kissed a while, and they would talk a while. John told Patti all he had planned: marriage license tomorrow, wedding on Saturday.

"Do you want to see the church?"

"Do I have any say in this?"

John looked a little disappointed. "Sure, I didn't mean for it to sound that way. I meant when do you want to see the church? I didn't have enough to do to keep my mind off of you, so I thought I would do some looking around. Let me start over. Would you like to see the options we have?"

Smiling, Patti said, "I can see now you are going to be the best husband. Yes, I would love to see the options."

"Let's go now, but you are going to love this church."

They drove to a beach, a few miles away from the hotel, in the opposite direction of Susan and Jeff's house.

"What's here, John?"

"The church. It's right over there." John pointed to a large building with a thatched roof of palm leaves, opened on all sides and supported by poles.

"How did you find this place?"

"I got the idea from Adam, our morning waiter at the Hilton."

"You know, I didn't know his name."

"Adam said he missed us. I went back to the Hilton for breakfast, and Adam asked if you jilted me. I shared my good news and asked him if he knew of a church. Adam brought the concierges with all the information, to my table and put the idea into motion. I thought the structure was a pole barn on the beach when I first saw the building, but there was a difference. This structure had benches, a pulpit, and a choir loft." They walked over to the building and from inside, the view was picturesque.

"This is a church?"

"It surely is." John sat on the front pew and watched Patti. She daydreamed as she walked around the front of the altar and touched one of the pews. John was beginning to worry; he didn't know if she liked it or not. She was still pondering over the possibilities when a man came up the aisle and asked, "May I help you?" John stood, "Oh, it's you, Mr. Reed, and this must be the bride?"

"Yes, it is. Patti, this is Brother Wells, the pastor at this church."

Patti walked over to shake his hand, "Nice to meet you, Reverend Wells."

"John tells me that you two are about to enter into holy matrimony. Taking Patti's hand, he turned to John, "You have asked her, or you wouldn't be here? Right?"

"Yes, Brother Wells, I've asked and better yet, she accepted." John was grinning from ear to ear. He could not take his eyes off of his bride to be.

"Yes, John was showing me the set up. Is this for weddings only?"

"No, actually we have church services here weekly. This building is very much a part of our church's physical plant," pointing to other buildings near by. "We use this building for our main sanctuary unless the weather isn't cooperative. We have canvas panels that we unroll at times. It's a very nice way to sing and worship. You might even notice there are no instruments. Because of the humidity, we use electronic keyboards and prerecorded music. We have tremendous budget needs, so we offer weddings to help offset the money we need to carry on the Lord's work. One bad thing about the islands is the enormous cost of real estate."

Patti said, "Reverend Wells, I love this setting. What do we need to do if we are to have our wedding here?"

"Nothing, unless you want something more than the usual service we provide, and please call me Brother Dennis. That's what everyone calls me. We are busy this week, and the first opening I have for this weekend is at ten on Saturday morning. John took that time slot. We do have eleven open also, but the weddings work back to back for a reason. Some couples need witnesses. We give each couple one hour to exchange vows and take photographs. We do ask the newly married couple to stay and witness the next wedding, if possible. It makes for an interesting event, but it isn't mandatory. We can always get two witnesses.

We don't have another morning wedding after yours so unless you want to come back at one that afternoon, that lets John off the hook. He said you would want to come back, but he didn't. I also want to sit down and talk with you both. There are many places on the island that will marry anyone with a marriage license, but I feel it's my place to talk with everyone when I perform the ceremony. To make sure it's not something they are rushing into." He laughed, "That's a joke. John has informed me of your courtship. Most of the weddings I perform come in from the mainland for a wedding and a honeymoon all in one package. John and I have your meeting set up for tomorrow also at ten. Plus, I have given John some details, but you should get your marriage license tomorrow morning. We do have a twenty-four hour waiting period."

Brother Dennis and Patti wandered over to John. Patti took John's hand as she thanked Brother Dennis.

"Then I will see you tomorrow?" Brother Dennis asked.

"We will be here at ten sharp," was Patti's answer.

Patti and John left the church in the sand and went back to the Hilton for dinner. They talked and planned their next couple of days. Patti suggested they stay at the Hilton, and she would have her room changed to a honeymoon suite. Patti would find a photographer. They were set. Tomorrow would be wedding bands, the meeting with Brother Dennis, and license. Everything after tomorrow would fall into place.

Friday evening after dinner, John and Patti were sitting opposite of each other in the hotel lobby. John asked, "Patti, are you nervous?"

"Why would I be nervous? I have never been any busier than I've been in the last few days. My mother has called me and left messages, at least ten times each day." She changed from a serious look to a big grin and said softly, "Yes, I'm nervous, but I'm ready. I wish we could have married today."

"Me too."

"Why don't we call it an evening, John?"

"No. Let's stay up all night and talk about our future."

"Now, John, we have to get some rest, and you know you can't see the bride until she comes down the aisle. When I was a little girl, I planned my wedding over and over again. My vision of that day has always been so far in the future I couldn't see it. To me, it has truly felt like waiting on Christmas. When I was little, I would go to bed as soon as I could on Christmas Eve. The faster I could go to sleep, the faster Santa would come."

"I've tried that too; that's why staying up will be better. I would toss and turn all night. Then Christmas morning my mother would have to wake me. I can't wait for tomorrow, and I can't wait for Christmas. It will be great this year."

Patti said, "I can't wait until I have to wake up our little boy or girl on Christmas morning."

"I can't wait to show you off to all my folks back home. Patti, am I rushing you? You said you planned your wedding over and over. Am I taking something from you?"

"No, John, not on your life. I couldn't be more pleased. When I was a little girl, my parents wouldn't let me ask Santa for more than one thing at Christmas. Dad always said, 'Santa can't bring every boy and girl all they want.' I had to choose one thing, but every Christmas Morning I would always have a surprise from Santa. I looked for that surprise first every year. Sure I had planned my wedding, but this is going to be my surprise. I can't wait until morning."

"Where are we going to live, Patti?"

"I want to live with you, John. I don't care what region." Patti stood and held out her hand to John who was still sitting. He took her hand, and she pulled him off the sofa.

"I'll walk you to your car if you will go home."

"No, I will walk you upstairs and say goodnight for the last time because I never have to leave you again."

John tossed and turned like he said he would, but unlike his childhood, he did not have to be awakened. It was 8:15, and he was dressed with his black tie. The coat to the basic black tux he bought for his wedding was across the end of the bed. He walked over and checked the pocket again to make sure Patti's ring was where it needed to be. This had to be his hundredth time to check for the ring. The ring was there, and he would not check again. He loaded the clothes he would need in the Jeep last night. Now all he needed was his coat, and he thought *why wait*. He was to meet Patti at the Chapel in the sand as Patti named it.

John pulled into the parking space before the nine o' clock wedding started. He sat in the Jeep and watched the ceremony. The thought hit him. He knew Patti was coming in a limo. The plan was to take the limo back to the hotel. He didn't want to start his car with the wedding already in progress, and it would push him to park the Jeep and have a cab bring him back. He would have to leave the Jeep and come back later. He let out a sigh; this was not a problem after all he had accomplished in a week. John let the window down in the Jeep. Although he could not hear from the Jeep, he knew what was happening. Both brides wore short dresses. The previous bride and now attendant had netting in her hair and the new bride had some ribbons in hers. Both men were dressed in casual wear, slacks and white shirts. It was odd how closely they matched. John wondered about Patti's dress. He had not told her he was wearing a tux, and she had not breathed a word about her dress. The newest married couple kissed and ran down the church aisle. They stopped at the back where they had a small cake set up on a table. They posed for pictures with each other and then with the attending couple. John left the Jeep and walked the few feet to the area in the front of the church and back of the sanctuary. He stood out away from the group until there was a break in the photo segment.

"Congratulations, I'm John Reed."

"Hi, John, nice to meet you. We are Joanne and Richard Thomas, and this is Joanne's sister Trish and her husband Derrick. We are making this a family affair. Are you next in line?"

"Yes, I can't wait. Our wedding is at ten." John looked at his watch 9:15. "Man your wedding didn't take long."

"We are going to witness your wedding. Would you like some cake?"

"No, thanks. I better pass."

"We are going to take a few photos, and we will be ready at ten."

The two couples posed in the front of the sanctuary for pictures. The two brides hugged for a picture, and there was a handshake between grooms. Then as soon as possible, the first couple Trish and Derrick left. John watched the happy couple enjoy their moment when he heard a car approaching. He turned to see a white limousine approaching. The driver parked as close to the church walk as possible. The car remained running. The tinted windows prevented John from catching a glimpse of the occupant, but he knew it was his bride. His heart raced! His stomach turned flips! Could the other couples be as happy as he was? They certainly did not act as anxious. John walked over to Brother Dennis and informed him about the need to leave his Jeep.

As John and Brother Dennis were talking, a couple of young men parked a Jeep Wrangler next to John's Jeep. The two men began pulling camera equipment out of the back and carrying it to the church. One had a couple of video cameras with tripods. The other had two cameras he put around his neck. Both men, assembling a zone for the different kind of cameras they would use, carried bags and tripods to various places in the church. One video camera was placed in the choir section and offset to the bride's side of the church. He tested the camera with a remote device and was soon pleased with the performance. Then he walked to the rear of the sanctuary behind the last row of pews on the groom's side. He placed another video camera on a tripod. Again he adjusted the camera with a remote control and left the camera pointing toward the limo. He asked John, "Are you the groom?"

"Yes, I am." The photographer placed a wireless mic on John's lapel. He did the same to Brother Dennis. He ran up the aisle to the limo and opened the back door. He entered not only to place a mic on Patti, but also a sensor that would take over the direction of both the movie cameras. Almost unnoticed, his partner placed a digital SLR camera on a tripod behind Brother Dennis and to the groom's side; he placed another camera on a tripod and laid it on the back pew out of the way. The gentleman with the still cameras, alternating the two cameras hanging from his neck, started snapping a few shots. The two attendants were asked to come to the front, and the photographer took several candid shots of the two newlyweds with John and alone. John thought the photographer offered a nice thing to the couple. He asked for their address so he could send pictures of the wedding to them. He overheard him say, "The bride wanted to include you in the pictures and wanted to make sure you had copies. She also wanted to know if you wanted any special picture taken." They both thought that was great and wanted some pictures. John thought how lucky he was. A bride should only think of herself on her wedding day, and his bride was thinking of others.

"We are ready when you are preacher," announced the young man holding another video camera.

Brother Dennis touched John on the shoulder as a flash went off. "If everyone will take his or her place we will start. Mr. Reed, whenever you are ready; it's ten."

John said nothing but nodded as he took his place. The music started playing. The video camera in the front turned automatically to the limo at the start of the music. Focusing on the limo, the young cameraman who signaled Brother Dennis walked to the side of the church. The other cameraman, signaling to the driver to open the door, walked to the limo. The driver did as directed, and the camera flashed away. John's new friends took their places. Richard, standing by John and Joanne, waited for Patti at the back of the church pews. Both attendants looked like old pros. Patti emerged from the limo to a barrage of flashes. John could tell it was Patti by the way she moved. She had a heavy veil covering her face. Her vintage dress was beautiful and fit her perfectly. The cameramen worked proficiently with their cameras as all eyes were on Patti. As she made her last few steps, John could see her face under the veil. With everyone in place, the music stopped. Patti was standing within arms reach of her groom. Their eyes were fixed on each other as Brother Dennis started the ceremony.

"Friends, we have come today to start a new life. This ceremony will take two different lives and join into one life. John and Patti have come to this point in their lives with anticipation. Each has a preconceived idea of what the future will be yet they don't know the outcome exactly. You stand before me as new friends, but you stand also before God. God performed the first marriage in the Garden of Eden. The Bible speaks of the love Christ has for the Church. The Church is the Bride of Christ, and like today where John has come to take his bride home, one day Christ will come for his bride. If there is any reason that these two people should not be joined together, let it be known at this time." A brief pause, "John, will you take Patti's hand?"

John said, "Gladly."

Brother Dennis smiled at him, "Do you, John, take Patti to be your lawful wife, and do you promise before God and everyone here today that you will love her, honor her, and comfort her? You will keep her in sickness and in health, through good times or through bad times, for as long as you both shall live?"

John, looking into Patti's eyes, swallowed hard. He turned to the preacher, then back to Patti. He glanced for a moment at Brother Dennis. John said, "Brother Dennis, can I say something?" Not waiting for an answer, John continued, "I have known Patti for only a few days." He looked at Patti and said, "Patti, I love you with all my heart. I can only hope you know how much. I was taught by my parents to put the most effort in everything I do and if I did, God would bless me. Many times in my life, God has blessed me far more than my effort. I stand here today, and I can't believe that I'm holding onto the most precious gift I've ever received. I am so glad we found this place. This church is open to the world, and I make a vow here today to love, honor, and comfort you, to keep you in sickness and in health. I do, I will, each day for the rest of my life."

John didn't know if his hands were shaking or if Patti's were. His speech caught Patti and everyone else off guard. Even the minister had to regroup. Brother Wells, performing ceremonies many times each week, had been reciting most everything from memory, but now he needed to look back to his book for help.

"Patti, do you take this man to be your lawful wedded husband? Do you promise before God and these witnesses to love him, to honor, and comfort him in sickness and in health, through good times or through bad times, for as long as you both shall live?"

Patti could not speak. She laid her head on John's chest. After another short pause, she lifted her head and said softly, "I do."

"John, if you will place the ring on Patti's finger and repeat after me. With this ring, I thee wed."

"With this ring, I thee wed."

"And with all my worldly goods, I thee endow,"

"And with all my worldly goods, I thee endow,"

"In the name of the Father, and of the Son, and of the Holy Ghost. Amen."

"In the name of the Father, and of the Son, and of the Holy Ghost. Amen."

"Now, Patti, if you will place the ring on John's finger and repeat after me. With this ring, I thee wed."

"With this ring, I thee wed."

"And with all my worldly goods, I thee endow,"

"And with all my worldly goods, I thee endow,"

"In the name of the Father, and of the Son, and of the Holy Ghost. Amen."

"In the name of the Father, and of the Son, and of the Holy Ghost. Amen."

"What therefore God hath joined together, let not man put asunder. As an officer of the law and a minister of the gospel, I declare that you are husband and wife. John, you may kiss your bride."

John would not let go of Patti's right hand. He took his right hand, lifted the veil, and kissed her. John looked at her, hugged her, and kissed her again. He picked her up and carried her away, down the aisle and into the limo.

CHAPTER 24

Patti shut off the water to the shower. She reached to get a towel to wrap around her hair, took another and dried her body. She slipped into her robe and then used her towel to clear the mirror. She thought of her husband. She always dreamed someone would love her like John did. She felt so good to be with him. She unwrapped the towel from her hair and started blow-drying her hair. Her head was full of the memories of the past few weeks. Their wedding, the honeymoon, and even moving into this borrowed house with John. She finished drying her hair. Putting away the dryer, she looked into the mirror as she brushed her hair. Thoughts of her wedding day always seemed to bring tears to her eyes. Patti set the brush aside and reached for a tissue. She was startled to hear John shout her name loudly.

"Patti! Patti!"

She rushed to the bedroom door to find John sitting up in bed; he called out again, "Patti!"

The morning sunlight gave dim light to the room. John swallowed and took a deep breath as Patti opened the door to the bedroom. The light from the bathroom shadowed the figure that stood in the doorway. John blinked to focus on her image. Patti switched on the light to the bedroom. The light made John blink his eyes repeatedly to adjust to the light.

"John, what's wrong?" She asked.

"I guess I was dreaming. I was chasing the plane at Marshall's as it was going down the runway, and I couldn't stop it. I was yelling your name and waving my hands, but you took off and left me standing there."

In a condescending tone, Patti said, "That's sweet, but I'm here, and why are you still in that bed? I thought you were the early riser." Her soft brown hair hanging limp, although the robe was tied at the waist, John could see her long bronze legs as she made her way to the bed.

John said, "I've never had a reason to stay in bed before now."

"Well, if you're not getting up today, John Reed, then I'm getting back in bed. I guess I won't be having an early breakfast after all?"

"What do you say to a one month anniversary brunch?" John asked.

Patti pushed John over to lay beside him, "Sounds great to me. Oh, by the way, I talked to my mother yesterday, and she said she received five dozen red roses. The note that came with them said, "Thank you. She's perfect. Can't wait to meet you. Love, John.""

John wrapped his arms around Patti. "Somehow I feel breakfast will never be the same."

The next few months flew by. John's work on the house was completed, and Patti was settled into her new job. Both where ready to go home. Patti and John boarded a plane with a Jackson, Mississippi, destination. It was the weekend before Thanksgiving. Susan and Jeff would follow in a few weeks to be home for Christmas and stay until after the New Year. John and Patti planned to arrive unannounced. They traveled on a night flight that was scheduled to land at 5:51 a.m. Mississippi time. John arranged for the Suburban to be left at the airport. He had most of Patti's clothes and things she had accumulated shipped, but he knew he would have plenty luggage also. They wanted to slip into town and surprise John's parents.

Patti and John would stay through mid-December, and then go to Chicago for Christmas with Patti's family. Patti was excited to visit her new home for the first time. John had Patti put her hands over her eyes before he topped the last hill approaching their home. He slowed down and told Patti he was about to turn into the drive. As they turned and slowly made their way up the drive, John gave the command.

"Okay, Patti, you can open your eyes now." He stopped in front of the house, "What do you think?"

"Oh, John, I love it!"

They walked up the walk to the front door. John unlocked the door and pushed it open. He pulled his wife toward him and picked her up. "I'm going to carry my wife across the threshold."

Everything was like John left it. Nothing was different, except the grandfather clock in the foyer had stopped. Yet the home was different, and John could feel the difference. John released Patti to wander through the house. He could give her a guided tour later. She didn't ask any questions, and John didn't offer any details to her new home. Later, John took her hand and walked to the back porch. The mild weather would place the temperature in the mid-sixties, which was a typical Mississippi fall morning. It was overcast, and the wind was blowing, making a rustling sound as it took the last of the fall leaves from the tree's branches. From the back porch, they could see the pond below their home. On the opposite side of the pond from the house was a small cabin.

"John, you told me about the pond and cabin, but I didn't visualize how close they were to your house."

"Correction, Patti, our house." John, putting his arms around her, he stood behind Patti.

"That sounds nice, our house."

"The cabin was my uncle's first home. He moved it here after he built a new house to serve as a retreat. He told me many times the house had too many good memories to throw away. I built this house because I loved the view. You know Uncle Andrew kept rose beds in front of that cabin until he died. Before I built this house, the only way to get to the cabin was a narrow trail off the main road that ran to the left of the pond back in the corner of the pasture." John pointed, "You can see the trail if you look closely in the wooded area. Oh well, you will soon know this place as well as I do. Coming up that trail, I literally had to be at the pond to see the cabin let alone the roses."

"Let me guess, all red."

"Yes, you're right. You were listening."

"John, you told me one time there had to be a story behind the roses, don't you have any idea why all red?"

"I've always thought it had something to do with his wife."

"I bet you're right. I would surely like to know the story behind the roses."

"Why don't we try to find an answer? Let me call my mother, and I'll invite us over for breakfast. She makes wonderful biscuits, and then we can go buy some groceries of our own."

"It's all about food, isn't it, John?"

"Yeah, I guess so. I just realized something. I've never had breakfast in Mississippi, with you before." John, giving her a hug, placed his cheek next to Patti's turned his mouth to her, he whispered in her ear, "I love you, Patti. Welcome home."

CPSIA information can be obtained at www.ICGtesting.com

225403LV00001B/2/P

9 781615 077366